DIRTY HUSBAND

CRYSTAL KASWELL

Copyright

This is a work of fiction. Similarities to real people, places, or events are entirely coincidental.

Also by Crystal Kaswell

Dirty Rich

Dirty Deal - Blake

Dirty Boss - Nick

Dirty Husband - Shep

Dirty Desires - Ian - coming 2020

Sinful Serenade

Sing Your Heart Out - Miles

Strum Your Heart Out - Drew

Rock Your Heart Out - Tom

Play Your Heart Out - Pete

Sinful Ever After – series sequel

Just a Taste - Miles's POV

Dangerous Noise

Dangerous Kiss - Ethan

Dangerous Crush – Kit

Dangerous Rock – Joel

Dangerous Fling – Mal

Dangerous Encore - series sequel

Inked Hearts

Tempting - Brendon

Hooking Up - Walker

Pretend You're Mine - Ryan

Hating You, Loving You - Dean

Breaking the Rules - Hunter

Losing It - Wes

Accidental Husband - Griffin

The Baby Bargain - Chase

Inked Love

The Best Friend Bargain - Forest — coming 2020

The First Taste - Holden - coming 2020

Standalones

Broken - Trent & Delilah

Come Undone Trilogy

Come Undone

Come Apart

Come To Me

Sign up for the Crystal Kaswell mailing list

Chapter One

JASMINE

I *shouldn't be here.*

This chapter of my life is over. Done. No matter what he thinks.

Sure, we've only spoken ten words in the last five years, but I still know how Shepard Marlowe operates.

It emanates through the building. Bounces off the shiny silver sign. The clean grey carpet. The glass walls.

The one thing that inspires him: money.

The receptionist taps her headset, putting her conversation on hold. "Right this way, Ms. Lee."

She stands and leads me through a busy hallway. Straight to the corner office.

"Can I get you anything?" She rattles off a list of espresso drinks.

I nod a yes to something. I don't need the caffeine—I'm already shaking—and I'd prefer tea. But I do need something to occupy my hands.

Something to keep me from touching him.

It's been so long since I've seen him in person. Longer

since I've heard his voice, smelled his soap, felt the softness of his lips.

But then there isn't a softness to his lips. Not anymore.

I sit in the expensive leather chair. Cross my legs. Smooth my skirt.

It's wrong. Too tight. Too normal. Too unsophisticated.

Most days my business attire—button-up shirt, pencil skirt, practical pumps—feels like a shield.

Today, knowing he's on his way?

My heart thuds against my chest.

My head screams *leave now, before it's too late*.

But my body?

It shares none of my caution.

I cross my legs the other way. Uncross them. Try to shift my thoughts to practical places.

It doesn't work. My head fills with memories.

His lips on my neck. His hands on my waist. His voice in my ears.

You feel so good.

The opening door draws my attention.

I turn, expecting the assistant or a lawyer.

But it's him.

"Jasmine." His voice is as cold as his clear blue eyes. He looks down at me with vague familiarity. Like I'm a colleague he hasn't seen in a few years. A colleague who irritates him. "I'm glad you made it."

I bite my tongue so I won't snap.

He moves into the room, but he doesn't take a seat. He stands next to the big leather chair beside mine. "I wasn't sure you'd come."

His eyes meet mine. It's a different stare than the one he had when we were kids. That boy was sweet, loving, soft.

This man—

He's cold, angry, hurt.

God, his eyes are still so blue. So beautiful. But that coldness—

It makes my heart ache.

I try to hold his gaze. Try to think up something to say. Some small talk to convince him I'm ready for this. Whatever it is.

Nothing comes.

His gaze is too intense. I have to look away. To the clean carpet. The supple fabric of the chair. The shiny patent of his shoes.

Eventually, the door opens. The assistant—she has a name, but I can barely remember mine at the moment—steps inside. Holds up two tiny espresso cups.

"Ms. Blackstone will be here shortly." She sets both cups on the expensive oak desk. Nods *enjoy*. Disappears.

She's everywhere and nowhere at the same time. Never imposing, always friendly, always smiling. Skills I recognize. Skills I mastered a long time ago.

Skills I need right now.

I take a small sip. Bright espresso. Creamy milk. A hint of softness. But not enough to dull the bitterness.

Shepard looks down at me, the tiniest hint of curiosity in his eyes.

He wants something.

I shouldn't be here. It echoes through my head again, but it's too late. My body is already buzzing. It's already screaming for him, remembering every kiss, every touch, every fuck.

I uncross and recross my legs. It does nothing to ease the ache below my belly button, but it does draw his gaze.

His eyes flit to my tan skin.

He swallows hard. Steels himself.

"I'm on my lunch." I'm not sure what he wants. Only

that he's confident he'll get it. Which is ridiculous. He's the one who hurt me. Why does he think I want anything to do with him? "I don't have a lot of time."

I know why. It's money. It's always money.

All the men I work with think the world revolves around them. Because it does.

Shep's family was well-off when we were kids. But now?

Now he owns half of Manhattan.

He can destroy me with the snap of his fingers.

Of course, I'm here.

Shepard takes a seat across from me. He folds one leg over the other, making a four with his limbs. Then he leans just a little closer. Just close enough I smell his soap.

Rich. Earthy. Money.

He's every part the distinguished professional. Navy suit, turquoise tie, brown dress shoes.

But there's a tiny hint of the boy I loved in his clear blue eyes.

"I have a proposition for you." His voice stays even.

I pretend as if I'm more interested in my drink. "Yes?"

His voice just barely softens. "I need a wife."

"A wife?" My heart thuds against my chest, drowning every thought in my brain. "You need a wife?" I repeat the words. They make even less sense this time.

He's twenty-five. He owns the hottest tech company on the market. He screams of power, money, control.

Filthy rich and incredibly handsome.

The body of an Olympic swimmer. The face of Prince Charming. There are ugly parts to Shepard, yes, but those scars are hidden beneath the surface.

They're—

"I need you, Jasmine," he says. "I need you to be my wife."

Chapter Two

SHEPARD

J asmine sinks into her chair. She presses her lips together. Brings the espresso cup to her mouth.

Takes a tiny sip.

Her lipstick—something red and rich that drives me out of my fucking mind—doesn't stain the glass. The kind of lipstick that stays on. That won't mark my skin.

Why is she drinking a macchiato? She hates coffee. Always talks about the superiority of tea.

She's a smart woman. Maybe she's doing it to drive me mad. So I spend the entire meeting wondering if her lipstick will stain my cock.

Or maybe I don't know the woman she's become.

The thought makes my stomach twist. But I don't have time for these kinds of considerations.

I certainly don't have time to focus on how badly she wants me.

It's written all over her face. The flush of her cheeks. The heave of her chest. The shudder of her thighs.

Fuck, those thighs—

It's been too long since they've been pressed against my cheeks. Since she's been under me, clawing at my skin, begging for my mercy.

You should know better, princess. I don't have a single scrap of mercy.

I try to focus on my espresso, but it's not nearly as interesting as her almond eyes.

She turns a few inches toward me. Finishes her drink. Sets the ceramic on the massive desk.

An expensive oak. The perfect height to turn her over and fuck her senseless.

God dammit. I'm better than these impulses. I don't care how long it's been. I don't care how desperately I need to erase my thoughts.

I'm not letting my cock steer this conversation.

It doesn't matter that she's the most beautiful woman in the world. It doesn't matter that she's the only woman I want.

Right now, I don't have a choice.

I need to win her heart in the next thirty days.

Either I convince the world she's in love with me. Or that bastard takes everything that matters.

Slowly, she smooths her pencil skirt. "You know where I stand, Shepard." She refers to the ultimatum she gave me six years ago.

"I do."

"Why do you think I'd marry you?"

"Your father's treatment can't be cheap."

Her dark eyes fill with concern. Over her father's health. Or my knowledge of it. "I have it handled."

"I know how much you make." It's barely enough for rent and groceries in her neighborhood.

"I have it handled."

"It's not enough."

"Our health insurance—"

"Don't be ridiculous." I turn my body toward hers. "Don't play this game, Jasmine." *I have a better game, princess. Where I command and you obey. Take off your panties. I want to watch you come.*

"What game is that?" Her voice hardens. Her posture goes with it. She folds her arms over her chest. Presses her heels together.

"Don't pretend you don't put your family first."

"Just because you—"

"You'll do anything for him."

"Not anything." She stares at me, daring me to spell it out. To make her a whore. Offer money for her body.

Which is ridiculous. I wouldn't insult her like that. "I'm not paying you for sex."

"You aren't paying me, period, Shep." She grabs her purse. Stands. Moves toward the door. "I'm leaving—"

"A million dollars."

She stops dead in her tracks. "A million dollars?"

"Yes."

"What if I want two?"

"I'm negotiable."

"Why not make it ten? Or twenty? As long as we're living in a fairy tale."

"Seven figures."

"Why do you even—"

I can't explain that. I can't even think about it. "You need the money."

"I have money."

"Not enough." I stand. Place my body between her and the door.

Fuck, she's as beautiful as she was the first time I kissed her.

No longer an innocent girl. No longer full of hope, love, passion.

We've been broken in different ways, but we're both there. Cracked. World-weary. Hiding behind masks.

I need to unpeel hers.

The way her body responds to mine—her blush spreads to her chest, her fingers dig into her thighs, her hair falls over her cheeks.

She wants this. Some part of her does. Even if the rest of her isn't willing to admit it.

Her eyes meet mine. Something passes between us. A memory of what used to be.

Then she steps backward, shakes her head, repeats her claim. "You can't buy me."

She turns and marches out of the office.

But we both know it's only a matter of time.

Maybe she won't hand me her heart willingly.

But she will do this.

The rest is up to me.

Chapter Three

JASMINE

By the time I slide into my expensive ergonomic chair, I'm the picture of a confident, together assistant.

Steady limbs, smooth skirt, easy smile.

My heart is beating so fast I can barely hear my thoughts, but I look the part.

As soon as my boss requests something, I nod *of course, sir*, and let work take over.

I've been an executive assistant for the last half a decade. Since I put college on pause to help my family.

It wasn't what Dad wanted, but he didn't really have a choice.

I've worked in half a dozen offices. Some are quiet. I sit, wait to be called upon, constantly ready, rarely engaged.

Here, I'm busy. Mr. Billings is a venture capitalist. He's always running to a meeting, requesting research on a company, planning a trip overseas.

He brings his personal assistant on trips. She's seen

every major city in the world, though she claims she spends most of it jet lagged inside of conference rooms.

I shouldn't covet her life. Sure, once upon a time, I wanted to see the world. I wanted more than my family's tiny shared apartment in the Bay. I wanted to defy my parents' expectations. To go into a creative field instead of a practical one.

But that was before Mom died.

Before Dad got sick.

Before paying bills became my greatest challenge.

Now, I want to survive. Everything else is gravy.

When I was still in high school, I had time for myself. I studied enough to ace my classes; I worked at my aunt's restaurant, and I nabbed the lead in the school play.

My parents didn't mind my afternoons with Shepard.

Even when it became evenings and weekends. And every single Sunday.

I thought they'd object—school is more important than boys—but they saw something I didn't.

Another ticket to success.

He wasn't richer than sin then. Just the son of a successful family. And the smartest guy in the math class at our very expensive private high school (I was there on scholarship).

He was smart, funny in a direct way, sweet in a Shep way.

It's hard to imagine now.

It's hard to remember.

I sneak a glance on my cell phone. The details of our meeting, in an email, sent by his lawyer's assistant.

No personal touch.

No signs of weakness.

But there, in the photo buried in an old folder, the two of us at homecoming dance.

His arm around my waist, his smile wicked, his blue eyes bright.

And me, in a red dress that matched his tie, struggling to stand in my uncomfortable heels, bursting with happiness.

He was so charming.

We were so happy. Yeah, we were kids with big dreams and small scars.

Or maybe that was just me. I always knew Shep was hiding a darkness. Before I even met him. He had a reputation at our school. For brooding behavior and fits of anger.

He was gentle with me. Most of the time. But sometimes…

He got angry for no clear reason. Or he avoided me for days. Then he turned up like nothing had happened. Like we'd spent all that time madly in love. Or he snuck his parents' liquor. Stayed at parties until he was wasted.

Then it wasn't sometimes. It was always.

He drank. A lot.

I used to think that was it. His only secret. He didn't want me to know he was out of control. He didn't want to admit he was out of control.

But now…

I'm not so sure.

Now, Shep is sober.

But that darkness of his is still there. It's closer to the surface. Stronger than ever.

And now he wants me as his wife.

No, what was it he said?

He needs me as his wife.

But why? He's been sober for a year. He's had every chance to approach me, apologize, ask me to dinner.

Why does he suddenly need to marry me?

———

THE SECOND I'M FINISHED WITH WORK, I TAKE THE SUBWAY to the hospital.

It's the tail end of visiting hours, but no one stops me from heading straight to my father's room.

He looks up at me with his usual weary smile. "Jasmine, sweetheart, don't worry about me." He calls me by my American name now. He has since I started dating Shep.

"I'm not worried," I lie.

He shakes his head *of course, you are*.

I set my bag on the scratchy green chair. Lay my rain-coat over it. It's May now. The weather is getting warmer, but the sky is unpredictable. Sometimes, the grey clouds fade to sun. Other times, they break into heavy rain.

"You're working too hard," he says.

"Only as hard as you would."

"It's seven. Have you eaten dinner?"

"I'll eat at home."

"You're getting too thin." He motions toward the cafe-teria. "You need to eat."

"Or I won't attract a good husband?"

He smiles softly. "Your mother would say that."

"She'd be delusional. Everyone in New York is thin."

"Men like a little something to hold on to."

"We are not discussing this." I appreciate the intent—I need to eat eventually—but I don't need anyone's opinion on my body. Especially not my father's. Ew.

He shifts tactics. "I understand. Your standards are high now. She was such a great cook." His eyes get fuzzy. Far away. Like he's lost in dreams of Mom. "Nothing compares to her food. But you have that in you too. You can learn. If you cook. And eat."

I choke back a memory. Thinking of Mom makes Dad

happy. It's not the same for me. It hurts too much. "Do you have enough to read?"

I look over the sparse room. It's decorated as much as the hospital will allow—the gold Buddha Mom kept on her dresser, a single framed photo of our family, a stack of trashy historical thrillers—but it's still sterile.

Free of warmth.

"Too much." He motions to the book sitting on his tray. "Mariah brought this yesterday." He calls the nurse by her first name. "Her husband spoke highly of the author. Said he's the next Dan Brown." He shakes his head *in his dreams*.

"Nothing about Da Vinci?"

He laughs and goes into one of his speeches about the wit and majesty of *Angels and Demons*.

It's as familiar as the taste of my morning tea. Funny, because I've heard it so many times. Because it's everything Dad believes.

I laugh along with him. Then we move into the great Dan Brown's next masterpiece.

For a while, I forget about the day, about Shepard's strange offer, the reason why we're having this conversation in the hospital.

Then a woman in a cheap suit enters the room and forces a smile. "Ms. Lee, we should talk."

Worry spreads over Dad's face.

I steel my expression. To convince him everything is fine. It's possible, isn't it?

It's possible we're not totally and completely fucked.

Chapter Four

JASMINE

The head of financial aid pushes her glasses up her nose. "We want to help. We do. But we don't have the budget to do any better than this."

"Of course."

"It's still experimental. The insurance company won't pay. And we're spread thin as it is."

I press my lips together. Call upon my friendly assistant smile.

She means well. She does. She has to deliver bad news all day, every day. Of course, she keeps her feelings out of it.

Dad's prognosis is bad. If we do nothing, he'll be dead by the end of the year.

That's what the current medical science supports.

At this point, we make him comfortable. Or we seek out an experimental treatment option.

Those are new. Unproven. Expensive.

Of course, the insurance company won't cover it.

"Thank you." I use my assistant voice. Even. Calm. *I'll get right on that, sir.*

"This is the last appeal." She pulls up the paper on her clipboard. Taps the highlighted phrase. Legalese that means *sorry, you're fucked, Trong Lee is going to die*. "Dr. Rodriguez will still take you. But he'll need a deposit upfront."

"Okay."

"That's doable?" She sets her clipboard down. Picks up another. A bill. With the total circled in red. "Twenty percent?"

Twenty percent of a lot is still a lot. Five figures. Five figures I don't have.

"I'm sure he'll hold your appointment until Monday," the administrator says. "But he'll need the deposit by the end of the business day."

"I understand."

Her expression softens for a second. She pats my shoulder. "It will be okay, Ms. Lee. You'll get through this." She offers me a soft smile, then she turns, heads back to her office.

I want to believe her.

But I don't see how I'm going to get through this.

———

By now, I have a familiar routine. Stay until a nurse asks me to leave. Take the subway to our place in Flushing. Fix an easy dinner. Leftover stir-fry and fresh white rice.

It's sad fixing rice for one. The minimum portion is too much. Like the rice cooker is mocking me.

All alone, again. Will your father ever come home? Will you ever invite anyone else here?

I try to shut it up by piling the entire portion onto my plate. But it still echoes through my head as I sort mail.

All alone, again.

With Dad in the hospital, we're relying on my salary alone.

I'm good with money. Smart. But I'm not a miracle worker. Even if I did max my credit cards, I wouldn't have enough to cover Dad's treatment.

I run the numbers a dozen times. Then a dozen more.

Maybe if I cut my cell phone. Or the electricity. Maybe I could stay with a friend. Only all my friendships have faded. I don't have time to stay in touch. Any request would be taking advantage.

I stack bills in a neat row. Junk mail in a pile. Magazines on the coffee table. I'm not sure who paid for these subscriptions to Cosmo and The Economist, but they make a hell of a contrast.

Thirty new ways to please your man.

Guess what: the world is falling apart. Again!

At the moment, I feel both in my core.

My world is falling apart.

Unless I find help from someone, I'm screwed. And Shep is the only one who's offering.

It's right there, in the Manila envelope between the magazines.

Jasmine in black marker.

That's Shepard's handwriting.

Not his lawyer's assistant. His.

I undo the clasp. Pull out a stack of stapled papers.

A folded paper falls from a legal document.

A note. From him.

He has something to say.

Knowing Shepard, it's not:

I'm so sorry, I was rude. I know, six years ago, you finally had enough and said "I can't do this anymore, Shep. I love you, but I can't be with you if you keep drinking. This is it. If you don't check into rehab, tomorrow, I'm leaving. I'm walking away and never looking back."

I know, the day after, you left. And I kept drinking. But I can explain. I was a kid. Barely nineteen. Too stupid to see what I had.

I can explain why, a year and a half ago, when my brother black-mailed me, and used this tiny clause in my contract that said "get sober or lose the company," I did go to rehab. There's a perfectly good reason why I chose booze over you. Then money over booze. It's not that I love money more than I ever loved you. It's not that money is the only thing in the black hole I call a heart.

I really am sorry. I should have written to you after I got out of rehab. Apologized. Made sure you were okay, surviving New York on your own.

I should have written when your dad got sick. Sent help. Or at least a Get Well Soon Card.

I'm sorry I didn't. I'm sorry I let you feel like you weren't enough. I'm sorry your love wasn't enough.

I suck a breath through my teeth. Try to wade through my thoughts. Whatever this is…

It doesn't matter how much I hate Shepard…

Right now, I need his help.

And he is right. My pride isn't worth more than my father's life.

I unwrap the letter.

Seven-figures. The rest is negotiable.

- Shep

Chapter Five

SHEPARD

J asmine: *I have terms.*

My body gets light. My head fills with the image of her fingers sliding over her cell. Her red lips parting with a sigh. Her dark hair falling at her shoulders.

She wants the money.

No, it's worse for her. She needs the money. If it was only a want, a desire for a better place or nicer things, she wouldn't give me the time of day.

She's fucked without my money.

I have plenty of it.

But other men have money. A lot of other men. And who wouldn't want her? Who wouldn't offer her the entire world?

I have to ask fast. Before someone else sees this opportunity.

Before I lose any chance at winning this fucking game.

Shep: Come to my office.

Jasmine: It's the middle of the night.

Shep: It's eleven fifteen.

Jasmine: I have to be at work at eight.
Shep: You know that isn't true.
Jasmine: What's the address?
Shep: I'll send a car.
Jasmine: And you already know where I live.

Is she smiling or rolling her eyes? I don't know anymore. I can't read her the way I once did.

She hates that she needs me. I understand that much.

Once upon a time, I hated the way I needed her. Even when I loved her. It made me too vulnerable.

Weaknesses are exploitable.

I can't afford any more.

Only this—

I don't really have a choice.

Shep: My driver will be there in ten minutes.

Fuck, I need a drink. Something aged and strong. A bourbon so sweet it tastes of honey.

I hold on to the memory as I message my driver. Then he replies that he's on his way. She'll be here, in my office, in less than twenty minutes.

She lives too far into Queens. It's not a nice neighborhood. It's not good enough for her.

She should be here.

She should be naked on my couch.

She should be groaning my name.

My eyes close. They go to her. A memory from long ago. The two of us in my bedroom. Her hands on my neck. Her voice in my ear. *Are you sure it won't hurt?*

Footsteps. That loud voice. My blood going cold.

I can't think about her anymore. I can't think about that time in my life. She's a spot of light, but the darkness is pure black.

This is a bad idea. She's too close to those memories. It's too hard to stay in control.

Only I don't have a choice.

If I don't convince her to marry me, I lose everything.

No, it's worse. I need more than her hand. I need her to fall in love with me.

If I fail, that bastard wins again.

That's out of the question.

Of course, he made it her. Of course, he made that a term.

This would be easier with someone else. With someone who mistakes security or money or orgasmic bliss for love.

Some woman who's interesting enough for a little conversation, a few fucks, a sweet goodbye, and nothing more.

I haven't exactly been a monk. Yes, I drank a lot. According to everyone in my life, I had a problem. Maybe I wasn't happy. Maybe I wasn't healthy. But I was functioning.

When my brother forced me into rehab, he took that away. I needed a replacement. Cigarettes reminded me of ugly things. Coffee didn't do enough.

That left one thing.

A woman under my command, bending to my every wish, begging me for release.

It was the only way I felt in control.

It's still the only way I feel in control.

I fucked a lot of women after I got out of rehab. Too many to count. It never meant anything to either of us. We got in, got off, got out.

Then I went to New York and I saw Jasmine again and—

I couldn't. My body refused. It only wanted her.

It only wants her.

My head knows better.

My heart—

There's nothing left. Only this empty space in my chest.

No doubt she's thinking the same thing right now. Sitting in the back seat of my limo, asking herself if there's any point in appealing to my mercy.

Under different circumstances, I'd pay for her father's treatment. I'd make sure someone was taking care of her.

Right now, I don't have the luxury.

I have to convince her. Whatever it takes.

Worse, I have to stay sober while I do it.

Nothing to dull my thoughts. Or my aches. Or that voice in my head reminding me exactly how powerless I was.

It's no use dreaming of bourbon.

Jasmine made her stance clear six years ago. When she gave me that ultimatum, I thought she was bluffing.

I did what I always did in negotiations. I called her on it.

But she wasn't bluffing. She walked away.

I respect her for making good on her promise. But I don't forgive her.

Jasmine: This is really overkill.

She's on her way. Almost here. Almost in this space that's mine and mine alone. The only place that makes sense.

Work is easy. A set of rules to manipulate. Victory conditions to obtain.

No subjectivity. No interpretation. No quests for truth.

Mom always went on about art and truth. For a long time, I thought it mattered. Now—

There's only one thing that matters.

Jasmine Lee as my wife.

———

My phone buzzes with my driver's alert. She's downstairs.

In the lobby.

At the security desk.

The elevator.

My gaze shifts to the decanter on the glass table. A dark amber. Almost as dark as her eyes.

Only it's not a whiskey that will warm my throat.

It's iced tea.

Lock's idea. His full name is Aalock Oza, but I call him Lock, what with his role as the keeper of my sobriety.

He thinks it's adorable. Chuckles every time. Says something about how he always wanted a name that suited his personality, not one that means light.

I would respect him for not taking shit if it didn't make my life so difficult.

There's whiskey in the cabinet. The locked cabinet. Everyone on my staff has a key. Everyone has a clause in their contract. They lose their jobs if they allow me to drink.

I can thank my brother for that. He's the one that blackmailed me into rehab last year.

Maybe I should. She's only here because I'm sober. I have to find a way to do this.

I pour a fucking iced tea. It's too warm. Too weak. Too astringent.

Mom always loved tea, but I never saw the appeal. Coffee is stronger, richer, more potent. I don't need a gentle meditation. I need a wake-up punch.

Something powerful enough to overwhelm me.

The oversteeped, room temperature Darjeeling—

It's doesn't sate me.

The elevator dings. My mouth gets dry. Then my throat. From the tea. Not her footsteps.

The click of her heels. A soft knock on the door.

"Come in." I set my glass on the table. Slide my hands into my pockets.

Jasmine steps inside. Presses the door closed behind her.

She's wearing the same heels and a tight red dress that hugs every inch of her soft body.

Her chest heaves with her inhale. The pendant between her breasts catches the light. A gift from me. For her sixteenth birthday.

She kept it all this time. She wants me to know she kept it all this time. That must mean something.

I stare into her dark eyes, trying to find the meaning. I can't. She's too stiff, too hurt, too unyielding.

This won't do. I need the upper hand.

It's not fair, but I don't have the luxury of sportsman-ship at the moment.

"Would you like to take a seat?" I motion to the leather couch against the wall.

Her gaze shifts to the empty glass. The decanter of amber liquid. Me. She raises a brow. *Really?*

"You'd like some?"

She barely laughs. "Is that how we're starting?"

"Would you?"

"Sure."

I pour her a glass.

Her fingers brush mine as she takes it.

She brings the cup to her lips.

This time, her makeup stains the cup. Crimson on glass.

Her eyes close as she sips. They burst open. Fill with surprise. "Oh."

Again, I motion for her to sit.

This time, she does. "I shouldn't have assumed."

I sit next to her. Place my hand over hers. "I know what you think of me."

Her brow furrows. She drops the glass in my palm. Places her hands in her lap. "I'm not marrying an alcoholic."

"Understood."

"That's it? Understood."

I nod.

She stares into my eyes.

I stare back.

"Six years ago—"

"You proved how much it matters to you."

Her brow softens. Her eyes go to the floor. "So why didn't you… no, it doesn't matter. You're sober now."

I nod, even though it's not a question.

"For how long?"

"Thirteen months now." I got out of rehab a year ago. I've been in New York for a year. But I've barely spoken to her.

"Congratulations." Pride slips into her voice. Just barely. "That's quite an accomplishment."

"I'm not going to offer a cliché about taking it one day at a time."

"One woman at a time, the last I heard."

"You've heard things?" I ask.

"Your name travels fast."

"And what have people said?"

Her guard drops. The tension in her shoulders eases. She shoots me that *really* look. Her classic when we were kids. When she couldn't believe the things my family did. Or bought. "I guess you're living in a cave."

"The straw bed is particularly uncomfortable."

"And it makes a mess of your hair." She pretends to pick something out of my hair.

I shrink back, reflexively.

Her eyes turn down. "Oh, I—"

Fuck. I'm past this. I am. "It's fine."

"Don't want me messing up your style?" she offers.

I nod *of course*. But it hangs in the air. That tension. I flinched when she tried to touch me. I'm going to offer to fuck her senseless, but I flinch when she tries to touch me.

I'm sure it makes no sense to her.

It barely makes sense to me. No, it doesn't. But I don't have the luxury of sorting it out.

She smooths her dress. "You're sober."

"Yes."

"And you'll stay sober."

"Yes."

"For how long?"

"They're still selling the old chestnut about life."

"No." She presses her palms into her thighs. "How long do you want to stay married?"

I can't start at a month. Or a year even. I need room to work my way down.

She wants this to be easy. She wants to forget the last six years. The ultimatum. The months before it.

I turn my body toward hers.

She shudders as my knees brush hers. She wants that too. Wants my body over hers, my lips on her skin, my hands between her legs.

"Until I decide to call it off," I say.

"Forever?"

"Yes."

"So you… what do you think is going to happen? I'm going to see your bank account and fall in love?"

"You know what's in my bank account."

"Your—" She motions to my crotch.

"My cock."

26

Her cheeks blush. "Are you... expecting that?"

"I'm not paying you to sleep with me."

She stares at me with that same *really* expression. She wants to keep this light. To shrug this off.

Part of me does. But the other part—"I'm not paying for your body, Jasmine."

"You pay me to sleep in your bedroom and while we're there—"

"No. I'm not going to touch you until you ask." And I'm not inviting anyone into *my* bedroom.

"I won't."

"Until you're so desperate you're on your knees, begging for my cock." I slip my leg between hers.

She groans as my knee brushes the inside of her thigh. "I won't."

"You will."

"No. I won't."

"Let's say you don't. For the sake of argument." She will. But no sense in debating now. "Then I won't touch you."

"You can't be with someone else," she says.

"You either."

"So we're just going to... not have sex."

"If that's what you want." I keep my voice firm. So it screams *we both know what you want*.

"A lifetime without sex?"

"You have a counter?"

"Three months."

"For two million dollars?"

"One." She swallows hard. "Three months for a million dollars. And you pay for my father's treatment. Right now."

"Two years."

She shakes her head. "Three months."

"One year."

Her eyes meet mine. "And you pay his treatment right now?"

"You'll move into my apartment tomorrow."

Her eyes fill with surprise. "Tomorrow?"

"I'll have my team find you a dress. We'll arrange every-thing. Marry right away."

"I'm picking my own dress."

"Sure."

"You can pull strings to have it rush ordered. But I'm in charge of my look—"

"I'll arrange a personal stylist."

Her lips press together.

"To advise. You have final say."

"And the wedding itself?"

"You have something in mind?"

"My dad… I don't want him to know why. I want him to believe we—"

"Of course." Better for me. When people pretend, they start to believe it. "If you'll convince my colleagues."

Her eyes flare with surprise. It flashes over her face, the realization that I need this as much as she does. Still, she nods. "I'll have a lawyer look over the contract."

"There are a dozen lawyers in your office."

"You're okay with them having this information?"

"It won't be so specific." I smooth my slacks. Let the back of my hand brush her thigh.

"How"—she sucks in a deep breath—"specific will it be?"

"A standard prenup. After one year of marriage, you get a million dollars. With an extra million every year. Until we hit ten and you get a quarter of everything I've gained in the decade."

"Is that supposed to be some sort of bribe?"

"Insurance." I rest my hand on her thigh.

Her legs part. Her eyes follow. She stares at my hand like she's begging it to move forward, but she says nothing. "What for?"

"Insurance isn't for any purpose."

Her eyes find mine. "I need another clause."

I nod *go on*.

"You have to stay sober. Or I get the ten million."

"Okay."

"Okay? That's it?" Her voice says everything. *Why wouldn't you do this for me?*

"Do you need more?"

"No. Ten million will be enough."

"I have my own clause," I say.

She holds my gaze.

"No cheating."

"I'd never—"

"Even so," I say.

"For you too. And I want more for that." Anger seeps into her voice. She tries to stay calm. To use that awful, fake assistant tone. But she doesn't quite manage it. "Twenty million."

I almost smile. "Twenty million." I hold out my hand.

"That's it? I can marry you next week, send a sex worker your way, walk home with twenty million dollars?"

"If you think that will work, go ahead."

Her eyes stay glued to mine. "Are you going to tell me why?"

"No."

"What if I make that non-negotiable?"

"You won't." I stare back at her. This is it. We're almost there. I just have to push her a little further. I pull out my cell. Tap out an email. Place the phone in her palm.

Her eyes go wide as she reads the email. "You'll really—"

"I can do it right now, Jasmine. I can erase every problem in your life. All you need to do is say yes. Say you'll marry me."

Chapter Six

JASMINE

My stomach flutters. This is it. The moment where I seal my fate.

Either I give up on my father.

Or I give up my freedom.

No, it's only a year. Three-hundred-sixty-five days. I survived ten months at this job. I survived a year working full time and going to school.

Yes, I eventually broke. I dropped out so I could find a better paying job, so I could support Dad. But I survived that too.

No matter what he thinks—and, honestly, I'm not sure anymore—I'm a survivor.

I can endure this too. Hell, I'd suffer worse for a slimmer chance to save my father.

Whatever it takes.

"Yes." I extend my hand.

Shepard takes it with a firm grip. "I'll send the paperwork tomorrow."

I nod. "And my father's treatment."

"Of course." He holds up his cell. A transfer from his

bank account. Six figures to the hospital for Trong Lee's treatment.

The end of the albatross around my neck.

A chance.

"That first." I firm my grip. It's supposed to be a sign of strength, but my body gets the wrong idea. My fingers melt into his. My heart races. My sex clenches.

He's right.

I want him.

Standing here, two feet from him, smelling his shampoo, feeling the pure power emanating from his blue eyes—

I want him so badly I can barely stand.

But I can.

So I watch as he finalizes the transaction. Then I shake his hand again. "Thank you."

"Lock will drive you home."

It's too late for the subway—the trains only run once or twice an hour. Until that money is in my account, I can't afford a cab or a ride share. I'm not walking in these shoes.

I should be grateful for the ride. I am.

But it's not like he's asking. He's telling.

For the next year, I'm his. To pose, bend, break.

Dad is safe.

That's worth a thousand years as Shepard's.

"Thank you." I shoot him my customer service smile.

He catches the fakeness. Frowns.

I have my cards to play. There aren't many of them. But I do have them.

———

At home, I change into my pajamas, fix a cup of chamomile, check my cell.

Even though it isn't business hours, it's there. Some strings Shep pulled, no doubt. I thought he was rich and powerful before, even as a teenager, but now?

He has everything.

He has all the power in the world.

The power to destroy me like *that*.

Only he can't. He needs me. I'm not sure why. Only that he does.

I read the message again.

Payment received. Trong Lee is scheduled to begin treatment Monday.

This is it.

Dad has a chance. He really has a chance.

The weight on my chest lifts. My limbs get lighter. The tension in my stomach eases.

This is going to be okay.

There's actually a chance.

There's a chance he's going to make it.

Chapter Seven

JASMINE

Despite my lack of sleep, I skip to work. It's a beautiful day. Bright blue sky, shining sun, blossoming flowers.

Spring in New York. It's gorgeous. Why is it I've never noticed?

I step into the lobby of my office building. It's buzzing with men and women in suits. The click-clack of designer heels against tile. Conversations about deals and weekend plans.

I guess it is Friday. I usually keep better track. The weekend is a chance to see Dad. Sometimes, I can even take him out of the hospital for a few hours. We can go to the park. Or take a walk along the water. Go to that restaurant in Chinatown he loves.

It's been so long.

The voices blur together during my elevator ride. All the way to the thirty-eighth story.

The office is half full. All the assistants are here, at their desks, setting up, making calls, checking schedules.

I turn left outside the glass-walled conference room.

March to my desk—the one outside the biggest corner office.

But it's empty.

The framed photo of my high school graduation, that tin of tea Mom loved, the tiny gold Buddha that matches the one in Dad's room—

They're gone.

The desk is already clean. No computer, no files, no pens. Nothing.

I move closer. To inspect the damage.

The desk has been wiped down. It's already dry.

It's already cleared of any hint of me.

"Oh my God, Jasmine. I'm so sorry. I tried to tell him it was wrong, but you know how he is." Amanda, Mr. Billing's personal assistant, moves toward me. She rests her hand on my shoulder.

I turn, breaking the touch.

She presses her hand to her heart. Makes that *I'm sorry* face. Her blue eyes fill with sympathy. Then with something else. Something happy.

She's… excited.

"I know losing this job is rough. But you must be over the moon. A whirlwind affair with your ex-boyfriend. And now you're getting married! Why didn't you tell me you knew Shepard Marlow?"

I motion to my cleared desk.

"Mr. Billings is upset you didn't tell him."

"It's really none of his business."

She scoffs. "You're engaged to a competitor."

Shep is hardly a competitor. Sure, he owns part of a venture capital firm, but they focus on business-to-business application development, not consumer technology.

"Seriously, Jasmine. It's so romantic. When did you see him?" She touches my shoulder again, this time a little more gently. "When did you first know? Did you look into his eyes and just fall in love?"

"Something like that."

"I didn't realize he was so handsome. Those eyes… is he as intense as he looks?" She raises a brow, so I know she's talking about sex.

My face flushes. The heat trickles down my body an inch at a time. I try to hold it off, to keep my thoughts in clearer places, but I can't.

His hands on my thighs.

His lips on my neck.

His cock driving deep inside me.

Shep was always caring, attentive, skilled. But it felt like he was holding something back.

Stopping himself.

Refusing to share some part of himself with me.

At the time, I didn't notice. Now that I've been with other men…

God, it's been awhile. Too long. I still think of him sometimes. Lots of times. The firm touch. The sure posture. The way his voice got low and demanding.

It scared me back then.

Now…

It scares me how much I want to hear that tone again.

"Oh my God, he is!" she shrieks. Looks around, at the other assistants turned our way. Lowers her voice. "I'm sorry. I know it's not the time. But, really, Jasmine. This is amazing." She holds out her arms, offering me a hug. "I'm so happy for you."

I let her squeeze me.

"Things are really looking up, huh? I expect great things for you."

That makes one of us.

———

I skip the file box. Put everything in my knock-off designer bag. The one Dad bought for me two birthdays ago.

He still beams with pride every time he sees it. He still reminds me about the deal he got in Chinatown, the way he haggled the price down from fifty dollars to twenty-five.

It's not the most well-made. The stitches are crooked. One seam is peeling. The red is faded.

But it's still my favorite handbag. I love it for his love. I love it more than I'd love the real thing.

Everything fits. Not that I have much. A few pictures, an oolong tea, a toiletry kit, spare makeup, extra under-wear. For long nights. Not illicit ones.

Now that Shep—

My body buzzes at the thought of his firm hands. That low voice in my ear, whispering dirty promises.

I'm going to get you on your knees, Jasmine. I'm going to make you beg for my cock.

How can something so wrong be so hot?

He is not going to make me ask.

He is not going to make me beg.

He's certainly not going to get me on my knees.

Not that I—

I mean. I want that too. The feel of him in my mouth, his hands in my hair, his low groan as he spills—

Ahem.

That's so far beyond my point. I don't care how much I miss sex with Shep. Or how much I miss sex, period. There's no way in hell I'm begging him.

I suck a breath through my nose, but it does nothing to cool my cheeks. I'm hot all over.

And I asked him to pretend with other people. He's going to kiss me, touch me, hold me—

He's going to kill me. I'm going to die of pent-up desire. I'm going to be the first person to die from sexual frustration.

At least I'll go out swinging.

I step out of the building. Onto the sidewalk. It's not as busy a little past rush hour, but it's plenty happening. Heels and dress shoes tap the pavement. The sun bounces off the glass buildings, turning the ground bright white.

"Ms. Lee?" A smooth voice asks.

I turn and see Shep's assistant. Aalock, though he prefers Lock. An Indian man with a British accent, a sleek suit, and gorgeous brown eyes.

I'm not sure which is sexier—his voice or his broad shoulders. I try to hold on to that. To fill my head with images of his hands on my skin, his voice in my ears, his body over mine.

It doesn't happen.

My head goes to Shepard.

My thighs clench.

"Mr. Marlow sent me the news." He motions to the car behind him. Not the limo from last night. An expensive sports car. The kind of toy that screams Shep. "Would you like a ride home?"

"Home?"

"Or you can offer us the key. I have a team ready to pack your things and move them into Mr. Marlow's penthouse. They're ready to remake your room." He opens the door for me. "There's already a room furnished. But, to be honest—" He looks over my outfit. "It's not your style."

"My style?"

"You're a beautiful woman, Ms. Lee. And a modern

one. Mr. Marlow… he had a different idea about the spare room."

I raise a brow.

Lock's laugh is hearty. Full-bodied. "He doesn't know you as well as he thinks, does he?"

"Are you allowed to say that?"

He runs an invisible zipper over his lips. "I have an idea." He offers his hand.

I take it.

Lock takes my coat. He walks me around the car. Lets me into the passenger seat. "Tell me what you'd like in your room and I'll take you somewhere you can find it."

"What if I'd like to go to Ikea?"

He clinches my seatbelt, closes the door, gets into the car on his side. "Ms. Lee, I enjoy your company already, but I won't allow you to bring Ikea into our home."

"You have something against the Swedes?"

"God forbid, you want to go there and eat some of those awful meatballs."

"They're better than they look."

"Thank God I'm a vegetarian." He shakes his head.

"They have veggie meatballs."

Mock horror streaks his expression. "Ms. Lee, please, spare me this pain. Tell me you don't want an Ikea Modern style." He says the words with an eye roll in his voice.

I can't help but laugh. Yes, he works for Shep, but he's funny. Warm. Kind. And, as the manager of Shep's personal life… I guess he works for me too. Or he will soon. "Do you have something else in mind?"

"Of course, love." He turns the key, bringing the car to life.

Damn, it has a kick. It's been a long time since I've been in the front seat of a car. Longer since I've driven. I always take the subway. Unless I'm running late or traveling when the train schedule is a crawl.

"If you're not sure, I know just the place. Totally you."

"How do you know it's me?"

"Trust me. I have a feel for these things."

———

WE HEAD STRAIGHT TO A FURNITURE STORE IN MIDTOWN. I've never heard of it. Never seen it before. But it's perfect. Just my style.

I pick out a bed, a desk, a dresser. Frames to hold posters I haven't bought yet.

The decorator discusses color scheme, theme, feel. I rattle off a few buzz words. Bright, vibrant, alive.

A place that's exciting yet safe. A place that's mine. A place that's filled with the things I love.

Tea, family, classic films, Broadway icons.

Lock overhears me. Offers to purchase tickets for me and Shepard. For tonight.

It's a sweet offer, but I can't say yes just yet. I can't agree to extra time with him just yet. It's enough I'm living in his apartment, at his beck and call, for some reason he can't explain.

Shepard is many things. Patient isn't one of them. Even if he was waiting until he was sober, he's had a year. He's had chances.

He's been in New York all this time. Sure, we haven't talked, but we've locked eyes. I've felt all that unspoken history pass between us.

If he wanted to do this to prove he could, to have some hold over me, to win me back—

He would have done it a long time ago.

There must be something else.

Yes, I need money now more than ever. But I needed it last month and the month before. I don't believe he's been biding his time, waiting until I was desperate enough to accept his offer.

Maybe I'm naïve. Maybe I'm blinded by memories. Maybe I'm a damn fool.

But I do believe there's good in him. I do believe he wants the best for me.

I finish with the decorator. Let Lock drive me to Shepard's penthouse.

A new building in a gentrifying neighborhood. Hell's Kitchen. Far west, right along the Hudson.

We park in an underground garage. Next to three other cars Shepard owns. The color is a dead giveaway. Bright red.

His favorite color on me. The color of everything he owns.

I should get used to it.

A million dollars buys a year of my life.

So when I hear his voice on the intercom outside the elevator, I steel myself.

He wants something from me.

Maybe it's something I can give him.

But he won't get my love.

That's not for sale.

Chapter Eight

JASMINE

L ight streams through the wide windows. Bounces off the shiny tile floors. The clean walls. The expensive furniture.

A leather couch with soft edges. A long dining table in cherry. Chandelier lights with sparkling accents.

And Shepard, standing in the middle of the room in a sleek grey suit.

He really is handsome. He always was, but now that he's older and broader, he's a full-blown hunk.

"Jasmine." He says my name like it's his favorite car. Something he adores. A possession he adores. "Please. Sit. We have a lot to discuss." He nods to Lock.

Lock understands immediately. "I'll leave you to it." He bows and moves along the sleek hardwood, through the hallway, down the spiral staircase.

This place is beautiful. Modern and antique. Like an updated castle. I didn't believe Lock at first. I didn't believe Shep would live somewhere with quaint charm. But he does.

"Would you like something to drink?" He motions to

the gold tray sitting on the table. The two espresso cups, both filled with dark liquid.

"Are you going to make it?" It's hard to picture Shepard fixing his own tea. The man has a driver, for goodness' sake. When was the last time he thought about boiling water?

"I can call Lock, if you think he'll do a better job."

"He is English."

"I prepared something for you."

"You personally?"

"I arranged for it." He picks up his espresso cup. Takes a sip. "I never could bake."

"Or cook."

He just barely smiles. "It's important to know your strengths and weaknesses."

"And your enemies?"

"Yes." His voice is matter-of-fact. Like it's oh, so obvious. Like everyone knows. "You still prefer oolong?"

"Anything is fine."

"Do you?" His voice drops a little lower. Gets a little harder.

"Does it matter?"

"Yes." Shep places his ceramic cup on the tray. Then he closes the space between us. Rests his palm on my wrist. "I know this isn't what you want, Jasmine. It's not an ideal circumstance for me either."

That should make things clearer, but it doesn't. Why would he ask me to marry him—pay me an outrageous sum to marry him—if it's not what he wants?

I stare into his eyes, trying to find his meaning, but they're still so deep and impenetrable.

How can they be such a clear blue when his intention is so murky?

God, his eyes are gorgeous. I want to get lost in them. To watch them fill with joy, pleasure, demand.

You're going to beg for my cock.

I swallow hard. "You're going to fix our awkward circumstance with tea?"

"I know I can't fill *all* your needs. But you are going to be my wife. I am going to take care of you."

"Tea isn't true love."

"Not what Mom would say."

My heart aches for him. And for myself. We both know what it's like, losing a mother young, struggling to pick up the pieces. "What would Olivia say?" I knew his mom for a while. She was an amazing woman. Even when she was ill, she was full of life. An artist who saw the good in everything.

"Jasmine?" His voice softens as he runs his thumb over my forearm.

The touch is comforting. Too comforting. And too familiar. He's a different person now.

He's not the boy I loved. And I'm not the girl he loved either.

That girl had big ambitions. She had dreams. Now, my biggest dream is for Dad to survive.

I'm not sure I can have that. But I can have him walk me down the aisle. That's something.

A lot even.

"What would Olivia say?" I let my hand fall to my side.

He watches our touch break, but he doesn't mention it. "Tea is sunshine in a cup."

I can't help but smile.

"No matter how awful or wonderful your day, it will get a little better with a cup of tea."

I nod.

"Now, don't frown," he says, still in his mom's voice. "You'll get wrinkles."

A laugh falls off my lips. I can remember her saying that to him. It was always half teasing. "She was right."

"I don't see any lines."

Is it that obvious my life is more frowns than smiles? "About the tea. It does make every day better."

"Allow me." He motions to the table.

I sit next to the tray of espresso. He nods a *thank you*, finishes the last sip of his coffee, takes the tray with him to another room. The kitchen, I guess.

I stay busy looking around the room. The walls are new, a freshly painted ecru. Covered in modern paintings. I recognize one from his house in the Bay. His mother's work.

All of these are his mother's. Abstract shapes in bold colors. Somehow, she tells a story or creates an emotion with only a teal triangle and a mint circle.

How is that possible?

Visual art isn't my expertise. I try to learn more, to understand brush strokes and styles, but it doesn't come naturally.

My parents always pushed me toward math and science. They wanted better for me than a career as a seamstress or a restaurant owner. I never did understand why that was such a terrible fate. Aunt Mai works long hours, but she loves her restaurant. And it's hers. She's always the one in charge.

But I didn't question them. Like a good Vietnamese daughter, I aced every class. Science was hard for me. Math too—though Shep helped. English though… that came naturally.

My parents praised my skill with language. I didn't seem like a first-generation girl. I spoke with the sort of vocabulary of a normal American girl. No, an intellectual, well-educated American girl.

I never asked if I could pursue a career in acting or writing. I knew it was out of the question.

Yes, I convinced them the school play was a good idea —it looked great on college applications and it helped with my fluency—but I knew it came second. After AP Chemistry and Algebra Two.

Now… I use my math skills every day. And my English ones. The acting comes in handy too. I know how to fake a smile.

For a while, I let myself believe it was possible. That I could participate in community productions once my career in statistics settled down. That I could write in my spare time. Or, at the very least, stay busy watching every play in town. The Bay doesn't have the best theater scene, but it is flush with avant-garde stuff. One-man shows. Burlesque. Drag.

Now…

I don't know what to think, honestly. Mr. Billings is an ass for firing me, but I'm sure every other executive in the industry will make the same decision.

If I want work, I need to move in a different direction.

Shep is providing me a place to live. He's paying for my father's care. That covers all my necessities. I don't need a job. But the idea of not working?

It's wrong to my very core.

My entire life, I've worked. I've studied. I've tried to achieve.

Am I supposed to spend the next year lying on his fancy leather couch, sipping oolong and eating cookies?

I'm sure it will be nice for a few days. A few weeks even. Then what?

I can't even imagine how I'd fill my days. The idea of free time is too foreign.

Time to relax, to focus on myself without Dad's treatment hanging over my head—

What would that feel like?

I don't know. I really don't.

The sound of footsteps calls my attention.

Shepard moves into the main room holding an antique silver tray. It's shiny, freshly polished. Real silver probably.

He sets it on the table. Removes a clean white teapot and two matching mugs. Then a small plate of scones and raspberry jam.

"Key tells me the flavor profiles are complementary." He motions to the thick red jam. "Something about the complexity of this blend of oolong and the mix of tart and sweet." Vulnerability bleeds into his voice.

"Key?"

"My chef. You could call her the household manager."

"Your staff is called Lock and Key?"

"They find it amusing." He pushes the plate toward me.

It matters to him, whether or not I accept his offer of tea and pastry. It matters to him, whether or not I like it. "Thank you." My stomach growls as I study the scones. They're dotted with little pieces of fruit. More berries.

He pulls out my chair.

I rest against the leather couch. I should sit. Accept his gift. It looks delicious and I'm starving. Honestly, all that talk of Ikea inspired a strong craving for lingonberry jam.

I'm sure the idea would horrify Shep as much as it horrifies Lock. I suppose it would horrify plenty of normal people.

Ikea doesn't exactly have a reputation for delicious food. More amazingly cheap.

Shep normal. It's a funny thought.

How long has it been since the term fit him?

"Jasmine?" He lifts the pot and pours amber liquid into one cup. Then another.

Damn, it smells good. Still, my legs stay pressed against the leather couch. I can't give in yet. I just can't.

Then his tone shifts to that low, deep one. "Sit," he commands.

My legs move on their own. Before I know it, I'm in the chair, my hands folded in my lap, my thighs shaking. *Say something like that again. Right now. Please. Only make it much, much dirtier.*

My hands steady as I pick up my mug. This is tea and scones. Nothing more. It doesn't mean I appreciate him trying to buy me.

"Thank you." I take a long sip of the oolong. It's good. Floral and sweet. A tiny bit astringent.

"You're welcome." His eyes fix on mine. "It's not perfect."

"It's fine."

"So, it's not perfect."

"A little over-steeped." I swallow another sip. The astringent note is more noticeable the second time. Tea is one of my few breaks. Ten minutes of time that's all mine. Ten minutes to brew a delicious beverage, soak in its warmth, let the comfort fill my belly.

"Next time, I'll lower the temperature."

"It could be the brew time."

He nods a *yes*. Holds up the plate of scones *would you like one?*

I'm tempted to say no, to see if he'll offer one anyway, but my body answers for me. My stomach growls.

He half-smiles as he places a scone on my plate.

"Thank you." I use my assistant voice.

He frowns but he says nothing about it. Just watches me cut my scone and cover it in raspberry jelly.

Mmm. It is perfect with the tea. The sweetness of the jam and the richness of the scone bring out the notes of honey in the tea. I let out a groan as I swallow.

"Good?"

"Yes, thank you."

His frown deepens. "Don't do that."

"Do what?"

"Use that voice."

"Which voice is that?" I stay as even as possible.

"That one. Like you're an assistant dealing with a difficult boss."

"How would you describe this arrangement?"

He frowns.

"I'm here. If you want me to be happy about it—"

"If you don't want to be here, your room is that way." He motions to the hallway, as if his offer is some kind of generosity.

"Is that supposed to win my favor?"

"No." He takes a long sip of tea. Rests his hand on the table. "I only mean that you aren't required to sit here with me."

"What if I'd like to sit here on my own?"

"You can ask me to leave."

"Really?"

"Yes." His voice shifts from an even tone to a shaky one. "Though I would prefer if you didn't."

"Oh?"

"I enjoy your company."

The surprise registers in my stomach. That's it? He enjoys my company? I don't expect this kind of sincerity from Shep. "Oh."

"I guess I don't have to ask if that's news." His eyes drift to my lips. He watches as I take another sip of my tea. "I know you don't think well of me."

"Yes." That's one way to put it.

"I won't ask you to forgive me."

"I won't." Maybe if he apologized. If *he* got on his knees and begged. Dad says forgiveness is good for the soul. That holding onto resentment, frustration, anger only hurts the person who's angry. But Dad never dealt with Shepard Marlowe.

He nods *I know*. "I won't try to erase the past. But I will ask you to give this a chance."

"You buying my time?"

"Yes. I'm going to try to make it as comfortable for you as possible."

"You won't even tell me why."

His gaze shifts to the window to our right. The bright afternoon light. The sun shining on the Hudson. "I wish things were different, but they aren't. Now. We need to talk about tonight."

"Tonight?"

"Your father. We're visiting the hospital in"—he checks his watch—"an hour and a half."

I swallow hard.

"What are we going to say to him? How are we going to convince him this is real?"

Chapter Nine

SHEPARD

Her dark eyes fill with surprise. She holds my gaze for a moment, then she looks down at her tea. Stares into the liquid like it has all the answers to the universe.

"I understand it's uncomfortable." I take another sip. Let the drink warm my lips and throat. It's not the same as bourbon, but with her here, it's comforting in a different way.

This is Jasmine. A quiet afternoon with a fresh pot of tea and heartfelt conversation. We spent a million lazy Sundays like this.

Sundays were easy. My mother and stepfather went into the city for brunch and gallery showings. It was the only day I could relax. The only day that was easy.

And now I'm thinking about that bastard. Because she's here. Because all those bright memories of her are surrounded by an ocean of darkness.

It's not too late to call this off. Pay her the money I've promised and send her on her way.

My stomach twists.

My heart refuses. I'm not sure how that's possible—since it's been MIA for years—but it is.

"I am sorry. About your father." That weight on my chest grows. It was awful, watching my mother fall ill. Watching her lose her spark. By the time she died, she was so frail she could barely hold her fork. She could barely smile.

If she'd known the truth—

I'm glad she died believing someone would take care of me. I'm glad she died happy. If I can offer Jasmine the same comfort—

She doesn't want to hear it. She doesn't want to face the possibility of her father dying.

I understand that.

I don't want her to experience that pain. If there was anything I could do, I'd do it. But there's not. This is out of my hands.

"Thank you." Her voice drips with hurt. Her expression stays calm. All that emotion, whirling beneath the surface.

Her poker face is perfect. It's hard to believe.

Yes, she was a talented actress when we were in school. Especially for her age. But she wore everything all over her face. In theater and in life.

I guess things have changed.

"I don't need to tell you how scary it is." She takes another sip. Lets out a low sigh. "And how little time there is to consider that."

"Is he doing well?" I pretend as if I don't have all that information. Residents are underpaid, especially considering the cost of living. It shouldn't have been so easy to find a source, but it was.

"As well as he could. But…" She breaks off a piece of her scone. Places it on her tongue. For a moment, her eyes close and her features relax. Then she swallows and that pain is there. "He always liked you."

"He liked my parents' success."

"Yes, but that's the same thing. Good family, good manners, good future. All the traits necessary in a husband."

"Good father?"

Her eyes fill with surprise. "We never talked about that."

"We were young."

"I do wish things were different… I wish he could meet his grandchild."

My cock whines. Some primal urge to pass on my DNA. But the shit in my head—I can't go there. "Is that what you want?"

Her tension eases enough for her to shoot me a *seriously* look. "Pregnancy and child-rearing aren't included in our arrangement."

"No, those are perks."

She half-smiles. "I don't think you're getting past my IUD." Her cheeks flush. "I mean. We're not going to have sex. So it's a moot point."

"We'll see."

She clears her throat. "We're not."

"I am safe."

"You're what—"

"I don't have any STDS—"

"That's not…" She clears her throat. "We're not."

"Have you been tested?"

"Yes. And I'm safe. But that doesn't matter." Her blush deepens.

"Okay. We won't. But if we did… we wouldn't have to use a condom."

Her blush spreads to her chest. "I suppose that's true."

"Unless you feel differently."

"No. I prefer… without. But it doesn't matter. We're not." She clears her throat again. "It won't happen."

She takes another bite of her scone. Then another. She chews and swallows a little too fast. Coughs.

She's nervous. She's not convincing herself.

She won't. She can't. There are certain things in life we can't deny. Her desire for me is one of them.

I break off a piece of pastry. It tastes of flour, butter, fresh fruit. Homemade. Expensive. But then everything I eat tastes expensive and homemade. Key makes sure of that.

I'm pretty sure Lock hired her solely because her name was Key. He loves the pun.

I can't complain. She's a talented chef. She keeps the house spic and span. Stays during work hours. Leaves at all other times. Rarely offers explanation as to her where-abouts or inquires about mine.

She understands discretion.

Everyone I hire understands discretion. It's essential.

For a moment, I let my eyes close. I try to focus on the flaky scone. But it's no use. It doesn't interest me.

Food has never interested me. There's nothing appealing about different cuisines or flavors. Food is like clothing. A need I fill so I can move onto other things.

Once upon a time, I appreciated pairing wine and pasta, bourbon and steak, tequila and tacos.

With water, coffee, or tea? It's all the same.

Only, right now, watching Jasmine attempt to hide her desire behind her pastry—

I do appreciate it. The tart jam, the sweet tea, the flaky pastry. Something changes when I watch her. When I see her eyes fill with delight and hear that moan roll off her lips.

It's easier to experience little pleasures.

She finishes her last bite. Then her last sip of tea. She stares at the empty cup, willing it to fill.

Her eyes flit to mine. Her expression gets sheepish.

"I can make more," I offer.

"No." She pushes her cup forward. Rests her hands in her lap. "We're leaving soon. Or do you have a helicopter that will help us beat rush hour traffic?"

"What if I did?"

"Will they let you use the heliport at the hospital?"

"If I offer a big enough donation."

She just barely laughs. "They probably would." She looks around the apartment. "Where would you keep a helicopter?"

"At a heliport."

"Do you have one in the basement?"

"Why would a helicopter be in the basement?"

"Some secret Batcave thing?"

I can't help but laugh. "No basement helicopter. But I can have one brought to the helipad on thirtieth street."

She looks out the window, trying to place the location. It's only twenty-something blocks south, but it's not visible. We're facing west. From this angle, it's hard to see anything except the Hudson and New Jersey beyond it.

"You'll need to move closer to the window to see it."

"You won't really."

I wasn't planning on it, but she's right—"It's the fastest way."

"Will the hospital really…" She looks at me, trying to figure out if I'm serious or not. "You're kidding?"

I'm not sure. It's been a long time since I've joked with anyone. I try out a shrug.

She raises a brow, not really buying it. "The subway will be crowded in an hour."

This time, I arch a brow.

"What? Too rich for the subway?"

"If I am?"

"It takes longer to sit in traffic."

"Yes, but in the back of a limo, there's plenty to do." I let my voice drop.

She pretends she doesn't understand my implication, but she still blushes. "I'll consider that."

"Or the helicopter."

"Or the helicopter." Her eyes go to the pot.

"I'll make more."

"No… I will."

That's a good idea. She'll be more comfortable fixing tea. And she—

Fuck, I don't know how I convinced her to love me the first time. That was a million years ago, before all this baggage between us.

How am I supposed to do it now that she hates me?

I stand. Offer my hand. When she takes it, I lead her into the kitchen.

Her eyes go wide as she takes in the expansive room.

It's enormous by New York standards, with a style rare in this part of town. Most new buildings have modern, utilitarian kitchens, all stainless steel and high-pressure appliances.

This kitchen is something Mom would have loved. Black and white tile, wide windows, pots and pans hanging over the ceramic sink.

Jasmine moves straight to the electric kettle. She fills it with water and sets the temperature to one hundred ninety degrees. Then she looks around the counter. Looks for something. "Don't tell me you threw out the leaves."

"They're finished."

She shakes her head. "They're better on the second

steeping." Her gaze shifts to the cabinets. "Sometimes a third or fourth. With some green teas, a fifth or even a sixth. If you're using a pot this small. That's the Chinese way of brewing tea. Less water, more steepings."

I nod as if I appreciate the nuance.

"The leaves unfurl as they steep. They have different flavors every time."

I point to the one on the right.

She rises to her tiptoes to open it. Reaches for a tin of tea. Doesn't quite find it.

"Here." I place my body behind hers. For a moment, I feel her against me, feel all her warmth and softness. Then she shifts out of the way so I can grab the tin.

My hand brushes hers as I offer it to her.

Her chest flushes. She stammers something then stays busy scooping tea into the ceramic pot. "This is really meant for black tea."

"Is it?"

She nods. "You need a gaiwan, ideally. Or a small ceramic pot, at the very least. So you can go through multiple infusions more easily."

I can understand the numbers in a twenty-billion-dollar deal. But, right now, I have no idea what she's saying.

She stares back at me. "You know what… I have an idea, actually."

"Do you?"

"My dad has a set in his hospital room. Ask him to explain it. He'll love that." Her lips curl into the world's tiniest smile. "He'll get so caught up that he won't ask too many questions about why I haven't mentioned you."

"Will he?"

"Ask questions?" The kettle interrupts her. She doesn't wait for a response. She continues as she fills the pot with hot water. "Of course. I see him a few times a week. More if I can."

"Do you tell him about your life?"

"There isn't much to tell."

"No rich men vying for your attention?" I try to say it casually, but I don't get all the way there. I hate the idea of her with someone else. Anyone else.

My brother—

They were always friendly when we were kids. He was a cool, older boy. I always worried about women noticing him.

Jasmine didn't see him as more than a friend. But when he moved to New York, he offered her a job. They worked together for a year. They had every opportunity.

He says nothing happened. He says he had no interest. But he says a lot of things.

I haven't trusted him in a long time.

"Some." Her eyes flit to me. She notices my jealousy. Smiles at it. "Nothing like the harem you've acquired."

"I don't have a harem."

"Just a lot of available women jumping into your bed."

"And you've been celibate all this time?"

She sets the kettle down. Turns her body to face mine. Studies my expression like this is the last hand of poker in a high-stakes tournament. "No."

My blood pumps faster. It's ridiculous. It's been six years. Of course, she's been with someone else. But hearing it on her lips is different.

"There were a few men."

I swallow hard.

"Some I barely remember. One who… well, I'm sure any stories I have pale in comparison to yours." She clears her throat. "Your reputation precedes you."

"Does it?"

"Were you always… curious?" She tries to keep her voice casual, but her body betrays her interest. Her chest heaves with her inhale. Her fingers curl into the tile counter top. Her gaze shifts over my lips, shoulders, hands, cock.

"Not always." My eyes flit over her body. It's already doing something to me, taking in her interest. It's already driving me out of my mind. "It was still new then. I didn't quite realize it."

"Oh." She turns to her tea to hide her blush. "This should be done."

"It isn't the only way I play." I move a little closer. So I can lower my voice. "But it is my preference. If you're curious…"

"We're not having sex, remember?"

"I remember what you said."

She pours tea into two tiny ceramic mugs. They're a shade of copper that matches the pot. And they're small. Barely two shots worth. "I don't think we're going to tell my father that." Her hand brushes mine as she hands me a cup. "Though it would distract him from the other questions."

"He knows about the other men?"

"Well…" She takes a small sip. "Not anyone recent. I've been focusing on easier things. Mostly Dan Brown." She lets out an easy laugh. "I don't understand how he reads those books over and over again, but he does. He adores them."

Dan Brown's popularity is somewhere on the very long list of things I don't understand.

It would be easier to make a short list of things I do understand.

Negotiations. The upsides of alcohol. How to make Jasmine come.

"I guess… we don't have to tell a complete lie," she says. "We could say we got back in touch. Had a—"

"Whirlwind romance?"

"Does a helicopter count as a whirlwind?"

I can't help but laugh. I forget how funny she is.

I sip my tea. This one is better. Sweeter. And knowing she fixed it—that warms me more than anything.

"We can tell the truth," I say. "I made you an offer you couldn't refuse."

She raises a brow *really*.

"For a date."

"Our meeting at your office was a date?"

"We had drinks."

She laughs *sure*. "Why not?"

"I made you an offer you couldn't refuse. Then one thing led to another. And I knew I had to have you. I knew I had to ask for your hand."

She considers it for a moment. Nods *okay*. "How did you do it?"

"Like this." I set my mug down. Pull the jewelry box from my pocket.

Her eyes go wide as I pop it open. "Shep, that's huge."

"You don't like it?"

She stares at the ring. It's perfect for her. An antique emerald cut stone between two smaller ones.

They call it a forever ring. One for the past, one for the present, one for the future.

The sentimentality is another item for the long list of things I don't understand.

But it does move her.

She doesn't want to melt over the ring. She doesn't want to stare with wide-eyed wonder. She doesn't want to sigh as I slide it on her finger.

But she does.

Then she looks at me like she really does want to marry me. And for one sweet moment, I remember how things used to be. I'm there on an easy Sunday afternoon, holding her on the couch, whispering dirty promises in her ear.

Before that bastard ruined everything.

He's not ruining this.

I take in her smile until realization spreads over her face. Then I take her hand. Offer my own smile. "Ready to meet the world as a newly engaged couple?"

"Are you?"

No. But this is going to have to be enough.

Chapter Ten

JASMINE

H oly shit. He's not kidding.

Lock drops us at the waterfront park. Right as a helicopter descends.

The gust blows my hair, my coat, my dress. It's like something out of a movie. The couple rushing to get out of town.

Shepard looks to me with a cocky smile. He holds out his hand. Motions *after you*.

For a moment, I see the boy I fell in love with so many years ago. A confident boy with a lust for life as big as his ego. The wonder and charm that defined him.

They didn't seem boyish at the time—I was barely fourteen—but they do now.

Is that part of him still there? It's hard to imagine Shepard looking at anything with wide-eyed wonder. But it's there in his gorgeous blue eyes.

He's looking at me like I'm the most interesting things in the universe. Like I'm an uncharted island he wants to explore.

My heart races as I take his hand and follow him to the helicopter.

The pilot helps me up the stairs. Into the tiny cockpit.

Shepard places headphones over my ears. At once, the overwhelming whir of the blades quiets.

The pilot's voice comes through the speakers. A deep voice with a British accent. "You must be Jasmine." He turns enough to shake my hand. "I'm Ian. A"—he winks at Shepard—"friend of your fiancé's. Congratulations by the way."

Shepard returns a knowing look.

"Now, buckle up, kids. You don't want to die before your honeymoon." His smile lights up his dark eyes. They're gorgeous eyes.

He's a tall guy. Broad and muscular. Dark skin. Short hair. Winning smile.

I try to close my eyes and imagine him over me, under me, behind me.

It's no good. My head still goes to Shepard.

Then the helicopter moves and my thoughts disappear. It's actually…

Woah.

I reach for something steady. Get Shep's hand.

My eyes go to his.

His baby blues are still full of wonder. But they're comforting too. His touch is comforting.

I squeeze his hand. He squeezes back a little harder. Just hard enough I know he's there. Just hard enough I feel safe.

I hate that I feel safe from his touch, but I do.

The helicopter rises slowly. Then we're moving forward. Over the city.

It's a different view. The tops of skyscrapers. Rooftop gardens. People drinking at a balcony bar.

It's not like a plane. We aren't that high up. People aren't ants. Cars aren't the size of toys. But they're still far away. Smaller. Like they don't matter. Like we're so far above it all, none of it matters.

Shepard points to our right.

It's beautiful. The sun, sinking into the horizon, streaking the sky orange, casting its glow over the Hudson.

The pilot says a few things about the city and the view. But I don't catch any of them. Only the orange glow of sunset reflecting off Shep's smile.

It's such a beautiful smile. I miss it. I miss him. The person I was with him.

But that was another lifetime ago.

And this—

The helicopter jerks forward. Shep squeezes a little tighter. The pilot says something about it being normal. All clear. It's just a bumpy ride.

Don't think about the helicopter crash in that *Jurassic Park* movie. Which one was it? And when did I find time to watch it?

Dad wanted to see it. Something about the dinosaurs. And the views of Hawaii. And wouldn't it be great to live there one day, on an island where our biggest concern is the best waves?

Or maybe that was me. I'm not sure. Neither one of us knows how to surf. We barely ever see the beach. Once or twice a summer, if his health allows. Lately—

Maybe I can take him out to Montauk on the LIRR. The coast is beautiful.

Or maybe we can fly there in a fucking helicopter.

My heart thuds against my chest. We're so far up. It feels so dangerous.

I should be terrified. But I'm not. The thrill is exhilarating.

New.

When was the last time I felt this kind of excitement? I'm not sure. I'm not sure what I'm trying to do here or what I'm going to tell my father.

I'm only sure of one thing, I want more of this feeling. And Shep is the only one who can give it to me.

Chapter Eleven

JASMINE

Sure enough, we land on the roof of the hospital.

Ian bids us farewell. Helps an EMT climb into the helicopter. Apparently, he's a colleague of Shepard's who does rescue missions in his spare time.

Another rich man with the world at his fingertips.

I suppose I shouldn't judge. The guy is using his free time to volunteer. Sure, his volunteer method requires all sorts of money. But he's still offering his spare time.

That's more than I can say.

Once upon a time, I dreamed of volunteering at community theater productions. Or even teaching high school students theater. I've never had time. Or knowledge.

It's been forever since I've read a play, much less practiced acting.

How would I teach a thirteen-year-old the basics when I barely know them myself?

I guess this is my chance. I'm unemployable in the world of venture capital. Wherever I work next, it's going to take a while to find a new gig. To find an industry where my status as the future Mrs. Shepard Marlowe doesn't hurt me.

Or maybe I should live more like Amanda. Fall in love with the life of luxury. Spend my days fixing tea and taking private acting classes. Spend my nights attending every play in the city. And, while I'm at it, why not fly to London once a month to take in some theater in the West End?

Shep can find a helicopter like *that*. A first-class ticket to London is nothing. Probably not enough for him. He probably demands a private jet.

It's ridiculous. But then it's more ridiculous to deny his wealth.

If Dad knew I was rejecting Shep's generosity, he'd shake his head. *We have limited resources in life, Jasmine. You need to take advantage of them when you have a chance.*

It's smart. Smarter than letting my pride rule my decisions. I'm not too good for Shepard's money. I've got the paperwork to prove it.

And now…

I suck in a deep breath. Press my lips into my best smile.

It's not good. Too customer service. Too *I will not allow you to ruffle me*.

This is my father. I don't want to lie to him.

I may not be happy about my current circumstance, but I'm happy Shep paid for Dad's treatment. That's something. That's huge.

I try to focus on the weight no longer on my shoulders. It's bigger than that. A noose no longer around my neck.

An ability to breathe again.

I take Shep's hand and follow him down the hallway. All the way to Dad's room in the corner. "I'll go first. Explain the surprise."

Shepard nods *sure*.

I take a deep breath. Exhale all the tension in my shoulders. Dad's treatment is covered. That's what matters. That's the only thing that matters. I turn the handle. "Hey."

Dad lights up as I step into the room. "Jasmine. You're early today."

"You don't want to see me?"

"Mariah promised she'd bring me tea from that shop down the street." He motions to the tin in the corner, next to Mom's statue. "I'm out of Oolong." He smiles that same warm smile. A happy memory. He's so positive, even after everything. "She's not as pretty as your mother, but she's a looker."

"Isn't she wearing a wedding ring?"

"I still have a chance."

A laugh spills from my lips. "You are her type." I motion to the stack of historical fiction, all secondhand, courtesy of Mariah's husband. Because we can't afford new books.

Though now… I can buy my dad a new book. One of those hardcovers that goes for some ridiculous twenty-dollar-plus price. I can buy an over-priced tea from the bookstore while I'm there.

I can probably buy the café.

At the very least, I can book an expensive afternoon tea for two at some hotel that charges four-figures a night.

My chest warms at the thought. This is good news. For him. For us. Maybe not for me. But that's okay. It's a sacrifice I'm willing to make.

"I have something to tell you," I say.

"You've finally finished *The Da Vinci Code*?" He smiles. "Jasmine, I'm so proud of you. Finally seeing the light."

"No." My laugh is easy. I pull a chair next to his bed. Take a seat. "I'm still struggling."

He shakes his head. "One day, you'll see the brilliance."

"One day." I have time now. I can read anything. Everything. I can build a library of historical fiction. Or especially smutty romance. Or literary classics. Or every play in the English language. "I've been busy."

He waves his hand *psh*. "You're always busy. You work too much."

"Actually." I bite my lip. Try to find the best way to phrase this. One with the fewest lies. "I've been spending my time on other things."

His interest piques.

"An old friend." I motion to the door. Raise my voice so he can hear outside. "Come in."

Shepard opens the door and steps inside. "Mr. Lee, it's nice to see you again." He moves close enough to the hospital bed to shake Dad's hand.

Dad looks at me funny, but he still shakes. "You too, Shepard." He turns his attention to Shep. "I haven't heard about you in quite some time. And what I did hear wasn't the most complimentary."

"Yes." Shepard nods. His voice gets soft. Sheepish even. "Your daughter and I didn't part on the best terms. That was my fault. I didn't realize she was willing to go to such great lengths for the people she loved."

Dad raises a brow. *What is he talking about?*

There's no easy way to say it. And I'm not about to open up the whole *Shepard is an alcoholic* conversation.

Dad is old-fashioned about these things. He doesn't buy into the idea of addiction and sobriety. If you drink too much, you learn some responsibility and drink less. End of story.

Rehab and addiction are problems for spoiled white kids.

Which…

Sure, that's true a lot of the time. But addiction doesn't discriminate. We know plenty of people who'd benefit from a twelve-step program. And that whole hardworking immigrant, the only problems that matter are the practical ones thing—

It can be good, in certain ways. It keeps us from taking ourselves too seriously. But it denies our emotions too. Grief isn't as big a problem as poverty.

And the tools for dealing with it?

We don't talk about therapy or medication or even acupuncture. We don't talk about it, period.

I've held this grief on my own for such a long time. I've kept things together for such a long time. I don't mind it, exactly, but I am tired.

I'm tired of pretending there isn't a hole in my heart.

"Are you okay, sweetie?" Dad rests his hand on mine. "Did you skip dinner again?"

"It's early." Earlier than I usually visit, at least.

He shakes his head. Motions to Shepard. "Are you going to talk some sense into my daughter? She's never eating enough. She's getting too thin."

Shep smiles. "She looks beautiful."

"But thin?"

Shep's eyes flit over my body. It's quick. Too quick for Dad to notice. But it screams of him picturing me naked.

"I'll make sure she eats something after this." He smiles at Dad. "She doesn't always take care of herself."

Dad nods *she doesn't*. "She has the tea covered though."

"Actually, I was thinking." I clear my throat. "Shep is terrible with tea. He threw out the Gaba Oolong after the first steep."

Dad shakes his head *so horrible*.

"I was thinking you could show him how it's done. Give him a little lesson, maybe," I say. "Trust me. He needs it."

Shepard laughs. He's seamlessly playing the part of doting boyfriend. Or maybe that's how he feels. Maybe he misses this kind of familial exchange.

He only has his stepfather now, and last I heard, they aren't in touch. Besides, it's hard to imagine the two of them having this sort of easy conversation.

"You haven't said why you've brought your ex-boyfriend to visit me," Dad says. "I may be a sick, old man, but I'm not a fool. I can't imagine he's here just because." He turns to me, searching my expression for an explanation. "It's been a long time."

"Yes," I say.

"But he has been in New York awhile now," Dad says.

I do nothing to hide my surprise.

"Sweetie, like I said, I'm not a fool. I read the news," Dad says. "And Nick still visits sometimes."

Shep's smile disappears. He's still angry with his brother. For the whole *go to rehab or you're out of the company* thing? Or because he believes I fucked Nick?

I should explain *no, I didn't, I'd never*. I should erase those fears. But there's something inside me that refuses. Something that wants his jealousy.

I spent the last year hearing rumors about him tying up models. He can spend a few weeks wondering if his brother fucked me senseless.

Though… From what I hear, Nick has a similar taste for domination. He tried to keep things quiet when he was sleeping with an intern at Odyssey. But he never was as discrete as he thought.

Nick and Lizzy are together now. They're happy. Engaged even. We talk every so often. Sometimes, the three of us have dinner. I love them like family. But it's hard to see them. To see him, at least. He reminds me of Shep. He reminds me of everything I've lost.

Now… "I didn't know Nick visited. That's sweet of him." I fold my right hand over my left. Dad still hasn't noticed my ring. Or maybe he just hasn't said anything. He's usually aware of these things. "When did you last see him?"

"He didn't mention anything about Shepard." Dad raises a brow. "Because he didn't know?"

"We've been keeping this to ourselves," Shepard says. He sells it with a big smile. He's the picture of a happy boyfriend. "I hate to admit it, but I'm greedy. I've been taking advantage of your daughter's time."

"He is greedy." I can agree there.

Shep shoots me a knowing look. His smile shifts to something real. Teasing even. "I hate to do this so awkwardly, but I'd like to make a request."

"The tea?" Dad raises a brow. "I can teach you, but there are some things you learn here." He presses his hand to his heart. "You learn how to feel it. You learn through repetition. Like playing an instrument. It's more than following the scales. It's letting them sink into your bones."

Shep just smiles. "I see where Jasmine gets it."

"Come here." Dad sits up straight. He motions to the electric kettle in the corner. Smuggled in. Not at all regulation. Only allowed because he fixes Mariah green tea on her breaks.

Shit, maybe he does have a chance. Maybe Mariah and her husband are a modern couple with some kind of open arrangement. Or maybe they're like me and Shep. Married for some other purpose.

Well, what we'll be like. And, oh my God, I'm not thinking about my father sleeping with a married woman in an open relationship. Yes, I want him to be happy. I want him to move on. But I don't want to hear about it.

Besides, he deserves better than other man status.

I mean—

Ahem.

I try to tune into the room as Dad walks Shepard through the steps to fixing oolong.

Shep listens closely. He nods along, even as Dad steers into asides about the mountains in China or Mom sipping a cup before dinner, every single day. He studies the way Dad scoops the tea, holds the kettle, pours.

They finish the first steeping. Pass a cup to me.

I hold it up. "Cheers." My glass taps Shep's. Then my father's.

Dad's eyes stay on me. He knows something is happening. Knows something is different.

But maybe he'll believe this story. It's easier to convince someone of something they want to believe. And he wants me to be happy. He wants to know someone is there to take care of me.

He wants to walk me down the aisle and meet his grandchildren. He wants to believe that's possible.

I swallow a sip of my tea. "Good." It is good. Perfectly steeped. Strong but not astringent. Shep is a fast learner. And Dad is happy teaching.

"Tell me about multiple steepings," Shep says. "Your daughter was quite poetic about it."

"I get that from him." I take another sip. Let it warm my chest. Let myself believe this ruse.

"Yes, she does." Dad smiles. "Most teas can take multiple steepings. Some are meant for it. The typical way of preparing tea, here"—he points to the gaiwan, a small cup with a lid. Then he takes off the lid—"we use more tea and less water. So we can go through more steepings. Because each time we add water to the tea, the leaves open a little more." He motions to the unfurling leaves.

Shepard nods with understanding.

"They offer a different flavor. See." He uses the lid to strain the tea into a small glass. Offers the glass to Shep.

Shep takes a long sip. "Sweeter."

"And now, the leaves are even more open, so we'll taste even more of the flavor. It takes patience and love to coax every note of flavor from the tea, but it's worth the effort." Dad looks to me. He's saying something. Talking about more than tea.

But I'm not getting his meaning. "It is." I finish my cup. Offer it to him, so he can strain another for me.

Shep takes a long sip. He sets his cup down. "My mother always said tea is sunshine in a mug."

"Olivia was a wonderful woman. I'm sorry you lost her," Dad says.

"Thank you." Shep nods. For a second, his facade breaks. Sadness creeps into his eyes. His lip corners turn down. Then he forces a smile. "She said it was like love. If you're patient and you treat someone well, they'll give you all this happiness. If you don't give them what they need, they'll be bitter or sour."

Dad nods *true*.

"That's why I'm here, Mr. Lee. I hate to cut to the chase, but I have to." Shep turns to me and holds out his hand. "I know I should have asked first, but I'm asking now." He motions for me to place my hand in his.

I do.

Dad notices the light bouncing off the massive rock.

"I'd like your daughter's hand in marriage," Shep says. "I'd like your blessing. Will you allow me to marry Jasmine?"

Chapter Twelve

JASMINE

"**L**et me talk to my daughter alone." Dad turns to me with a knowing expression.

It's funny. I've spent so much time trying to protect him. Trying to hide the ugly truth. I've almost forgotten what it feels like to have someone trying to protect me.

"Of course." Shepard squeezes my hand. He pulls me a tiny bit closer. Then he leans in. Presses his lips to mine.

My body responds immediately. Electricity courses through my veins. Collects between my legs. A blinking neon sign flashes *must have Shepard*.

It's bright enough it belongs in Times Square.

It's loud enough it would actually get attention in Times Square.

Of course, Shepard could afford that kind of thing. What does it run, a billboard asking for marriage, announcing love, telling the world *she's mine*?

I pull back with a sigh. Focus on the taste of oolong. It's no good. I can taste him. And I want more. My entire body is screaming *more, more, more*.

My cheeks flush. My chest too. I brush my hair behind my ear. Offer my best smile. This is supposed to look real. So Dad doesn't ask questions.

"I'll find something to eat," Shepard says.

"Take her somewhere nice after this," Dad says. "You can afford it."

I can't help but laugh. Shep does too. And Dad. It's easy. Like old times.

Shep nods *take your time* and lets himself out.

Dad motions for me to move closer. He turns the kettle to a hundred ninety degrees. Lifts the gaiwan's lid.

He focuses on fixing oolong, pouring the water, stirring the leaves, straining the tea, letting my anxiety build. The same thing he did when I was younger.

It worked so well. He always got me to confess. Not that I did a lot that needed confessing. I've always been a model daughter. I've always known what was expected of me. My parents didn't leave Vietnam so I could waste my potential.

"Dad…" I try my best assistant smile, but it's awful.

He sees through it immediately.

I used to act, didn't I? It was just high school, but it was something. I found a way to believe my words. I found my character's motivation.

I can do that now.

No assistant smile. No fakeness. Only the reality.

Shepard is making my life easier. I'm moving into an amazing apartment half a dozen blocks from the river.

Beautiful view. Plenty of tea. Lush leather couch.

And time. The one resource I haven't had in so long. The one resource that isn't renewable. The one resource I've been clinging to.

That's all I want, more time for Dad. This is my best chance. Even if treatment doesn't work, I have more time.

More time with him.

"I should have said something sooner," I say.

He doesn't reply. He just hands over a cup and motions *drink*.

I do. Better on the third steep. More guilt inducing too.

Is this something they teach in classes in Vietnam? Or is it a skill parents learn on the way to America? Maybe in Aunt Mai's restaurant. Or Dad's office. The temple where he practices. He never was all that religious until Mom died.

Ahem.

"I wanted to say something." I try to find the truth in my words. I wanted to tell him how bad the situation was. How many hours I was working. How far I was falling behind. But I didn't want to burden him. He did so much for me. Gave up an entire life. A long work week is nothing. "But I didn't want to worry you."

He makes that *mm-hmm* sound parents love.

"Things didn't end the best with the two of us. I know I never shared the details, but I could tell you didn't approve."

He does it again, but louder and lower.

"I wasn't sure if it was my decision. Or if you didn't approve of his behavior. I know you think I overreacted moving to New York, but that wasn't about Shep." That was only part of it. "I wanted to be here. To go to Columbia." To get away from all those reminders of Mom. To somehow fill the hole in my heart.

I swallow the words that rise up in my throat. I still can't talk about Mom. I can't face how much I miss her.

I turn to Dad. Try to place his expression.

It's pure parental *I'm waiting*.

I clear my throat.

He makes another *mm-hmm*. He stretches this one out, so it just barely hints of distaste.

"The truth is, the first time I saw him here, I knew. That I missed him. That I'd always love him. I tried to deny it. I tried to believe something else. I was too proud to admit it. It's not that I made a mistake. I was right to walk away. But things have changed. I need him."

Dad stares at me.

I go to sip my tea, but my cup is empty.

Dad takes it, fills it, hands it back.

I down it in one gulp. Shit, that's hot.

I try to wait for him to respond. For another *mm-hmm* even. But there's nothing.

When I can't take it anymore, I set my cup on the table, and look him in the eyes. "Are you going to say something?"

"Does he make you happy?"

"What?"

His voice softens. That paternal tone he used when I would hide under my bed, terrified of thunderstorms. "Does he make you happy?"

"Does Shep make me happy?" I repeat the question without thinking. It's absurd. When did Dad get all these American values? "What do you mean?"

"Jasmine, sweetheart, it's a simple question. Does he make you happy?"

But…

I…

He…

What?

Of all the questions he could ask, that was the last one I expected. I take a deep breath. Turn over the words. Does Shep make me happy?

He did once. Now? I barely know the man he's

become. I only have the last forty-eight hours. The strange offer. The limo ride. The meeting at his office. That throaty dare. *You're going to beg for my cock.*

My sex aches. So not the time. And not what Dad means. But that is something I miss. Something I need.

There have been other men. I've tried dating since Shep. There was one guy my sophomore year of college. An artist who saw the beauty in the world. He took me to museums and shows and made me feel like some kind of creative goddess, even when I was reading lines for a 101 class.

I thought I loved him.

Then Dad got sick and things got hard and he couldn't deal. Or maybe I pushed him away. I'm not sure anymore.

Even when things were good, when I thought I loved him—

There was always something missing. The sex was good. But only good.

I didn't shake the way I shake at Shep's voice.

That's not what Dad's asking. But it's the truest thing I have.

"He does." I let my head fill with thoughts of Shep's deep voice. His cocky smile. His inability to make tea.

"Are you sure?"

Maybe Shep hasn't made me happy yet. And, yes, I'm always going to resent this obligation. But maybe I can appreciate all the perks. Maybe I can focus on all the problems he's solved. It's not a conventional idea of happiness, but it's something. "I am."

"Then I'm happy for you."

———

After a short talk about the virtues of marriage,

commitment, and grandchildren (I should wait, but not too long), Dad calls Shepard to the room. Makes him promise to take care of me.

Shep's smile is so broad I almost believe it's real. He beams. Acts every part the doting boyfriend.

Then we leave the room and something changes. He slides his arm around my waist. Pulls me a little closer.

My heart thuds against my chest. His touch is comforting and that's terrifying.

I want his love already.

I have another year of this. A year I have to survive without falling for him.

He doesn't have love to give. He proved that six years ago.

I try to repeat the mantra as we drive home. It's a limo this time, not the helicopter, but it's still fast.

New York is beautiful at night. The illumination of the city kills the stars, but it softens the sky too. Turns it to a shade of blue that only exists here.

The skyline comes into view.

God, I do love this city. I know I shouldn't, as a native Californian. I should hate the snow and the humidity. I should complain about the lack of fresh air and the inferiority to San Francisco.

But I can't. I love New York. I love the hustle, the no-nonsense attitude, the endless possibilities.

I always have, but I haven't thought about it in so long. I've been so busy, so distracted, so overwhelmed.

Living this tiny life. My office in the Financial District. The subway to Dad's hospital room. Three more stops and one long walk to our apartment. Rinse. Repeat.

Now that I have time…

I still can't call this freedom. But I have to admit, I do have possibilities.

I let my mind wander to easier times. Tea at the Japanese Garden in San Francisco. A bike ride across the Golden Gate Bridge. Dinner in Japantown, at that over-priced Indian place.

Shep laughing at my *holy shit* reaction to a super spicy dosa. *I thought you could take any amount of heat.*

An acting class in high school. My theater teacher applauding my monologue. Marveling at the nuance I brought to the character.

We pull into the garage. Take the elevator to Shep's floor. The penthouse, though it's technically the top two floors. The highest is only accessible via the spiral staircase.

It really does feel like a modern castle.

Here, looking at the Hudson, I almost forget I'm in the most populated city in the country. I almost forget I have no choice in this.

Shepard hangs his trench coat on a rack by the door. It's the only hint to his San Francisco side. Or maybe I've watched *Vertigo* too many times.

Aren't trench coats from London? Plenty of people wear them here. In early spring, when it's cool and rainy, they fit the bill.

He flips a switch. The expensive chandelier illuminates.

Footsteps move in the kitchen. "Is that you, Mr. Marlowe? Is the future Mrs. Marlowe with you?" A woman's voice asks. It reminds me of Shep's. Strict. No nonsense.

"Yes, but I'm retiring for the evening." He nods a goodbye to me. "Key will take care of you."

Key will take care of me?

"Lock manages things outside the house. Key manages the house." He motions to the light coming from the kitchen. "She'll fix your dinner. Or, if you prefer, you can order something." He turns to Key as she moves in from the hallway. "On me, of course."

Key, a woman in her thirties with a tailored dress and a blond bun, smiles wryly. "Of course, Mr. Marlowe. I would expect you to take care of your fiancée." She turns to me. "Has Mr. Marlowe readied a credit card for you?"

"Not yet." He turns to me. "After we sign the papers tomorrow."

She raises a brow. It's not like Lock. He has a certain mischievous joy—the joy of a young Shep. She's more like a current Shep. Questioning his intentions, his competence, his right to breathe the same air she does. "Papers?"

"A prenuptial agreement." He waves away her objection. "I know how you feel about them."

"You don't like them?" I ask. It doesn't suit my image of her. I know we've just met, but she seems practical. Reasonable. A man of Shep's wealth would be a fool to skip a prenup.

"Some things aren't about money." She nods good night to Shep. "But it's Mr. Marlowe's choice. He pays me to cook, not to talk about his love life."

"It doesn't stop you," Shep teases her.

"I can't help it. You give me so much to discuss." There's the slightest hint of teasing in her voice.

He chuckles. "You and Lock…"

"Aalock"—she calls his full name—"and I have to keep ourselves entertained somehow."

"Entertained and losing money?" He raises a brow.

"We never bet money." Her smile is almost dirty. Then it's not. That normal *I'm ready for anything* assistant smile. "What would you like, Ms. Lee?"

"Jasmine. Please," I say. "Whatever is easiest."

"Nonsense, Ms… Jasmine. What's easiest is what you'd

like. If you're too tired to consider that, leave it to me. But if there is something you prefer, I'll make it happen."

"Some kind of grilled fish, maybe." Something Mom made that won't fill my stomach with pangs of nostalgia.

"Of course." She turns to Shep. "Are you sure you won't be joining us?"

"Send the food to my room." He looks to me, but he doesn't move closer. "I'll make an appointment for you. At my office. First thing tomorrow."

"No. Send it to my lawyer. I'll do it there." I press my lips together. He's already leaving.

What gives? He's been trying to talk me into adoring him all day. Now that I actually need a little comfort, he's leaving.

Maybe… if I ask… if I admit I'm terrified I'm going to wake up to the news my father is gone…

I try to find the words, but I can't. Maybe it's my pride. Maybe it's all the space between us. Maybe it's an inability to trust him after everything.

"Good night, Shep." I turn to Key.

She waves me to the dining table. Insists she'll bring tea. If I'd like to cook, fine, but she won't have any inter-ference.

So I sit and let her fix me a cup of ginger. It's good. Strong. Fresh ginger boiled long enough to extract every ounce of flavor.

The dinner she makes is fantastic. Almost as good as Mom's. Lacking only in that key ingredient. Love.

I guess I should get used to it. A million dollars buys me a year without love. It's not the worst fate in the world.

But, at the moment, in this big living room, all alone, with this secret on my chest—

Right now, it feels like it.

Chapter Thirteen

SHEPARD

E ven though I spent all night with my lawyer, trying to find a loophole in that bastard's agreement, I read the paperwork one more time.

The terms are clear.

Thirty days to win Jasmine's heart. To convince a board of trustees I'm a healthy, normal man who is capable of love.

Because the bastard knows he ruined it for me. And he wants to punish me for breaking free of him.

Of course, that's the problem.

The board is five men. One of them is the bastard who's pulling my strings. Another is the bastard's lapdog.

Which means there are three men who need to believe Jasmine and I are madly in love. Worse, they need to find her charming enough they vote in my favor.

They're the types who listen to their peers. If we convince the world, we'll convince them.

If we don't—

I can't consider that option.

It's not about the contract. It's not about losing the company I built from scratch. It's not even about the money.

It's about beating the bastard who's pulling my strings. He doesn't get to control me. He doesn't get to win. Not again.

I shove the papers in the bottom drawer of my desk. Turn the lock. No one else, and I mean no one—not my brother, or his fiancée, or my assistants, or Jasmine—is going to learn about this.

It's bad enough the lawyer knows.

It's bad enough it exists.

I suck a breath through my teeth. Straighten my tie. Smooth my jacket.

I'm exhausted. Coffee isn't enough, but it's all I have for now.

I move past my assistant's desk. Straight to the kitchen in the middle of the office. It's early enough I should be alone—the sky is still orange with sunrise—but I'm not.

Ian is in his office, at his computer. A few months ago, I would have been sure he was working. But recently, he confessed he's fallen for an online friend. Or maybe an online obsession is a better way to put it.

He follows her life from afar. She doesn't know he exists.

He swears it's not about her looks or some need to possess her. He swears he's only interested in her as an artist. A writer. A cultural scholar. Something like that.

Who can keep up with Ian's dalliances?

I suppose I can't lecture him about deception. Not that I would. I understand the way the world works. Nice people who play by the rules lose.

People who are willing to do whatever it takes—

They're the ones who win.

If he wants her, he needs to find a way to have her. No matter what. I'm not about to question his obsession. I have my own.

His eyes flit from the computer to me. He raises a brow. *Trouble in paradise* and shakes his head.

I try to ignore him as I fix a macchiato. Not my usual preference—I take my espresso with a hint of sugar, no milk—but I've been craving the drink since I saw one in Jasmine's hands.

I long to taste everything that's been on her lips.

Fuck, why am I trying to be a gentleman here? She wants me. She practically jumped into my arms in the limo.

I should act like a normal person. Pull her into my lap and kiss her.

But I'm not a normal person.

Yes, I could pin her to the leather seat, hold her arms over her head, kiss her until she moans against my mouth—

Fuck, I'm losing my train of thought.

The espresso maker whirs. Then it's a soft *drip, drip, drip*. Footsteps.

Ian's deep voice. That British accent that screams *I know better than you and I'm more sophisticated*. "Good morning."

Or maybe I'm in a shitty mood and I don't want to hear his opinion about my relationship. "You're here early."

"Is that for me?" He takes the macchiato from the machine. Brings it to his lips. "Still rubbish." He offers it back.

I don't want anything he's drank. I'm not a germa-phobe. It's a matter of principle.

I start fixing another.

He laughs. Takes another sip. Grimaces. "Is there trouble in paradise?"

"There is. Someone is stealing my espresso."

His low chuckle fills the room. He's not a happy-go-lucky guy, exactly, but he's not restrained either. He uses his money to fly helicopters, jump out of airplanes, surf the North Shore.

Ian in Hawaiian print board shorts. That makes me laugh. Not because he's black. Because he's British.

Key says he's like a younger, richer Idris Elba.

But then Key lives to irritate me with these comparisons.

"Always in a sour mood, aren't you, Shep?" He places the nearly full espresso cup in the sink. Fills the electric kettle with water.

"Should I switch to tea?"

"Of course. But I know your mother tried."

"Sunshine in a cup."

"And your fiancée?" He stresses the last word, like he finds it hard to believe I have a fiancée.

"Don't tell me your stereotyping."

"Tea's the most popular beverage in the world." He holds up a tin of English Breakfast. "Of course, in the states, you're still holding on to the taxation."

"Of course."

He shifts to the matter at hand. "That happened fast."

"It did."

"Unusually fast."

"And your *friend*?" I motion to his computer. "Still pretending you're someone you're not?"

"I should ask you that."

"Yes, I pretend I'm a functioning human."

He laughs that laugh that means *I know you think you're joking, but you're not.* "How is your brother?"

"Fine, last I heard. Do you need help with a tech issue? I'm sure he can stop fucking his fiancée for long enough to assist."

"Been too long?" His smile is knowing. "I've been there before." His gaze shifts to his computer. "There are opportunities, but they aren't as appealing as a woman you can't have."

"She's my fiancée."

"Yes."

"We're happy."

"Does she know you aren't in love with her?"

My stomach twists. It's not that simple. I'm not capable of loving anyone. If I were, it would be her. "Are you the relationship expert all of a sudden?"

"I have enough." He chuckles. "Even if they're short."

"I do too."

"Yes, but you're more discrete."

Of course, his taste is legendary. Young women who are new to sex. He'll introduce them to all sorts of things then send them on their way. He's clear about the rules, but something tells me the women expect they'll change his mind about that whole *this ends in sixty days* thing.

Maybe I should ask for advice. He has women falling in love with him, even when he doesn't want that.

Of course, it's the same for me. It's always the women who connect the least. The ones who can't see even a sliver of the man behind the scars.

"The meeting is in how long?" he asks.

"What does that have to do with anything?"

"You tell me."

Am I really this obvious? "Twenty-eight days."

"Interesting timing."

Sometimes, I hate having business partners. They learn things they shouldn't.

Ian is a genius when it comes to information. He can find anything, anywhere.

He found this.

He doesn't know the entire story, but he knows too much.

"What did you do to Lucien to fill him with this much ire?" Ian asks. "Or is he as much of a bastard as he seems?"

"He is a bastard."

"Fucking with you for the sport of it?"

"Something like that."

He shakes his head. "Distasteful." The water steams. He pours it over his leaves.

It makes me think of Jasmine, but then what doesn't?

"I don't blame you for playing the game. Sometimes, it's fun to see if you can win." He sets the electric kettle back in its spot.

I nod as if that's my only reason.

"Sometimes though… sometimes it's better to walk away. Sometimes that's the only way to win."

"I'll keep that in mind." I don't need the game theory lecture. But I know he means well.

"Look at us. Two rich men fixing beverages for themselves. Things change every day."

"They do."

"If you need my help…" He holds up his cup. "Or another helicopter ride."

"Thank you." The words are awkward on my tongue. I don't offer anyone gratitude. Certainly not someone as cocky as Ian.

But he's right about one thing, I'm not selling this story about a whirlwind romance. I need to change that. And I know how.

And I do need his help. "Actually, there is something."

He raises a brow. "I'm listening."

It's not going to be pretty, but it's going to work.

It has to.

Chapter Fourteen

JASMINE

There it is.

My fate summed up in ten pages and one dotted line. One year of marriage. No dalliances with other men, public or private. Nothing that looks like an affair. No kisses on the mouth or dinners where I sit a little too close.

For this year, I'm at Shepard's beck and call, twenty-four hours a day, seven days a week. If he requests my presence, I attend. If he insists I sit in my room, I sit in my room. If he demands I dance for his colleagues—

Well, I'm not actually required to dance. Just to attend, act the part of loving wife, keep all terms a secret.

Any misstep and I lose the seven-figure payout.

Worse, I lose this new term, the one I insisted on adding last night.

As long as I'm with Shep, he pays for my father's care. At home. Our apartment in Queens. I wanted to move him into Shep's place—there's certainly room—but it's too risky. I might break. Confess everything.

This is it.

Three hundred and sixty-five days for a million dollars.

I sign on the dotted line. For a moment, I feel that weight lift off my chest. I taste the freedom. I hear the fucking music.

Then a knock on the door calls my attention. Shepard's assistant. Lock.

What the hell?

My lawyer motions for him to enter. He steps inside with a *let's get this done* look.

"Ms. Lee." He offers his hand. "How are you this morning?" He holds up something else. A thermos. "Key prepared it before I left. It's supposed to stay warm for twelve hours, but I wouldn't bet on it."

"Thank you." It's there, my name on the dotted line, the notarization, the lawyer's signature. I'm officially his. "Have you come all this way to bring me tea?"

"If only, Ms. Lee," he says.

"Jasmine, please."

He nods *of course*. "If only, Jasmine. Unfortunately, my plans for the afternoon—knocking off work to put the city's most expensive champagne tea on your fiancé's credit card—have to wait."

I like the way he thinks.

I shake my lawyer's hand with a quick *thank you*, then I stand and meet Lock at the door.

He smiles as he hands me the mug. "Your fiancé has dinner plans. He needs you to buy a dress."

"What's wrong with this?" I smooth my pencil skirt. It's not fancy, but it looks professional enough. I guess that answers the question.

I look like an assistant. And who shows up to dinner with his secretary? That sends the wrong image. Even for Shep.

Better for me to look like a trophy wife.

"I believe"—he leans in to whisper—"the idea is to show off your lovely figure."

Oh. Of course.

"Make the other men jealous." He shakes his head *how silly*. "You are a beautiful girl. I understand the impulse."

I am an object for him to parade. And he can tell me what to wear. So many fun terms to this agreement. It's like Shep is trying to make earning this million dollars as painful as possible. "Yes."

"Men." He shrugs *what can you do?* "I have an appointment at a store you'll love. Unless you'd rather find something on your own." Despite his friendly tone, the implication is clear. I should take his help. I should allow him to dress me correctly. So Shep is pleased.

I suppose I should expect as much. He's specific about his home, his office, his suits, his car. Why not his wife to be?

————

Is moderation in Shepard's vocabulary? Subtlety? Temperance?

This is New York City. It's possible to find gorgeous, one of a kind clothes in a hundred different spots, at every price point imaginable.

There are knock offs in Chinatown, gorgeous vintage numbers in the village, trendy dresses in Brooklyn.

And here, at this exclusive boutique in SoHo, expensive designer gowns with four-figure price tags.

Do people really pay this much for a dress they'll wear, what, three times? It's ridiculous. My frugal nature screams *look online, there are better deals. That dress on display is gorgeous—a deep plum with a sweetheart neckline and a mermaid skirt—but it's not worth—*

Shit, is that really the price? My head gets light. My knees knock together.

"Jasmine—" Lock catches me before I can full-on faint. "Don't tell me Key prepared the tea incorrectly."

I can't help but laugh. He's good at his job. Assuming part of his job is keeping the wife in line. "No, it was perfect. But hot. I'm a little flushed."

"Shall I find you water?" he offers.

I nod *sure.*

"Look around. The manager is in the back. She'll be meeting us soon. If you need assistance."

If I need assistance. Or when I pick out something that isn't to Shep's liking.

It's hard to imagine Shep actually caring about what dress I wear. Sure, his intentions are still mysterious and vague, but since when does he care about clothes?

I do a quick walk around the shop. It's a normal size for the city. Small, but still open and airy. A podium in the middle of the room. Neat racks along the wall. Gowns sorted by design.

There aren't enough dresses to sort by color or style or size. No one wants something someone else is wearing. That's the ultimate embarrassment.

What is it like to have problems so trivial?

I shouldn't be dismissive, I know. I'm no longer a scrappy underdog. I'm already part of the elite. I shouldn't judge.

But it's hard to feel generous with these price tags surrounding me.

This dress is gorgeous—a deep rose and black floral print chiffon—and it could cover two months of expenses. Rent, food, water, electricity.

Two months of necessities or a gown for one evening.

But then I'm no longer a struggling assistant. I'm a rich man's fiancée. A year from now, I'm a millionaire.

Seven figures doesn't go as far as it used to, especially in a city this expensive, but it means never worrying about rent again.

Never fixing another peanut butter and jelly sandwich for dinner because I can't afford groceries.

Never camping out in front of a discount designer outlet on Black Friday because my work clothes are worn thin.

I never have to want again.

Not for material goods.

It should make me happy, relaxed, something, but it feels too unfamiliar. My whole life, I've been taught to be smart, savvy, frugal.

How can I spend five thousand dollars on a dress? Even if it is Shep's money?

I scan the racks for something cheaper. There. A coral with a distinct Marilyn Monroe vibe. Like the dress she wore in *How to Marry a Millionaire*. It's fitting. And the movie has a message I need.

What's wrong with a woman wanting a rich husband? Why isn't that okay if it's okay for a man to want a beautiful wife?

It's not my style, or my color, or what flatters my figure. And I'm certainly lacking the late Ms. Monroe's effervescent charm. But I like the idea of channeling her effortless smile and her adorable giggle.

Not me at all. But someone who can laugh and bat her eyes and stay above it all. That's what I want. The only thing, besides Dad being okay, that I want. Some way to survive this year without letting it affect me.

I check the sizes. Grab my usual, one smaller, one

larger. Look for the dressing room. Find a smiling woman in a designer suit.

"You must be Miss Lee," she emphasizes the Miss, like it's oh so important I'm not yet married to Shep. "I'm Alexa. I understand you need help finding a gown for tonight."

"I'm going to try this one."

Her brow furrows *it's not right* then her expression shifts to the usual assistant smile. "You should. But will you allow me to pick a few things that better suit your look?"

"My look?"

"You're a winter darling. This pink isn't the worst. It's saturated enough. But it's awfully light. And warm. I see you more as a dark winter. I bet you look gorgeous in scarlet."

Okay... the whole season thing is vaguely familiar. Aunt Quyen was obsessed for a while. Always talking about how she was a Spring, but no one would see it, because everyone assumed Asian women were winters. But look how great she looked in yellow—only a bright spring looks that great in yellow.

She does look great in yellow. She wears some unusual styles, but she always has the perfect color for her outfit.

Maybe there's something to the whole season thing. Or maybe Shep wants me in something demure and subservient.

Okay, a dress can't really be subservient. But the whole *I'm going to have final say over what you wear thing?*

That's weird. Even for him. He doesn't care about clothes. His mother picked his out when he was a kid. And now?

I'd bet good money he has someone craft his entire wardrobe. I bet he has someone in charge of laundry, socks, goddamn hair styles.

If I was a less stubborn woman, I'd admit he always looks put together *and* sexy as hell. I'd admit that whoever it is who curates his appearance is a genius.

But I'm not a less stubborn woman. And, besides, I'm not willing to give up this way of expressing myself. We've never had much money for clothes, but I always found a way to show a little flair.

"I'm trying this one," I say.

"Of course." She doesn't lead me to a dressing room. She motions to the podium in the center of the room. "Do you need a longline bra? That dress has a fitted bodice. You don't need one. But some women prefer it."

I'm going to change right here, in the middle of the room, on an actual podium.

"Don't worry, Mr. Oza is going to stay in the office until I call him in." She holds her hand over her mouth and stage whispers. "When I first met him, I assumed he preferred men. Since most men who come in here willingly do."

Is running an errand for Shep really coming here willingly? I'm not so sure. But I'm not going to correct her.

Her voice raises to a tone that can only mean *what I'm about to tell you is so scandalous you have to prepare yourself.* "It turns out he prefers anyone." She motions *only in New York.*

"I'm from the Bay." There are clothing optional parties in Golden Gate Park once a month, at least. New York may be a bigger city with more people, but it can't compare to San Francisco in terms of Queer Community.

She laughs *so you know.*

Not exactly. But I catch her meaning.

I'm trying on this dress. In front of her. I can do that.

She wheels over a rack. Takes the three gowns from my hands. Slides one off the hanger. "Whenever you're ready, dear." She motions to the podium. Then to a chair where I can set my clothes.

Okay, I suppose there's no waiting. I step out of my shoes. Unbutton my blouse. Then the skirt. The bra.

My underwear is a cheap cotton in a practical black. Not a fit for the luxurious atmosphere. But I'm sure Shep will change that soon.

I hate to give him credit, but, God, the thought of silk and lace. Of his hands on my panties. His fingers running over my sex, pressing the smooth fabric—

Shit. Not the time. Even if I'm buzzing with desire. Again.

I try to focus as Alexa helps me into the dress. It's a bit of a procedure, between the boned bodice and the fitted skirt.

She zips. Adjusts the top. Turns me to the three-panel mirror. "What do you think, darling?" She motions *one moment*. Moves to a rack of shoes. "What size?"

"Seven and a half."

She nods *sure* and picks up a pair of silver sandals with red soles. Louboutins. Those run in the hundreds of dollars. Sometimes closer to a thousand. "These might not be ideal for the outfit, but they'll give us an idea of the drape."

"Sure."

"For the next one." She sets them in front of me. Stands next to me. Even though she's on the ground and I'm on the podium, she's nearly at my height. She's taller than I am and she's wearing heels. "What do you think?"

"It's fun."

"Yes, it is fun."

I stare at my reflection. The dress is beautiful. And my boobs actually look like they exist. The pink fabric hugs them just so. Makes my figure look hourglass.

But I look more like I'm going to prom. An '80s prom. Or a Halloween party. It's just not me.

"Maybe something darker," she suggests. "This would be lovely." She pulls a black gown from the rack. It's a simple sheath with a halter top and a smooth skirt. "Or something more daring. I have just the thing." Her smile widens. Her face beams with excitement.

She moves straight to a rack on the right. Pulls off a dress in a deep shade of red. It's cut low. Very low. And the skirt has a high slit.

It screams *trophy wife*. Or maybe *I'm going to tear this thing off and fuck you senseless*.

My head skips over the earlier implication. Goes right to Shep's dirty promise.

I'm not going to touch you until you're on your knees, begging for my cock.

I can see his eyes lighting up. I can feel his hands running over the low neckline. I can feel his hard-on against my ass as he pulls me close.

"Miss Lee," Alexa asks. "Which would you like to try first?"

"The black." I'm not sleeping with Shep. I'm not. It's going to make things so much more complicated. And they're complicated enough.

Alexa helps me out of the pink dress. Then into the designer shoes. The black dress. Onto the podium.

My reflection takes my breath away. Sure, I don't have the makeup and hair to match the majesty of the dress, but I still look like royalty. Elegant, beautiful, rich.

"Gorgeous." She claps her hands together. "Maybe with an updo." She steps onto the podium. Stands behind me. Pulls my hair into a makeshift bun. "It's short, but we can work with that."

"We?" I ask.

"Shep provided a team. You'll go to lunch after this. Then hair and makeup while we steam and press the dress. Then dinner with your fiancé. It's a big event. A business event. A few colleagues will be there." She adjusts the straps. "Shall we try the red dress or are you set with this one?"

"Sure. Let's try it." I let her help me out of this dress and into that one.

Fuck. My eyes go to my chest immediately. Then my legs. I look like a Bond girl, but with the luxe fabric and my, ahem, less than ample chest, it looks more classy than trashy.

I should channel Ms. Monroe. Stay above it all. Giggle and bat my hand *oh you.*

I shouldn't let him affect me.

But that isn't what I want.

I want to drive Shep insane. As insane as he's already driving me.

This dress will do that.

"This one." I nod. "It's perfect."

She chuckles. "I'm sure Mr. Marlowe will enjoy it as well." She says it knowingly, like she's sure the dress will be on the limo floor the second we're alone.

And, well—

She's partly right.

I'm going to put that image in his head.

I'm going to drive him wild.

I'm going to make him beg me.

Chapter Fifteen

SHEPARD

"**A**re you sure you aren't in love with her?" Ian shakes his head *ridiculous*. "If you aren't, you wouldn't mind if I—"

"Fuck off."

He chuckles *you're too easy* and holds up his drink to toast.

"Isn't it bad luck?" I hold up my glass of sparkling mineral water. Other people opt for more interesting beverages, sparkling apple cider or iced tea or the appropriately named mocktails, since they're mocking anyone drinking one, but why bother? The only thing in the same league as alcohol is coffee.

"Only if it's plain water." He taps his glass against mine. His bourbon, neat, shakes. He typically prefers gin and tonic, but this place doesn't have the right tonic water. And, of course, there's the matter of testing me by consuming my drink.

My eyes go to Jasmine as she walks into the room.

Everyone's eyes go to her. She steals all the attention.

Fuck, that dress.

Right now I don't give a fuck about Ian's drink. About any drink. About anything except spreading her open and making her come.

He takes a long sip. "You really don't deserve her."

For the first time in forever, I'm barely interested in the alcohol three feet away.

I'm not thinking about the taste of bourbon on my lips.

The taste of her cunt is so much more appealing.

I always want her. And, according to my therapist (another requirement of an agreement with a family member, though this time I can thank my brother), I did a bang-up job replacing alcohol with sex. Only no matter how deep my craving for control, it never replaced my desire for a drink.

It's always there, in the back of my mind.

Only right now, it isn't.

Right now, there's only one thing in my mind.

Jasmine.

She stops at the host stand. Points to our table.

From across the room, her eyes meet mine. She holds up her bag—a tiny black thing with a silver clasp—then she holds it against her chest, daring my eyes to follow her movement.

They don't need the help. That thing is cut almost all the way to her belly-button. Soft silk skims her slim body. Shows off inches of tan skin.

She turns, points out something to the host. God knows what it is. God knows what my fucking name is.

The dress is backless. It swoops low, to the very top of her perky ass, then drapes over her long legs.

My gaze stays fixed on her as the host leads her to our table. Fuck, the way the fabric falls over her thigh as she walks. That slit is high. High enough I could make her come right here, under the table.

I should push her to the edge and leave her wanting. I should punish her for daring me. I should hate that she's daring me.

But I don't. I love it. That's the Jasmine I know. The girl who disarms people with a smile so they barely notice her fierce, defiant nature.

She plays nice on the surface, but underneath—

She's playing dirty with me. Which means I can play dirty with her.

Blood races south. I swallow another sip of sparkling water. I'll have her later. This is practically an admission of intent.

She wants to play this game. She wants to dare me the way I've dared her.

Which means she wants me to break and beg for her touch.

I won't. But it will be fun watching her try.

"Miss Lee." Ian stands and offers his hand. "Lovely to see you again."

She shakes. "You too." She sets her purse on the table. Turns to me. "Is it the three of us?"

"No." Ian shakes his head. "A colleague is joining us." His eyes go to his designer watch. "He's late, actually." He looks to me. "Aren't you going to help your fiancée into her chair?"

"Thank you, but I can handle it." Jasmine moves around the table, to the seat next to mine—

I stand. Stop her. "No. Allow me." I take her hand. Pull out her chair. "You look beautiful."

"Thank you." Her dark eyes fix on mine. "It was a long day, between the dress, the hair, the makeup." She reaches to her head. Pats her fancy updo. Then the clip. "I'm not sure I'll go through that whole song and dance every time I have dinner. But it was an experience."

"Oh," Ian interrupts. "You don't enjoy pampering?"

"Pampering, yes? Someone tugging my hair—"

"That sounds like a good time," Ian says.

She laughs knowingly, but I can't tell if it's a put on or not. "Yes." She looks to me and raises a brow. "It does."

My balls tighten.

"That is fun. This, not as much. More makeup brushes and hot rollers. I like the end results, but it's a chore getting there. I keep things more practical."

"Impractical is fun sometimes," he says.

Her eyes stay on mine. "Sometimes, yes."

I bring my hand to her waist. Right now, I don't care about Ian. I don't care about convincing Jeff. I don't care about anything but her body against mine.

Which is bad news. The worst news.

I need to stay on task.

I need to win.

My body ignores my protests. Without thinking, I pull her into a tight embrace. Her pelvis against mine, my hands on her hips, her chest raised with inhale.

She looks up at me.

I tear my eyes from her tits. Fuck, I need to push that dress aside. I need to see her, feel her, taste her.

Now.

Her expression gets curious. Unsure. Then she leans into her desire. Or maybe she leans into the fantasy. The pretending.

My eyes close. I pull her into a slow, deep kiss. My lips against hers.

She melts into me, slowly. Her soft lips part for my tongue. She groans against my mouth, inviting me into her body.

It's only a kiss. Only for appearances. But I feel it everywhere.

She pulls back with a heady sigh. Fake or real, I'm not sure. I suppose it doesn't matter. As long as she can convince that bastard.

That's all that should matter.

I help Jasmine into her chair. Then take mine.

Ian shoots me a *well done* look. I wave him away. Yes, I invited him here for his assistance. But the whole cocky charm thing—it's not helping.

"A drink?" Ian offers as the waiter passes. "Another round," he says to the waiter. "And for the lady?"

"Mineral water." Her eyes shift to my glass. "Thanks."

"That isn't necessary," I say.

"Even so." She nods a *thank you* to the waiter. Turns her attention to Ian. "Is this a social dinner or business?"

"I'm not sure your fiancé has social dinners. Not anymore." He refers to my reputation for romancing women.

Jasmine just barely frowns. "Yes. I suppose I've taken all that time."

"It's not hard to see why." He takes another sip. "Beautiful, smart, acquainted with helicopter rides. The total package."

She laughs. "What makes you think I'm smart?"

"Your dress," he says.

"Really? This dress." Her expression gets curious. "That's not the reaction I expected."

"Don't worry. I'm thoroughly distracted. And Mr. Pace will be as distracted. You understand why Shep invited you to this dinner. You're using your assets to your advantage in a way that won't threaten the fragile male ego." He holds up his glass, toasting to her. "Smart."

This time her laugh is deeper. Enough, it makes her tits shake. Somehow, the fabric of her dress stays glued to her skin. "I suppose that's one way to put it."

"If you were engaged to someone a bit more tolerable, then you'd really be a genius," he says. "At least someone who prefers tea."

"Not everyone can see the light." She turns to the waiter as he drops off our second round. Another bottle of Perrier. Another bourbon for Ian.

And Jeff Pace's drink. "White wine." The waiter motions to the entrance as Mr. Pace steps inside.

He's an older man. He wears it well, but not in a silver fox way (at least, not according to Key). More a distinguished grandfather way. Neat grey hair, smooth suit almost hiding his belly, stern expression.

He's not a saint, but he's no sinner either. I should know. I had Ian look for dirt on everyone on the panel. There was plenty of the usual—affairs, secret children with maids, apartments for the other woman, teens in rehab— but nothing worth using.

Not with the risk of that bastard discovering my blackmail and releasing those pictures. If he's caught, he'll be ousted from any respectable community, thrown in jail, forever an embarrassment.

But the pictures will be out there. Everyone will know the ugly truth. They'll look at me with pity. Whisper about the awful things I've been through.

That can't happen.

Besides, I know how the world works. He'll find a way to release the pictures without outing himself. He'll find a way to dishonor my mother's memory, fuck over my brother, and ruin my life.

Again.

He's the gift that never stops giving. He really is.

My eyes flit to Ian's bourbon. The white wine. Jasmine. She's still more interesting than the drink.

And I still want her more than I want alcohol. But I

want too much. Not just her sweet lips against mine. Her dress at her waist, her hands tied behind her back, her eyes filled with submissive desire.

She wants that too. I'm not sure if she realizes it, but she does.

"Mr. Marlowe, Mr. Hunt, always a pleasure." He offers his hand. Ian and I stand to shake, then Jeff looks to Jasmine. To her tits, though it's hard to blame him. "You must be the future Mrs. Marlowe."

"I must." She stands. Offers her hand.

To his credit, he shakes instead of offering some ridiculous hand kiss. Or some attempt to hug her so he can feel her soft body against his. "Jeffery Pace, but most people call me Jeff."

"Nice to meet you, Jeff," she says.

"Mr. Marlowe seems rather excited about your engagement."

"Can you blame him?" Ian chuckles. "I'd be excited too."

"You're going to settle down?" Jeff asks.

Jasmine's eyes go to Jeff's left hand. She eyes his wedding ring. Looks to me for insight.

Somehow, I understand what she's asking. Is he the kind of guy who really believes in true love and fidelity or the type who sees marriage as a business partnership and a status symbol?

The truth is somewhere in between, as far as I can tell. Like many rich men, Jeff has had affairs, but he's also devoted to his wife and children. He had all sorts of emails to his last mistress—a woman twenty-five years his junior, of course—going on and on about how he loves his wife and he'd never do anything to hurt her.

Maybe she knows. Maybe she doesn't care. Maybe she has her reasons.

It's not as if I can promise Jasmine a life filled with love. But I still judge Jeff for his decisions.

He has a devoted wife and a heart with a capacity for love. He should be faithful.

He should be honest.

I'm a hypocrite, yes, but I don't give a flying fuck.

I nod *about what you'd expect.*

She smiles *of course.* Turns to the conversation. Starts asking about Ian's type.

Jeff chuckles as I fill her in on Ian's reputation for inexperienced young women.

Her eyes go wide. She looks at Ian like she's not sure what to think of him. Or maybe she's playing her part. The devoted fiancée, who can simply not imagine her husband-to-be hanging out with a man so promiscuous.

The conversation shifts to business. She's perfect here too. Asking questions as if she's interested in the details. They aren't interesting to most laypeople. Zeroes on a merger. The conglomerate that owns this company has all sorts of say.

"Yes, sometimes, we have strange terms on our agreements." Jeff's statement pulls me back to attention. "Especially when it comes to one of our board members." His eyes flit to me. "He likes to test people. To see what he can accomplish."

"How?" Jasmine leans in, intrigued. Or pretending. Or sensing there's some hint to the truth here.

Ian clears his throat. "Typical things. A rehab stint here. A skipped vacation there. You know rich men. They like to throw their weight around."

"Yes," she says. "I do know the type."

"There have been some strange terms. Some rather demanding ones too. Most people don't play that game.

They just move on. But some do." He looks to me. "I don't like it myself. Life is too short."

"It is," Ian says. "It really is."

"But I suppose some people want to win more than they want anything." Jeff holds up his glass. "And it seems it's going well too."

"Hmmm?" Jasmine does her best to hide her curiosity, but she doesn't quite get there.

"One of his latest attempts. I had news about it today. It's quite silly. I'd love to tell you more, but I'm afraid I'm sworn to secrecy," he says.

"Of course." She smiles, demurely, then she looks to me. Asks for an explanation. "If you'll excuse me, gentlemen. I need to powder my nose."

"Of course," Jeff says.

I stand. Help Jasmine out of her chair.

Her fingers linger on my wrist as she picks up her purse. Then she moves away from the table. Around the corner. To the hallway with the restrooms and the coat check.

My heart races. My thoughts get loud. Too loud. That bastard is here again. He's everywhere.

He's always fucking things up.

"Excuse me." I don't wait for a response. I move toward the bathroom. Around the corner. To the dark, quiet space.

The weight of the wall is comforting. But it's not enough. It's not getting my thoughts straight.

I need a drink. Or a woman under me. Jasmine under me.

I try to find steadiness with my exhale.

Then the door to the women's room swings open. Jasmine steps into the hallway. Looks me dead in the eyes. "Are you all right?"

"No."

"Was he—"

I'm not answering that question. I can't think about that question. I can't think. Period. "Did you wear that dress for me?"

"I don't know what you mean." She plays coy. Moves away from the door. To the space on the wall, next to me.

I let my hand skim her wrist. "Yes, you do."

"Shep—"

"Tell me to stop."

Her eyes find mine.

"If you want me to stop, tell me to stop—"

"I thought you wouldn't touch me until I begged you."

"Am I touching you?"

She motions to my wrist.

I raise a brow *really*.

She nods *really*.

I pull my hand away. She's right. Rules are rules. Right now, I need rules. "You're daring me."

"I don't know what you—"

"Yes you do, princess."

The pet name makes her pupils dilate.

"You know what you're doing. But you don't know me anymore. You don't know how dangerous this game is."

"I can handle it." Her voice lifts to that proud, defiant tone. She thinks she can handle me. She thinks she can dare me and walk away.

She's wrong.

"You have no idea who I am now. You have no idea how rough I like it." I move closer. Close enough to smell her shampoo.

Her eyes fill with interest. "How rough?"

I don't answer her. Or touch her. Not yet. "Is that what you want, princess? Do you want to find out? Do you want me to order you onto your knees right here? To order you to open your pretty mouth so I can fuck it?"

Her chest heaves with her inhale. Her skin flushes pink. Then red.

"Or maybe you want me to pull your hands over your head. To pin you to the wall so you're helpless to resist as I split you in half."

"I…"

"What do you want, princess?" I'm done playing. I'm going to have her. On these terms. "It's a yes or no question. Do you want to come?"

Chapter Sixteen

JASMINE

Do you want to come?

My sex clenches. My lips part. My fingers curl into my purse.

My body screams *yes, yes, yes. More, more, more.*

I want everything Shep offered. All of it. All at once. I want his hands on my wrists. I want his body sinking into mine. I want him issuing dirty demands.

Something inside me wakes up. Some part of me that's been seeking attention for a long, long time. I've never played games like this before. I've barely allowed myself to consider them. Only when I heard rumors about Shep.

Even then, it was about him. I wondered what he wanted now. If he'd always wanted control. If he'd want to tie me to his bed.

Sure, the thought of his hands on my wrists made my sex clench, but I told myself it was something else. Memories of him. Loneliness.

Anything but a desire to be dominated.

I'm an independent woman. An independent woman from a country that's still under the thumb of an imperialist regime. In a place where everyone assumes Asian women are sex maniacs or docile housewives.

I can't want this. It goes against everything I believe.

But I do.

Right now, with his blue eyes fixed on me, and his voice low and deep—

Right now, I know. It's not simple curiosity. It's not memories of Shep taking my virginity.

It's the fire in his eyes. The threat in his posture. The heft in his voice.

I want him dominating me. I want it so badly.

"Yes," I breathe.

Am I being smart or foolish? Is it better to make him suffer from this pent-up desire or better to get what I want?

Holding out is stubborn. Giving in…

"Come here." His fingers curl around my wrist. It's a different touch than usual. Hard. Aggressive. Sexy as all hell.

He grips me tightly as he reaches around the coat check's half-door and unlocks it. He nearly drags me through it. Nearly pins me to the wall.

Then he releases me. Closes both halves of the door. Clicks the lock.

We're in a small room with a sparse silver rack. It's May. An especially warm day. Not many coats to check.

Still—"Is someone working here?"

"Do you see anyone?" He looks around the small space. It's smaller than his office. But that's not saying much. His office is enormous.

There's certainly nowhere for an attendant to hide. "No."

"Do you wish there was someone?" He slides his hand into the pocket of his slacks. "Do you want someone else to watch you come?"

My veins buzz with desire. It sounds so hot when he says it like that. Do I want someone else? "Maybe. But I do want… I want you to watch."

His pupils dilate.

His expression shifts to something primal and predatory, like he's a wolf and I'm a scared little sheep.

But I don't feel like prey. I feel like a fucking goddess. "They're expecting us at dinner."

"You'll have to be fast then."

My chest heaves with my inhale.

"Are you wearing anything under that?"

"Yes."

"Take it off."

I nod and bring my hands to my hips. The slit of my dress. It's cut high enough it's easy to slip my hand beneath it. To find the edges of my smooth black thong—Alexa insisted on something seamless.

I slide the garment to my knees.

Shepard keeps his back against the wall. "All the way—"

"Help me."

He shakes his head. "What did I say, princess?"

"You won't touch me until I'm on my knees, begging for your cock." At the time, it sounded absurd. Right now, I'm buckling. My body is screaming *now*.

He nods *yes*.

"At all?"

"Do you want to come on my hand, princess?"

"Yes." It's not a plea. I'm not begging. It's a statement of fact.

"My cock?"

I nod.

"My lips?"

"Yes," I say.

"Yes, sir," he corrects.

It's absurd. He wants me to call him sir. It's completely ridiculous. But it's also the hottest thing I've ever heard. The words fall off my lips with no regard to my inhibitions. "Yes, sir."

"Not yet." His eyes pass over me slowly. My eyes, lips, shoulders, chest, waist, pelvis. The panties at my ankles. "Even if you do get on your knees and beg me to fuck your pretty mouth."

Fuck.

"First—" He moves closer. He lowers himself to one knee and he reaches for me, but he doesn't touch me. His fingers go to my lingerie. He pulls it to my feet without touching my skin. "Raise your foot."

I do.

He pulls the thong aside. "The other."

I do that too.

He takes my underwear and slides it into his pocket. "You don't need this anymore, princess." He stands. Takes one step backward. Presses himself against the wall. Strong, demanding posture that screams *I'll give you want you want, when I've decided you want it badly enough.*

My body screams *yes, more, all, now, please.* I can barely stand. I try to find steadiness, but the rack is in the way. Between my shoes and my shaking legs, it takes all my concentration to stand.

"Pull up your dress." He motions to the slit. "I want to see."

Before my brain can think up a single objection, my body obeys. My hands go to the slit in my dress. I pull it up my thigh, higher and higher—

"Stop." His eyes go to my exposed skin. The tip of my thigh. The edge of my pelvis. He can't see my sex yet.

"Stop?"

He nods *yes*. "Hand on your thigh."

"The same one?"

"Yes."

My hand skims the smooth fabric. Cool silk. My skin is burning hot in comparison. Or maybe that's just Shep.

"Higher."

I drag my hand a little higher.

"Higher."

I do it again.

"Until you just barely feel the pressure."

"Yes."

"Yes?"

"Yes, sir." My sex pulses at the sound. It sounds right on my lips. And the demand in his eyes—

Fuck. My eyes close. I'm too on edge. Too needy.

I drag my hand higher and higher and higher. Until I'm almost there.

Shep's breath gets heavier.

Higher and higher—

There. I groan as my finger brushes my clit. My body is impatient. My hand acts on its own. Presses harder and harder. Until I'm right at the pressure I need.

"Look at me, princess."

My eyes blink open. Go to him. Those baby blues are fixed on me. Demanding every ounce of my attention, pleasure, obedience.

It shouldn't set me on fire, but it does.

Right now I don't care about should or shouldn't.

I don't care about anything but following his orders.

It's strange, intoxicating, thrilling.

Most of all, it's freeing. Right now, struggling to stand in this tiny coat room, staring at the man who has all the power to destroy me—

Right now, I'm not a woman under contract who's struggling to keep her head above water.

Right now, I'm a being of pure bliss.

"Is that how you touch yourself?" he asks. "Your fingers on your clit? Or do you drive those fingers deep into your cunt?"

"The first. Usually."

"Show me."

"Yes—" My eyes catch his. This time, I say it without reminder. "Yes, sir." I hold his gaze as I draw circles around my clit.

The heavy fabric drapes over my arm, adding drag, attempting and failing to cool my skin.

He can't see what I'm doing, but he's not looking at my pelvis. He's looking at my face. Watching my expression change like I'm the Mona Lisa. Or, knowing Shep, like I'm the zeroes at the end of a massive paycheck.

Right now, I'm the only thing he wants, and he's the only thing I want, and nothing else matters.

I hold his gaze as I make my touch firmer. Tension builds quickly. All that pleasure buzzing through my body collects in my sex. Winds tighter and tighter.

It's hard to keep my eyes open. His stare is too intense. My orgasm is too close.

Fuck, I can't remember the last time I ached like this. Not with someone else. Not on my own.

I touch myself plenty. Sometimes, I even think of him.

But it's not like this.

This is something else. His presence makes everything sharper.

The intensity in his eyes. The part of his lips. The hardness in his slacks.

He wants me so badly. But he's so calm and patient. Waiting. Watching. Staring like I'm his favorite movie.

I want that. I want to unzip his slacks, do away with his boxers, wrap my fingers around his cock.

I want to stroke him until he comes in my hand.

Even more, I want him to hold me against the wall, to order me to grip him tightly so he can fuck my hand.

To order me onto my knees so he can come in my mouth.

To order me onto all fours so he can—

Fuck. With the next brush of my finger, I come. My eyes flutter closed for a second. They beg to stay closed, but my body wants to follow his orders more.

My eyes blink open. All that tension in my sex winds so tight it hurts. Then it unravels.

A wave of pleasure rocks through me. My hands shake, my knees knock, my toes curl into my heels.

My world goes white, nothing but blinding light, nothing but the purest bliss in the universe.

"Beautiful." Shep's voice is a low growl. Equal parts demand, dare, appreciation. He takes one step toward me. Places his hand on my hips. Steadying me.

Then his arms are around me and I'm melting into his body.

He holds me closely for a long moment, then he helps me up, smooths my dress, presses his lips to mine.

It's not a kiss for show. It's not the peck of a friend. It's pure, deep need.

For my body? My obedience? My love?

I'm not sure. I'm not sure what I'm offering when I kiss him back. Only that I want all of it. Everything.

He pulls away with a heady sigh. "I'll go back to the table first. Wait a minute, then join me."

"They'll know—"

"Does that bother you?"

Maybe it should, but it doesn't. I shake my head.

He smiles. "Dirty girl."

Maybe that should bother me too, but it doesn't. It only makes me ache for him.

How can I be needy and satisfied at once? It defies reason. But then Shep always has.

I let him unlock the door and leave the room. Then I smooth my dress, check my hair and makeup in the bathroom, wash my hands.

I was wrong about the dress. I'm the one out of my mind. But I was wrong about caring too.

I'm going to take his dare.

I'm going to get on my knees and beg.

But that isn't losing. It's winning.

I'm going to get what I want.

I'm going to get every single thing I want.

Chapter Seventeen

JASMINE

S teady feet, subtle smile, effortless expression. I smooth my dress. Hold my bag to my hip. Walk casually, like I've been in the bathroom perfecting my lipstick, not in the closet touching myself.

There are eyes on me. People are staring. There's something in my posture, my smile, my ruffled hair. Something that gives me away.

Do people know? Does it matter?

I suppose it's better for Shepard this way. It adds credence to the whole *we're madly in love* thing.

There. I approach the table. Try out an aloof expression.

Shep does nothing to hide his satisfied smile. He might as well scream *that's right, I fucked my fiancée.*

"Long line?" Ian looks to Jeff and raises a brow. The restaurant is quiet. And more than half the patrons are men. It's clear there isn't a long line.

Jeff's expression shifts to one of contemplation. He makes that *hmmm* noise. Not the parental one. The *wow, that's a pickle* one.

It's strange. Jeff seems like exactly the type of guy who sneaks away for illicit trysts. Is he really judging Shep for this?

No, it's not a judgmental look. It's a curious one. Like he's not sure what to believe.

Huh.

Strange.

There's a reason for this dinner. A reason why we're meeting with Jeff and Ian and not just Ian. Shep didn't ask me to dress up to step into Ian's helicopter.

Sure, those weren't dress up circumstances. But he didn't give me any sort of instruction or warning. He's not trying to convince Ian of anything.

Jeff, on the other hand…

I make a mental note to look up Jeffery Pace. To find out what he has to do with Shep. He's on the board of a company Shep wants to buy. Or wants to sell. Or wants to buy something he has to sell. He must be.

The timing is too suspect. It must have something to do with this whole plan.

Or maybe I'm thinking zebras when I should think horses. Shep doesn't need an elaborate reason to bargain with me. There are plenty of reasons why marriage is a good idea.

It raises his status, ends those rumors about his extra-curricular activities, marks him as a normal, family man.

The chance to have me under his thumb—

My head hurts. I sit. Sip another glass of mineral water. Focus on my food. A sizzling steak topped with chimichurri and pickled onions. Tangy beets with creamy goat cheese and nutty pistachios. Rich chocolate cake with fresh raspberries.

A perfectly steeped pot of black tea to go with it. A

Russian Caravan that brings out the complexity of the chocolate cake.

With enough caffeine to keep me up all night.

I nod along as we finish dessert. The men talk business. Jeff says something gross, but no doubt well intentioned, in his mind, about how he likes a woman who eats, not one who's too skinny.

At once, Shep's face fills with fury. With a deep anger I barely recognize. It should scare me. It *does* scare part of me. But there's this other part that's thrilled, flattered, aroused even.

I place my hand on his. Motion *don't*. It's nothing. Not worth it. I hear worse all the time.

Men think they're entitled to comment on women's bodies. Especially women who work for them. Especially women of color who work for them.

"Does that mean you'll be paying the catering at our wedding?" I smile serenely, like I find his joke oh-so-amusing.

Jeff just laughs. "No, but I have a better idea. Have you ever had a personal tour of a chocolate factory?"

Shepard raises a brow *what?* He looks to Ian for help, but the charming Brit just shrugs.

"I can arrange it anytime. Before the wedding. As part of the honeymoon. Have you ever been to Paris, Jasmine?" he asks.

My heart skips at the thought of the city of lights. "Never."

"I think you'd prefer London, honestly," Ian says. "I know I'm biased, but between the tea and the theater—"

Theater in the West End. My nod is involuntary. "I'd love that."

"Did you just invite my fiancée to London?" Shep asks.

"Someone has to do it." He looks to Jeff. "You have Paris. I have London. Where will you sponsor, Shep? Rome? Madrid? Someplace the coffee is as dark as your soul?"

My laugh is real. Easy. I like Ian. He knows Shep. Knows how to push his buttons. Knows there's something unusual about our arrangement.

I'm not sure how much he knows, but it's enough he's helping us convince Jeff, not fighting for the truth.

"Please," Shep says. "There isn't any coffee in the world as dark as my soul. But I wouldn't expect you to know your beans."

Ian holds up his cup of tea as if to toast.

I raise mine to meet him.

Shep shakes his head *how ridiculous*. It's sweet. Loving. Like we're a real couple having a normal dinner with friends.

"Sounds like an invitation to Hawaii to me," Ian says. "Tour every Island looking for Kona coffee as dark as your fiancé's soul."

"I have to agree. It's not possible." My eyes meet Shep's. God, it's hard looking at him after that. I'm still buzzing. "But it would be fun to try."

"Think about it, Jasmine," Jeff interrupts. "Marcus and I own factories all over the world. He insisted on sending the two of you on a tour of one. Our treat. Think about where you'd like to go."

I guess this is a perk of marrying a rich man. The world is my oyster. I have to get used to it.

———

AFTER DINNER, WE TAKE A CAB BACK TO SHEP'S APARTMENT. Apparently, he gave Lock and Key the night off. Apparently, he wanted privacy at home.

"Don't they live with you?" I ask.

"Key has a room, yes," he says. "But she enjoys nightlife too."

"Really?" It's hard to imagine his buttoned-up assistant tearing up the dance floor. But then I'm sure it's hard to imagine me touching myself in the coat room. At least, for people who see me in my assistant gear.

"Yes. She loves jazz. Why? Would you like to attend a show?" His eyes meet mine. His voice stays curious. Like he really is interested in my feelings about jazz. Like he really does want to find an activity that will please me.

"Maybe. I can't say I know much about the genre." Or music, in general. I grew up on Mom and Dad's favorites. They were always exposing themselves to American culture, so they could feel more assimilated. The old and the new. Somehow, that ended up being some mix of the Beatles, the Beach Boys, and disco.

Lots and lots of disco.

Seriously, we could run a roller rink with all the disco Dad owns.

"Dad mostly listens to ABBA," I say.

"Really? Did you take him to see *Mama Mia*?"

"I did." I smile at the memory of our cheap theater seats. It was the first time, the only time, I saw him captivated by the stage. I'm sure it was just the familiar songs, but it still felt right, connecting over something I love so deeply. "He adored it. The movies too. The first. He didn't like the second as much. He wanted new songs. Though he did love the setting. He was surprised by how beautiful Greece was."

"Was he?"

"You have to see the movie to understand. It's all sun and sea and beautiful white houses. Like Greece is the happiest, easiest, safest place in the world."

"You liked the movie?" He helps me out of the car. For a moment, we're on the street outside his apartment on a beautiful May evening. The air is still warm. The breeze is light. It even smells like spring.

For a moment, we're a normal couple, coming home after a date, ready to kiss goodbye.

Then I reach for my key and realize I don't have one. I'm still leaving the apartment when he allows, returning when he says okay.

That can't be an oversight. More likely, he's testing me. Letting me prove I can behave with this much leash before he offers more.

I turn to the sky. That New York blue. A beautiful shade that only exists here. The light pollution dulls the stars, but it makes the sky so gorgeous.

"Do you mind if I take a walk?" I want to say *fuck off, I'll walk wherever I want*, but that's a luxury I don't have. I know better than to bite the hand that feeds.

If it was just me, my needs, my desire for a safe place to rest my head, I might do it.

But Shep is paying for Dad's treatment at home. Dad has Mariah three shifts a week. An aide, no doubt one who likes Dan Brown less, keeps an eye on him the rest of the time.

He's safe. That's what matters.

I motion to the river, half a dozen blocks away. "I need to clear my head."

His eyes pass over me slowly. "You shouldn't wear that alone, this late at night."

"This is a nice neighborhood."

"I don't care. I don't like it."

My cheeks flame. My chest too. I shouldn't like him being protective as much as I do. I should find it annoying. Imposing.

Typical Shepard, taking care of his possessions.

But I want him taking care of me.

I want him growling with jealousy.

I want him furious at the thought of other men touching me.

"Here." I take his coat. Sling it over my shoulders. It's too warm—far too warm—but it does the job of covering me.

His eyes meet mine. "Is that what you'd like, a quiet walk alone?"

"Yes."

"You can have the balcony to yourself."

"Even so."

He nods with understanding. "Think about what Jeff said."

"Huh?"

"He'll say the trip is just for us. Then he'll show up at the factory like it's a coincidence. Or he'll send Marcus. Jeff seems to believe us, but Marcus is… less easily impressed."

There's more there. Something he isn't saying. But I know better than to ask. "Sure."

"I've seen some of his factories. They're interesting, but not any more so than chocolate factories in Brooklyn. If you'd like to tour one sooner, I can arrange it."

"That's fine."

"We will need to accept his offer. Treat it like the gift he sees it as."

"Fly to Madrid?"

"I'm not sure you'll find much tea in Madrid. The paella might make up for it."

My chest warms. He's looking out for me. He's protecting me. But he's also treating me like a prisoner.

I don't know what to believe.

I repeat my mantra. *Dad is okay. Dad is okay. Dad is okay.*

That *is* what matters. "I suppose he won't appreciate it if we want to see his factory in Brooklyn?" I ask.

"Unlikely. But I'll see."

"Good."

"I think you'd like Paris. Even though—"

"No good tea there either?"

"So I hear." He offers me his hand. "Are you sure you don't want to come up now?" There's something in his eyes. Almost like he's pleading for me.

Not for sex or obedience.

For companionship. Comfort.

Which only makes my thoughts swirl faster.

This is strange. Confusing. I need to think. By myself. "Yes. Thank you."

"You can let yourself in." He pulls a key from his pocket. Presses it into my palm. "Lock the door behind you. And leave it on the table in the living room."

So he does know I don't have a key. And he wants to keep it that way. "This would be easier if I had a key."

"In a few days."

I guess that's a compromise. It's weird. But I can respect his caution. Mostly. "Thank you."

"Good night, Jasmine."

"Good night." I watch him move into the apartment. Then I turn toward the river and go in search of clarity.

What the hell does Shep want from me?

Why is he really doing this?

Chapter Eighteen

SHEPARD

From the balcony, I watch her walk away.

She's right. This is a safe neighborhood. And it's statistically unlikely a stranger will attack her. The real danger is inside the house. The people we know, love, trust—

They're the people who hurt us.

I know that better than anyone.

But I still watch her until her silhouette disappears. She *is* safe. There's a tracker in her phone. And another in my coat.

She's lived in New York City, in a far worse neighborhood, for years.

Even so, I fail to concentrate on work. My mind turns until I hear the door click open.

Her footsteps move closer. The click of her heels. Then the soft pads of her feet.

Jeff believes we're in love. At least, he believes it enough to vote in my favor. But he's also buying himself opportunities to spring other board members on me.

No doubt working up to the one I least want to see.

I guess there's no getting around this. At some point, I'll come face-to-face with that bastard. At some point, I have to keep it together as he gloats about his hold over me.

He's not going to vote in my favor unless I bend to him. But then I don't need his vote if I can convince half the board.

One down.

Three to go.

It should soothe me. It does, to an extent. But that fucking voice—

I can still hear that bastard.

I pull open the door. Move into the living room.

Jasmine is sitting at the long table, her red lips around a glass of water, her expression curious.

"How was your walk?" I try to make my voice calm. Even. Free of that bastard's influence.

"Warm." She motions to the coat rack against the wall. "I'm not sure you'll need it until the fall, but if you do."

"Are you comfortable in that dress?"

"More than you'd expect." Her eyes travel down my body. Stop on my pelvis. "Why do you ask?" She's daring me again.

But, this time, I'm out of patience. "Take it off."

Her eyes go wide. "I—"

"I said take it off. Don't make me ask twice."

Chapter Nineteen

SHEPARD

She stands. Reaches for her zipper. Pulls it down her back.

In one swift motion, the dress falls at her feet. "That's five thousand dollars of silk. Someone should hang it up."

She takes a step toward me.

Then another.

Not what I expected her to do.

"Are you going to remind me I'm supposed to beg?" Her voice is defiant. She wants to be punished for her insolence. Not what I usually enjoy, but when it's Jasmine—

My thoughts slip away. I should be more careful. Take more time to outline these terms. But I need this. Now. "Sit."

She does.

I move toward her. Drop to my knees to help her into her heels. The right. Then the left.

She shudders as my finger skims her ankle. I let my hand drift to the back of her calf.

I'm cheating, I know, but I'm too far gone to care about sportsmanship.

"Outside." I want to do this in the fresh air. Where someone might see.

I stand, move onto the balcony, motion *come here*.

She does. She looks down at her feet, almost surprised they're moving. Then her eyes go to mine. She holds my gaze as she closes the distance between us.

It's a beautiful night. Warm, clear, with that classic New York City blue. Barely dark enough to qualify as night.

The river is visible here. The moon bounces off it, casting subtle highlights all over Hell's Kitchen.

Casting a glow over her tan skin.

She's so fucking beautiful. With her heels, she's only a little shorter than I am. Our bodies nearly line up.

If I turn her around, pin her to the wall—

The angle is perfect. I should surprise her. I should take her now.

But she isn't ready for that. We've barely discussed terms.

"You've never played before," I say.

"I've read things." Her posture stays proud. She's naked, and I'm fully dressed, but she's still holding herself like she has all the cards. She's a natural.

"Some people use a stop sign. Red, yellow, green. I prefer a safe word."

She nods.

"Do you know what a safe word is?"

"I wasn't born yesterday."

"It seems easy, but sometimes, when people are caught up in the scenario, they don't want to use it. Or they're too scared. It's too much. Too real." My head goes there. Again. It always does. That reminder that I'm a sick fuck acting this out. But it's the only thing that works. "I don't usually play non-consensual scenarios."

Her eyes go wide.

"It's a common request."

"I don't think… that's not for me."

"I need to know you're prepared to use a safe word. That you feel comfortable enough."

"How am I supposed to know that?"

I guess I have to test her. It's been a long time since I've done this with someone inexperienced. Longer since I've done it with someone—No, I've never played with someone I fucked normally. Whatever normally means. "I'll start gently."

"I don't need gentle."

"What do you need?"

"I've never really thought about this."

"But you liked what happened in the coat room?"

"Yes."

I raise a brow.

"Yes, sir." She takes a half-step toward me. "I liked all your ideas too."

"I meant what I said."

Her chest heaves with her inhale. She stares at me, daring me to elaborate.

"I'm not touching you until you beg."

"Are you going to define touch?"

"No."

"Or beg?"

"No."

"So it's all by your terms."

"Our terms. My limits. Your limits. Everything is within those bounds."

She nods. After years working in finance, she understands contracts. "What are your limits?"

"I always initiate."

She nods in agreement.

"You only touch me if I demand it."

"Anywhere?"

"Anywhere." I bite my tongue, praying she won't ask me to explain. A lot of women do. The more eager ones understand immediately. They love the idea of letting go completely. Others find it strange. They're used to men begging for their touch. They aren't used to earning it.

"When we're playing or always?"

It's a good question. "When we're playing. With other people around—"

"We're pretending?"

"Yes."

Her expression gets curious, but she still nods. "This is all your demands?"

"You following my demands. Is that what you want?"

Her breath hitches. "I think so. I haven't done that before. But I like the idea."

"Good." My eyes drop to her chest. Fuck, I probably should have waited to order her out of her clothes. There are too many things I want to do to her. "It sounds selfish. I'm sure you think of me as selfish. Maybe I am. But not here. I'm reading you, making sure I give you what you need."

She nods with understanding.

"What about your limits?"

"I've never thought about it."

"Would you like to be tied up?"

Her eyes meet mine. "Yes."

"Slapped?"

"Not on the face."

"Will you crawl?"

"Crawl? Why would I crawl?"

I'm moving too fast for her. There's too much she doesn't know. "To show obedience."

Her pupils dilate. "Maybe."

I need to keep this simple. In terms more familiar. "Is there anything you don't like?"

"Nothing that will leave a mark."

Smart. I nod.

"I'm not sure I'm into pain."

"You're not? Or you're not sure?"

"It doesn't appeal right now. But I've never tried."

Pain isn't my preferred method, but I'm still hesitant to write it off. I want my options open. I want as much of her as I can have. "I'll keep it light." My eyes flit to her chest. "You like authority."

She doesn't quite follow.

"Calling me sir, following my orders, proving you obey like a good girl."

Her eyes go wide at the term.

"What about being a bad girl? Do you ever want spankings if you misbehave?"

"Maybe." Her chest heaves. "Yes."

My cock whines *right now*. Most people are like that. If they like being good, they love being bad. But then I'm already hard enough to tear my slacks. "Is there anywhere you don't want me to go?"

"Anywhere?"

"Your mouth, your cunt, your ass?"

Her eyes go wide. "Well, I… I haven't." She licks her lips. "I've never had anal sex."

"But you're willing to try?"

"Not right away."

Something to earn. My balls tighten. I want to earn every bit of her trust. I need to find some patience, but I'm struggling. "You need to pick a word."

"Coffee bean."

"Coffee bean?"

She nods *yes*. "Something I don't like."

I can't help but laugh. She's perfect. "Okay, coffee bean." I offer my hand.

She takes it. Shakes. Steps backward. "Is there some way we… transition."

"You'll know."

"How?"

I let my voice drop to the demanding tone that makes her shake. "You will."

She does. Her nipples tighten. Her head tilts with a nod. It's like her body responds before her mind does. Still, she fights me. "You really think I'm going to beg?"

"Yes."

"I'm going to beg you to touch me." She moves a little closer. "You're not going to beg me to touch you?"

I nod.

She stares back at me, waiting.

I like making her wait.

I let my eyes roam her body. I haven't seen her like this in years.

She's older now. A woman, not a girl. Still, as she'd say, a ruler. But curvier. Her breasts are bigger, her hips are rounder, her ass is fuller.

Her hair is shorter now. Usually, it's in a straight line at her shoulders. Right now, it's pinned back. That shiny clip is keeping her dark strands out of her face.

Perfect.

I take a step backward. Bring my eyes to hers.

She shudders. Her tongue slides over her lips. Her chest heaves with anticipation.

"What do you want, princess?" I ask.

Her nails scrape her hips.

"Do you want to come on my hand? Or maybe you'd like me to carry you to my bed, tie you to the frame, and fuck you until you beg me to stop?"

Her chest heaves with her inhale.

I sit on the beige couch. The fabric is too plastic, comfort sacrificed for water resistance, but it serves its purpose well.

I take an extra cushion. Place it on the ground in front of me.

Her eyes follow the green fabric.

"Kneel," I say.

"Kneel?"

"Don't make me ask twice, princess."

"Or?"

My head fills with thoughts of punishing her. Pulling her into my lap. Spanking her until her ass is red and her cunt is dripping.

I will.

But not yet. Not today.

"Or you won't get what you want," I say.

"And what do I want?"

I motion to the cushion. "On your knees."

She practically falls onto the cushion. Then sits back on her heels and looks up at me, waiting for her next order.

"This is what you want, isn't it, princess?"

Her eyes go wide.

"You want my cock."

Her nod is slight.

Blood races south. I need her already. I need her now. "Do you want me to pin you to the ground and fuck you? Or maybe you want me to come in that pretty mouth?"

Her tongue slides over her lips. "Yes."

"Yes?"

"Yes, sir."

I stand, so I can stare down at her. That's what she wants.

To feel like she has some modicum of control.

Or maybe she wants to feel like I'm using her. Maybe she wants to feel like a vessel for my pleasure. I'm not sure yet. But, fuck, it's going to be fun finding out.

"You want to feel my cock, princess?" I move close enough to take her hand.

Her fingers stretch forward, reaching for me.

I make my grip tighter. So tight she gasps. "When I ask you a question, answer me."

She looks up at me.

"Do you want to feel my cock?"

Her eyes meet mine. "Yes, sir."

I bring her hand a little closer. Almost to where it needs to be.

Fuck, I'm already shaking.

She looks up at me, her expression half confusion, half desire.

Then her gaze moves down my body and the confusion in her eyes fades.

All desire.

"Do you want to taste my cum?"

Her eyes fill with surprise, but she doesn't hesitate. "Yes." She licks her lips. "Yes, sir."

"Do you want me to fuck your pretty mouth?"

"Yes, sir."

"Ask me."

"Ask you?"

I nod. "Say, please, will you fuck my mouth, sir."

Her dark eyes go wide. It's like she's about to say *who the fuck do you think you are?* Or maybe *you're cheating, you asshole.*

I am. This isn't fair play at all.

But then I don't play fair. She should know that.

She sucks in a deep breath. "Please."

"Please?" I raise a brow.

"Please." Her eyes meet mine. "Sir." She says it like it's a dare. *I'm not going to beg that way. Resist me if you can.*

I bring her hand to my cock.

She sighs as she cups me over my slacks. She runs her thumb over my length, pressing the fabric into my skin.

Fuck, that already feels too good.

She sits up straight. Raises her chest, pointing it toward me in a gesture that's half pride, half *look at my perfect tits*.

I want to touch them, taste them, feel them around my cock, paint them with my cum.

I want everything with her.

After she obeys.

It's what she wants too. She wants to earn it.

I offer her my hand again. When she places her fingers in my palm, I repeat my request. "Say it, princess. Say, please fuck my mouth, sir."

She looks up at me. "May I please touch you, sir?"

A compromise. Maybe I should say yes. But I can't. I need her obedience tonight. "Say it."

Her eyes get brighter, more full of fire. She takes a deep breath. Exhales slowly. "Please fuck my mouth. Sir."

Fuck. I'm already too far gone. I'm not going to last long. But that's for the best. I don't want to push her too hard. Not the first time. "Open your mouth, princess."

She hesitates. "What if it's too much? Too hard?"

It's a good point. She won't exactly be able to use the safe word. "My watch."

Her eyes flit to the device.

"Tug on it."

She nods with understanding.

I shift back into the scene. Stiffer posture, lower voice, eyes fixed on her. "Open your mouth, princess."

She does.

"Wider."

She opens wider.

"Lips around your teeth. Keep your tongue on the bottom of your mouth. Keep it pressed against me. So I can fuck the back of your throat."

"Fuck," she breathes.

I bring one hand to the back of her head. I'm going to mess up her fancy hairdo. I'm going to make it clear she's been fucked properly. "Hands behind your back. Or on my hips."

I don't give her time to respond. I unzip my slacks. Push my boxers aside.

Pull her head to my cock.

Fuck. Her lips brush my tip. Then it's her soft, warm mouth.

I don't give her respite. I push deep into her mouth.

She groans against my cock. Her hands go to her thighs. Then to my hips.

I'll bind her wrist next time.

For now—

Fuck. I pull back and drive into her again.

My eyes fall closed. For a moment, I soak in the feeling of her sweet mouth. I give her a few seconds to get used to my length.

Then I pull back and thrust into her again.

She looks up at me with fire in her eyes.

Her nipples tighten. Her thighs shake. Her nails scrape her palms.

She's wet. She wants this as much as I do. She wants to be mine.

I can push her harder. Further. Closer to what she craves.

I tighten my grip on her hair. Toss aside a pin. Then another.

Her dark strands fall over her cheeks. I knot my hand in them. Tug her enough she groans.

Then I pull her head over my cock. Just barely. Just enough she feels it.

Then more.

More.

Fuck.

I hold her head in place with both hands. One to steady her. The other to tug her hair enough she moans.

I drive into her again and again. Hard, fast movements that stretch her lips.

She keeps her tongue pressed flat against me as I fill her with steady thrusts.

Her groans get louder. The vibration makes me shake. Fuck, she's already too good at this. And knowing she's mine. That she's obeying me.

A few more thrusts and I come. I drive into her, spilling into her pretty mouth, until I have nothing left to give.

Then I pull back. Watch her swallow hard.

"Good girl," I say.

Her pupils dilate. She likes the term. A lot. I'm going to have fun with her.

Too much even.

The rest of this might be a mess. I might not know who the twenty-four-year-old Jasmine Lee is.

I may not know her head or her heart.

But I know her body.

I know how to give her exactly what she craves.

Chapter Twenty

JASMINE

It's official. I'm an insane person.

No one in their right mind would do this. No one in their right mind would kneel on a balcony and beg their ex-boyfriend to fuck their mouth.

Only I did. And I'm standing here, in the shower, replaying it again and again.

Shep is in his room. We have separate rooms. He fucked my mouth, said a few things about our terms and tomorrow, a few things I didn't hear, then he sent me to my room. Went to his. To work or shower or fuck himself. I don't know.

I should care. Part of me does. Part of me is screaming *what the hell is wrong with me?*

The other part?

I slip my hand between my legs. The running water makes the friction strange. Too smooth.

It's not the same touching myself without him here. I want him here.

I want him watching. I want him ordering me onto my knees, or my back, or my stomach.

But he isn't here. I'm alone, in the shower, because he sent me away after he finished with me.

I'm alone, in the shower, washing off all the remains of today—the hair spray, the makeup, the tape that kept my dress in place—because he demanded I look the part.

I'm alone, in the shower, without all the rich girl accessories. And, sure, the shower is amazing by New York City standards. The size of my old bathroom, with shiny tile, ornate fixtures, and perfect water pressure.

Sure, the shampoo and soap are the best money can buy and the whole place smells like lilac.

But it's still a shower. Like any other shower. It's the most normal place I've been all day.

I should be thinking about my life and what's become of it, but instead, I'm closing my eyes and replaying the coat room and the balcony.

I'm picturing all those other dirty promises, stroking myself to orgasm.

I come fast. Too fast. The wave is so intense it makes my legs shake. I press my back against the wall to stay upright.

Even with all that intensity, it's not enough. I need him. I need him again and again and again.

When was the last time I wanted something this much? Something beyond food or safety or health? I can't remember.

I wash my hands. Soap my body.

Then shampoo, conditioner, a quick shave.

Even as I step out of the shower, wrap myself in a towel, move into my room—

I replay it again and again.

I should be more concerned about this recently redecorated room. It is, as Lock promised, much to my liking. Sleek furniture. Bedding in shades of red and purple. Scarlett. Violet. Eggplant. Crimson. White walls decked with black-and-white movie posters. Sheer curtains that let in the beautiful New York blue.

I don't know what the hell I'm doing tomorrow. I don't know what the hell I'm doing next week.

But, right now, I don't care.

I soak in the sensation of satisfaction. Hold on to it as closely as I can. For as long as I can.

Until I fall asleep and dream of all the other things I want Shep to do to me.

————

FOR THE FIRST TIME IN MY ADULT LIFE, I SLEEP IN ON A weekday. There isn't even an alarm to snooze. My cell is still in my purse, in the living room.

It's just me, this big, beautiful room, and the soft light of morning.

My room faces west. The Hudson. The sunset. New Jersey. But even that New Yorker cliché—anything but Jersey—can't harsh my buzz.

I'm still riding on last night's pleasure. All the other details are irrelevant.

After I move through my morning routine, I check my dressers. My clothes are here. As are some new items I didn't choose. Bought by Shep. Or his team.

I should be annoyed by the imposition, but my thoughts turn dirty too quickly.

Lace lingerie, silk sleepwear, basics that cost as much as my grocery bill. All things he can tear to pieces.

I don a crimson robe. It's soft and smooth, somehow warm and cool at once. Then I move into the main room.

Jazz music pours from the kitchen. I don't recognize it.

I can't find a pattern. But that's the point of jazz, isn't it? It defies other musical conventions.

Maybe Shep likes it. That would suit him. He defies classification.

"Miss Lee." Key's voice fills with surprise. "I didn't realize you were awake." She almost blushes. "I can turn the music off."

"Don't. I like it."

"Are you certain?" Incredulity streaks her expression. "I'll put on something you'd prefer. Aalock tells me you enjoy show tunes."

"Musicals, yes. Though it's more the energy of the theater. I prefer plays."

"The ones without singing?"

I nod.

"Can you believe people are still paying seven hundred dollars a seat for Hamilton? I know it's nothing to Mr. Marlowe. And nothing to you soon. But—"

"I haven't seen it."

She shakes her head *disappointing*.

"I haven't seen much recently. I used to go to the TKTS box on Sundays, to find a cheap matinee, but now I spend that time with my dad."

"Your father, of course. He left something for you." She motions *one moment*. Moves into the kitchen. Returns with a note. "Would playing a few songs from Chicago be too obvious?"

"That's a sweet thought, but I don't think I ever need to hear *All That Jazz* again."

Her smile is almost warm. Teasing even. "Amy Winehouse perhaps?" She offers another, more popular but jazz adjacent option. "Or do you prefer a different modern performer?"

"This is great. Really. I promise."

She places the note on the table. "What would you like for breakfast?"

"Anything is fine."

She stares at me, unblinking. "Of course, anything is fine, Jasmine. I can do anything. If you'd like me to decide—"

"Yes. Surprise me."

"Oolong, I assume?"

"Perfect." I nod *thanks* and pick up Dad's note. It's weird having an actual servant. Though I guess there's a more modern word for it. Assistant. Chef. Household manager.

Does it matter what you call Key's job? The title doesn't change the duties.

As long as he pays well, I suppose. It's not like I'm here out of choice.

But I am here. And I do have choices now. An entire day with nothing on the agenda.

What the hell am I supposed to do?

It's been a long time since I'd had options, much less a wealth of them.

My eyes flit to Dad's note. It's not a note, actually. More of a card. A thank you to me and Shepard for the treatment.

In his handwriting. He's doing well enough to write himself. My shoulders fall with relief.

I check my cell. A bunch of messages from acquaintances congratulating me on my engagement or digging for gossip.

Something from Dad, checking in. His usual check-in. Some normalcy amongst the craziness. Though, at this point, I'm pretty sure I am the craziness. Because thinking of last night—

Mmm.

Right on cue, my phone buzzes with a message from Shep.

Shep: There's lingerie in your drawer. Send me a picture of what you're wearing under your clothes today.

Jasmine: Or?

Shep: Or you won't get what you want.

That shouldn't be as hot as it is.

Jasmine: I'm going to visit my dad today.

Technically, I'm asking his permission. But I try not to consider that.

Shep: Lock can drive you. I've added his number to your cell. If he's running an errand for me, Key can call a car.

I guess that's a *sure, do whatever you want*. Or something close enough.

Shep: Send me a picture before you go.

Jasmine: Will you think about it at work?

Shep: Of course.

Jasmine: Will you touch yourself?

Shep: No, princess. I'm saving that for you.

Fuck.

I change the password on my cell. To something Dad won't guess. I don't want him reading this. Beyond embarrassing. And I'm not sure he'd really understand the whole… playing thing.

Key returns with a fresh cup of oolong. Perfectly steeped again.

Strong, nutty, just a little sweet. But strange. I'm not sure I like someone serving me tea.

I'd rather make it myself. I'd rather take care of myself. So I can feel self-reliant. Independent. In control.

No doubt, that means something, but I can't consider it right now. Only three hundred sixty-four days to go. After that, after I collect, then I can think about what this year means.

While I wait for breakfast, I stay busy looking at the current slate of productions on Broadway. Key is right. A seven-hundred-dollar ticket is nothing to Shep. He probably knows someone who will offer us their thousand-dollar tickets for free.

We'll sit at a private balcony. He'll ask me to take off my panties and slip his hand under my leg and—

As hot as the thought is, it's out of the question. Some things are sacred. Theater is one of them. I guess I'll have to add that to my limits. He'll laugh. Then smile. That smile he had when we were kids. When we actually understood each other.

Or maybe we never understood each other. Maybe that was an illusion. Youthful naivety. Something. It doesn't matter.

This time, I'm not getting the wrong idea. He can have my body.

And I can have his.

But that's all it is.

Love isn't part of the equation.

Chapter Twenty-One

JASMINE

The hallway smells like fish sauce. I'm sure the neighbors are annoyed, but I have to smile. It smells like home. Like happiness. Like Dad's well enough he's cooking something.

I'm stuffed with fresh raspberry chocolate chip pancakes—another perfect tea and food pairing—but I still feel a hunger. Not for food. For comfort. Love. Family.

The way things used to be.

I let myself in.

Dad looks up from his spot at the kitchen counter. "Jasmine, honey, taste this." He holds out his spoon. A sauce he's fixing on the stove. There are noodles draining in the sink. He's making bun cha. One of his favorites.

"Sure." I press the door closed. Nod hello to the aide who's here today, a tall man in blue scrubs, and move to the kitchen.

This apartment feels even smaller after being in Shep's place, but not in a way that's inferior.

Don't get me wrong. I appreciate the space in Shep's

massive Hell's Kitchen estate. But I appreciate the cozy feeling of family more.

I taste the sauce. It's strong enough I forget the fruity breakfast. "Wow."

"Wow?" He shakes his head. "You're too Americanized now."

"It's my fault you haven't cooked in five years?"

He doesn't bring up his illness, his reason for not cooking the last few years. He just nods *of course*. "You're old enough to cook for yourself now. You didn't even have fish sauce in your fridge." He shakes his head playfully.

"My neighbors complain."

He shakes his hand at them *ridiculous*. "Invite them over next time you make Pho. They won't complain anymore."

Probably true. But unlikely to happen. It's been a long time since I've attempted the all-day affair that is pho. Sure, the broth doesn't require a lot of active time, but I don't have the mental energy to plan a twelve hour beef bone boil.

Or a trip to the butcher for said beef bones.

I know Dad would mention some grocery in China-town, one through a strange alley, behind a corner, that you have to know to find. But that's too much effort.

Even the one ten blocks away is too far.

The place around the corner may not have a great selection, but it has good prices for the city, and it's the on the way home.

Good enough.

But then, there doesn't have to be any more good enough. I can ask Shepard's staff—the man has actual staff—to buy anything I want. I can make a mess crushing star anise with a mortar and pestle and demand someone else clean it up.

Not that I actually want to go through such an arduous task. They sell it crushed and it's nearly as good.

Mom would hate hearing that, but, hey, she's the one who loved The Beach Boys.

I smile as the song skips to "California Girls." Then I think about how Dad would always tell Mom how it was about his favorite girls now—*your real California girls now, sweetheart, are you going to learn to surf*—and my smile disappears.

I still miss her. But, more, I'm not ready to miss him yet.

Not that I need to consider it now.

He's up. He's cooking. Things are good. They can stay good. At least, for a while.

And the rest of my life… it's wide open. I can enjoy. Period. End of sentence.

I check my cell. Sure enough, I have both Lock and Key's numbers. I can ask them for anything.

Is that imposing? Or does it make their job easier if I'm specific?

After all, telling Key to surprise me with breakfast means she has to both come up with the idea and execute it.

I shoot her a text.

Jasmine: Can you find some Milk Oolong for later?

She replies immediately.

Key: Of course, Ms. Lee. Should I prepare an afternoon tea based on the flavor profile?

Why not?

Jasmine: Yes. Thanks. I'll let you know when I'm on my way home.

It's strange calling Shep's place home, but it's close enough.

Jasmine: Can you buy an extra tin? For my father?

Key: I'll have it sent over.

"Don't you have work?" Dad turns his attention to the pot on the stove. He stirs carefully, like he's fixing dinner for a king.

"Mr. Billings let me go."

He makes that awful *hmmm* noise.

"It doesn't look right, apparently. Me being engaged to Shep."

He does it again, only longer and lower.

"That's part of why we kept this quiet." It's a good explanation and it's almost true. "I like my job." Sure, my gig has its irritations. And, yes, I wouldn't do it for free. But there is something about getting things done. It feels good.

I want to be productive. Useful. Self-reliant.

I need to explain this in some way that will win Dad's approval. "I was worried about what would happen. I thought Mr. Billings would understand. But I guess there's no belief in love in business. Shep owns a competing VC firm. That's enough."

Again, he makes that horrible *hmmm* noise.

"I'm going to look for something else. But I'm not sure what. I don't think any other firms will hire me. Or... if they will, it will be because I'm engaged to the enemy, and they want to trot me out like a symbol. Look, it's Shepard Marlowe's wife. We can use her to get to him. We're important. Something like that."

He does it again.

I go to slide my hands into my pockets, but I'm not wearing a coat. It's warm today. Beautiful actually. My sweater dress—one I bought on sale at Nordstrom to treat myself on my twenty-first birthday—is already too thick for the weather.

But I like the thickness of the fabric. And the dark

color. They're shields. To hide all the things going through my head.

"I actually slept in today," I say. "I can't remember the last time that happened."

He finishes stirring the sauce. Turns the burner to warm. Goes to fixing the ground pork.

"How's the apartment treating you?"

"It must be expensive."

"Shep's covering it."

Again, the *hmmm*.

"He volunteered." Sort of. "I, um, I wanted to have an easier time visiting with you. Isn't this easier? We can walk to the park." We can't make it to Battery Park or Central Park or the Brooklyn Botanical Garden. But we can walk to Browne Park. Or something a little farther out.

"I like the apartment."

"Good."

"It's our apartment."

"Yeah."

"You should be here. Until you do get married."

I want to. So badly. But I can't tell him that. He'll get the wrong idea. "It's going to be soon. We're just getting ready."

"You're marrying soon?" He turns back to me, studies my expression.

I nod.

"Are you pregnant?"

"Dad!"

"Why else?"

I say nothing, but that doesn't matter. He reads it all over my face. Not the ruse or the deal I've made with Shep. The reason I agreed.

Because Dad is sick. Because he might die. Because I want him to walk me down the aisle.

"Jasmine…"

"You won't change my mind."

"He does make you happy?"

"Yes. But I'd be happier with a cup of tea."

He nods *of course*. Turns the water to hot and starts to wash his hands. "You don't distract me."

"I know."

"Tea doesn't fix everything."

"We'll see about that."

Again, that *hmm* noise. He stays silent as he fills the kettle, turns it on, scoops leaves into the pot. The same oolong. The one that was Mom's favorite.

I didn't like it at first. I always preferred the strength of black tea. The scented varieties. Earl Grey. Vanilla. Chai.

But, every day, Mom fixed me a cup of gaba oolong. And every day I liked it a little more.

"I actually… wanted to talk about something else," I say.

"Something besides your sudden wedding?" He heats a pan on the stove.

"Well… more about the planning." I pull my supplies from my purse. Two bridal magazines. Three catalog's. A tablet filled with boutiques, hair stylists, photographers. "I don't even have an idea about the dress."

The pan sizzles as a pork meatball hits the surface. Dad nods yes. But it's without his usual spirit.

He's thinking it too. That Mom should be here. That she should be the one helping me.

Instead of curling into himself, pushing some well of sadness as far down as it will go, he turns and offers a soft smile. "Thien would have insisted on a big, American wedding. A dress out of a Disney movie. Not the one you liked. Aunt Mai's favorite."

"*The Little Mermaid?*"

He nods *that's it*.

I pull up the image of Ariel in her wedding dress. Giant skirt with actual tiers and a touch of pink.

Dad smiles. "She would have encouraged you to feel like a princess. Or wear something modern, that you'd see on a celebrity. But, really, she would have been picturing you in traditional dress. Something red and gold with long sleeves and a matching hat."

I'm not so sure. Mom always pushed me to assimilate as much as possible. She would have wanted me to wear a very American dress. But it's easier for Dad to speak his peace when it's via what Mom would have wanted. "It would be beautiful."

"She always had high hopes for you and Shepard. She thought—"

"He was rich?"

He chuckles. "It's much easier, going through life with money than without."

That's the problem, isn't it? Shep has money. I need money. Which means I need him.

Money doesn't just buy rent, food, medicine. It buys freedom too.

The kettle steams. Dad washes his hands. Pours water over the leaves. Motions for me to sit.

I do. I start flipping through the first bridal magazine, but everything looks the same. Pretty blond women in ivory dresses on light blue backgrounds.

Key left all these in the car. For me. From her or Shep, I don't know. It is helpful. But it's presumptuous too. Like I can't handle this alone.

Who am I kidding? I *can't* handle this alone. There's way too much that goes into planning a wedding. Especially into planning a wedding that fits a man who owns half of Manhattan.

I should take Shep's advice. Let his team handle the details.

But not the dress. They can't take the dress.

———

Dad focuses on cooking until the meatballs are finished. He turns the burner to warm, fixes another round of tea, joins me at the table.

I'm already on my second catalog, but I haven't absorbed any of it.

Fabric flits through my mind. Lace, ivory, silk, tulle, chiffon. In ivory, white, cream, blush, and even the occasional baby blue.

So many different dresses. So many beautiful dresses. So many ornate details. Beads, sequins, feathers, chiffon flowers.

Does the dress need to mean something?

Can it just be a dress?

All this wedding information makes the same point.

This is the best day of your life. Never compromise. It's about what you want.

But it's not the best day of *my* life. It's another day where I'm under Shep's command. And the dress…

It's not about finding something that matches the occasion. Not exactly.

It's about holding on to the little part of control I have. Wearing something that proclaims *I'm Jasmine Lee and I'm more than a rich man's wife. I'm…*

Something.

Dad taps the page on the right. A silk sheath. "It would suit you."

Maybe. It's beautiful. Elegant. Sexy even.

Is that what I want to say about myself?

I haven't thought much about my wedding. Even when I was a girl, when Shep and I were teenagers in love.

My thoughts of the future were always college, my own apartment, shows in the city. Not love or kids or marriage. I knew I would have that. It wasn't even a choice. It was just what I was supposed to do.

Now…

"Drink your tea." Dad pushes the mug toward me.

I wrap my hands around the warm ceramic. Take a long sip. It is soothing. It always is. "Thank you."

"No offense, honey, but why ask me?"

"I'm not supposed to ask for my father's help with my wedding?" I try to recall friends' weddings or things I've seen on TV. It's usually moms, sisters, aunts even. "Are you going to call Aunt Mai?" Quyen would be better with clothes, but he admires Mai's practical streak. "Ask her to close the restaurant for a week so she can fly out here?"

He chuckles. "Shepard could afford it."

He could. And he would. It's not actually the worst idea in the world.

"You're inviting them to the wedding. Why not to the wedding planning?"

"I'll consider that." It's the best idea I've had so far. Though… knowing my aunts… They're two bossy, in demand ladies. They'll hijack the wedding as well as Shep's team will. They'll be on my side, yes, but they'll also be following their vision.

He takes a long sip of his oolong. "I know you love my fashion sense." He motions to his t-shirt and sweatpants. "But you must have girlfriends who are almost as stylish."

"I'm not sure anyone comes close, Dad." I can't help but smile. I wish I had his optimism. Maybe my kids will. Maybe it skips a generation.

Or maybe this is too much, too soon.

Last night was amazing. But jumping into a whole wedding—

It's a lot.

"Still, it can't hurt to have the moral support," he says.

I nod *true*. Flip the page to an over-the-top princess dress. It's the spitting image of Belle's dress from *Beauty and the Beast*, only cream instead of bright yellow. A little more subtle, but only a little.

He laughs and says something about American weddings. Which is ridiculous. Vietnamese weddings are huge status symbols. Maybe even more so than American weddings.

Everyone, everywhere wants the chance to show off. To say *look at my beautiful daughter, my beautiful wife, this beautiful life she's going to embark on.*

So far, Shep's team hasn't forced me into any specific appointments. I can spend the next two weeks—or however long I have to figure this out—trying on dress after dress. Or I can pick one out of a magazine. Or call a seamstress and ask her to create something from scratch.

But I understand the rush. I need to decide this, soon, or his team will decide for me.

"If you aren't going to call your aunts, bring a friend. It will help." His smile is soft. And a little sad. Because he's not well enough to help. Or because Mom isn't here. Or both.

"I will." Only I don't have any close friends. Not anymore. My first year of college, I bloomed. I met so many people who shared my interests. Who wanted to talk about film or theater or the wonder of New York City.

But after Dad got sick and I had to drop out to work full time—

It was too hard, explaining my decision, dealing with the looks of pity people offered. It was too hard, dealing with expectations. Even with other people in my position. Or worse positions.

They thought they understood because they'd been through similar hardships. Maybe they did. Maybe I was the one who didn't get it.

I'm friendly with lots of people. But there are only a few I trust for anything genuine.

Dad. And Nick.

That was complicated before Shepard asked me to marry him. Now…

"What about Lizzy?" He mentions Nick's fiancée. Who was once his subordinate. At the company where I worked as Nick's assistant. God, that was a minefield. "She was always stylish."

He's right. Lizzy is very stylish. And she's not the type of person who expects anything of me. She didn't take the normal path either. Went from Stanford to a New York school no one remembers, all to stay closer to her sister.

But she's also nineteen. Twenty now, maybe. A kid. A kid who's going to marry my fiancé's brother.

If we were normal people, that would mean she was my future sister, and we'd be skipping hand in hand. Or complaining about the in-laws.

"You know things are strained with Nick and Shep," I say.

"Life is too short, Jasmine."

"It's his life, not mine."

He shakes his head *it's ridiculous*. Sips his tea.

It's nice, him disapproving of my fiancé's life choices. He's looking out for me again. We're having a normal breakfast. Like we would if he wasn't sick. "I'm not going to get in the middle." It's hard enough dealing with this arrangement without Shep thinking I'm on his brother's side.

"Aren't you going to invite them to the wedding?"

"Of course."

He holds out his hand *sounds like an opportunity*.

That's true enough. "They need time."

"Why?"

I thought I knew. Now, not so much. Nick holds onto secrets better than anyone. And Shepard is as tight-lipped as they come.

"Was it because of rehab? How Nick forced Shep to get sober?" Dad asks. My surprise must be obvious, because he clarifies. "It was in the papers."

It was a few lines in a few business sections. But only the part about rehab. Not the rest. Even I don't know the details. Somehow, Nick did what I couldn't. He convinced Shep to get clean. And now Shep hates him with a fiery passion.

Is it as simple as a little blackmail? Nick taking away the one thing Shep loves?

Or maybe it has something to do with this arrangement.

No… Nick isn't the type. He's a straightforward, no-nonsense guy. Except for the whole sleeping with an intern ten years his junior thing, he's obsessed with propriety.

I rack my brain for some explanation that will tie these things together—Nick convincing Shep to get sober and Shep paying me to marry him—but there's only one thing.

Me.

I wouldn't do this if he was drinking. He must know that.

But it's been a year. There's no way he waited all that time.

"Jasmine?" Dad makes that *mm-hmm* noise again. "There's something you're not saying."

"Nothing important."

"I know I'm old—"

"You're not old." He's not even fifty.

"But I still remember things. And I remember your fiancé." His intent is clear. *He was always drinking. Always drunk. Even when the situation didn't call for it.*

I can't exactly deny it. But I can change the subject. "This isn't helping me pick out a dress."

He doesn't bite. "It will be your family soon. It will be your problem too."

Maybe. But I'm really not getting in the middle.

I pull out my cell to text Shep.

To say… something. I'm not sure if I actually want Lizzy's help, but I do want to know what he'll say.

Is he still furious?

Because he thinks Nick fucked me? Or because of rehab? Or something else, something I don't see.

There's already a message from Shep.

Shep: I just got word from a colleague. We need to have our engagement party on Saturday. Is that a problem?

Jasmine: No.

Shep: Good.

Jasmine: I was going to ask Lizzy for her advice on a dress.

Shep: You're in touch?

Jasmine: On and off.

That's an exaggeration. But I know the sassy programmer. She'll be jazzed to see me. And even more excited to offer fashion advice.

She defies that whole *nerds only wear jeans and graphic tees* stereotype.

Shep: Just Lizzy?

Jasmine: Who else?

Shep: You've been friends with Nick for a long time.

Jasmine: He's not a fashionista, last time I checked.

Shep: Just Lizzy. I don't want you seeing him alone.

So he does believe something happened. Or he's jealous.

I want to tell him to fuck off. To insist I'll see who I want.

But that's not what I agreed to. I'm not to appear unfaithful. Dinner with my fiancé's brother—

That will be a headache to explain.

Not that I have a choice.

I'm still Shep's to bend, pose, break.

But I'm not letting it get to me today. Today, I'm going to enjoy the spoils. To soak up every drop of freedom.

Even if there are only a few sips.

Chapter Twenty-Two

SHEPARD

My phone buzzes against my thigh.

Jasmine. Everything else goes through my assistant.

No doubt something else about my brother. To tempt me. Tease me. Drive me insane.

If he touched her…

I look to the woman sitting across from me. She's talking about her startup. Some medical technology that will save the world. It's a brilliant idea, but it's going to take a lot of money.

Even then, it's a long shot.

Still worth the risk. I make an offer.

She stares back at me, mouth agape, eyes filled with surprise. She's new to this world. Everything is still thrilling. Everything is still second to the mission.

"Of course, Mr. Marlowe. Just get the paperwork to our lawyer." She smiles, excited but careful.

I like her. If things were different, I'd invite her to dinner. Or to skip dinner and go straight to sex. I used to play a lot, yes. But I enjoyed normal sex too. Whatever normal means.

So long as women understand my terms—that I'm always the one who moves things along—I enjoy a lot.

Now...

She's intelligent, articulate, beautiful. A lithe brunette with trendy clothes and defined features. If she wasn't a medical student, she could be a model. I'm sure she turns every head that passes her. I'm sure most men picture her in their bed.

But I don't. I only see Jasmine. Already, my head is filling with thoughts of her soft groan. Her tan thighs. Her red lips.

I need that again.

I need her tied to my bed.

I need her writhing with pleasure. So much she's begging me to stop.

"Of course." I stand. Shake the start-up founder's hand. Walk her to the door.

My assistant says something about a next meeting, but I ask her to wait. She offers coffee. When I say no, she looks at me like I'm crazy.

It is crazy. I don't turn down coffee. I'm a walking cliché. The recovering alcoholic who turned to sex and caffeine.

But then I guess I already have my preferred fix.

"An espresso, yes." I wave a thanks. "In ten minutes. I have a call."

Her expression gets knowing. She's almost as bad as Key. God, when Key and Lock get together—

I'm sure Jasmine would roll her eyes at a third assistant. It is ridiculous. But I need to keep things separate. I need sharp lines between every segment of my life. It's the only way.

I lock the door. Lower the shades facing the floor. Turn to the window.

It's already late morning. Almost noon. The sky is a brilliant shade of blue. The sun is shining. The water is sparkling.

I'm far enough south I can see where the Hudson and the East River meet. I can see the lush trees of Battery Park.

They were a soft pink two months ago. Now, they're a bright green. A shade that screams of a coming summer.

Hopeful.

For once, I appreciate it.

I pull my cell from my pocket. But it's not another picture of Jasmine in violet lingerie.

Jasmine: Just Lizzy. But he might be there. To drop her off. Or at their apartment.

My blood boils. My fucking brother. I don't need the reminder.

It's bad enough that bastard is reminding me of the timeline. It's bad enough I'm rushing the announcement. The wedding itself. The fucking planning.

Now I have to picture my brother making Jasmine come.

As much as I doubt Nick's intentions, I believe he loves his fiancée. He would do anything for Lizzy. He would never consider touching another woman. Not now.

Before he met Lizzy—

I need to erase that time from my mind. It's not like I was celibate. I slept with plenty of women. If Jasmine slept with another man, even my fucking brother—

I don't have any right to complain.

But my body fails to listen. My palms clench, my ears flame, my stomach churns.

I need her on my desk, her skirt at her waist, her legs spread wide, her back arching as she comes.

Fuck, I'm not holding onto my thoughts for long enough. I need to get a grip.

This wedding should be a joyous occasion. Sure, I'll never love Jasmine, but I do appreciate her. If I was going to choose a wife, it would be her.

Only it's not my choice. And even the promise of her soft thighs against my cheeks every day, for the rest of my life, isn't enough to erase that.

Nothing can erase the truth.

That bastard is pulling my strings again. No matter what I do, I'll never be out from under his thumb. If I didn't think there was some way he'd hold this over me from the grave, I'd kill him myself.

He deserves worse. He deserves a life of abject misery.

But I haven't managed that. I haven't managed to repay an ounce of the pain he gave me.

One day.

One day, I make him hurt.

Right now, I destroy his bullshit challenge.

Jasmine: Will it be a dry party?

Shep: No.

Jasmine: Do you think that's a good idea?

Maybe not, but I'm not about to advertise my sobriety to the world. Especially not with the likelihood that bastard will attend. I don't need him thinking he's done that to me too.

Shep: Last I heard, you drink gin. Bombay Sapphire.

Jasmine: Should I ask how you heard that?

Shep: Ian is coming, so I'll have five kinds of tonic water.

Jasmine: That seems excessive.

Shep: Apparently, there are a dozen varieties of Fever Tree. And most bars in London have at least three.

Jasmine: Are you mocking him? Or is he mocking you?

Shep: A little of both.

Jasmine: Wasn't he drinking bourbon at dinner?

Shep: Like I said, a little of both.

Jasmine: I'm glad you have a friend you can tease.

Huh. I don't usually think of Ian as a friend. Friends aren't really my concern. But I guess the word fits him.

Jasmine: Will Nick be there?

It would look strange if they didn't come.

But that presents a problem. A big problem.

My brother responded to that bastard differently. My brother prefers honesty and disclosure, at least when it comes to the people he trusts.

He trusts his fiancée.

And he trusts Jasmine.

Which means—

There's a possibility I need to prevent.

Shep: We should meet with them before the party. For dinner.

Jasmine: I was going to suggest that.

Shep: Great minds.

I'm sure her reasons are different. I'm sure she wants Nick and I to become best friends again.

Friend is pushing it.

But I do need his cooperation. His agreement. His silence.

I will convince him to keep his mouth shut. Whatever it takes.

Chapter Twenty-Three

JASMINE

After a few games of Five Hundred Rummy, our millionth viewing of *The Da Vinci Code*, and Dad shaking his head at my inability to appreciate the brilliance of the movie—*how can anyone dislike anything with Tom Hanks?*—we take our lunch to the park.

The park. Outside. In the fresh air.

It's something else, seeing Dad walking on the grass. It's been a long time since he's been well enough to come here.

It's a beautiful day. Warm and sunny. I don't even mind my too thick dress. I don't mind overheating as I walk back to our apartment and hug Dad goodbye.

The car is waiting, of course. With the air-conditioning on high. By the time I'm back at Shep's place, I'm freezing.

And there it is. The afternoon tea Key promised, waiting for me. I guess Lock called to announce our ETA.

What's it like, having everyone else handle the logistics?

I guess I should get used to it.

The milk oolong is perfect. Creamy and sweet. With buttery tea cakes and fresh peaches.

It's almost relaxing, sitting on Shep's balcony, taking in the beautiful day.

No, it is, for a while. As I sip another pot and leaf through a play I read in high school. It's funny, looking at things as an adult. There's so much more in it. So much I never understood.

I no longer see *A Midsummer Night's Dream* as a silly romp. It is, but there's more too. After all this debauchery, everyone gets married. They commit to a normal, orderly life.

The characters pay a price for their adventures.

I guess I understand that well.

———

I TRY WAITING UP FOR SHEP, BUT I DON'T MAKE IT. IN THE morning, I wake to an empty apartment. He's already at work.

I enjoy a fancy breakfast—more pancakes, chocolate chip this time—and never-ending cups of tea. Another close look at a famous play.

A Streetcar Named Desire this time.

God, is all theater this depressing? Why didn't I notice in high school? I guess it fit my mood then. After I lost Mom, it was hard seeing the beauty in the world.

Now—

It's hard to believe I'm better at finding joy, but I am.

I ask Lock to take me to the Brooklyn Botanical Garden. No doubt, he checks with Shep for permission, but I push that aside. I walk and talk with him. Ask all about his life, growing up in London, and what made him decide to move to America.

And if the rumors are true, about his more... broad sexuality.

He's a gentleman. Teases me but keeps things professional. Even when he whisks me to a champagne tea. And an evening of shopping—I need something for our engagement party, apparently—he keeps bringing the conversation back to me.

What I want to do.

My favorite play.

If I prefer dramas or comedies.

When Mr. Marlowe is going to take me to see the latest and greatest. And, if not, maybe he'll take me.

He claps when I pick a dress, fills my ears with tales of Shep visiting London, teases me about my desire to stop at Dunkin Donuts.

Key can prepare something much better. And there's no way he's allowing a ninety-nine cent donut in this household. Especially when it's not even fresh.

It's funny. He's funny. And it feels like we're old friends.

The day feels easy. Until I get home to dinner and I eat alone.

This time, I'm up late enough to see Shep. But he barely says hello. Just nods, changes into his gym clothes, mentions something about needing to work out frustrations.

His eyes flit over me quickly. Like he's considering another way of working out his frustrations.

But he doesn't. He leaves.

———

Even after a busy, full day—lunch with Dad, afternoon tea, an off-Broadway play—it's impossible to sleep. Shep is right there. In the next room. Alone.

And I'm here alone.

Why is he avoiding me?

I try to put it out of mind, but I can't. I try counting sheep, but it's useless. I try reading one of the books Dad bought me, but it's not interesting enough.

The question echoes through my mind.

I replay our last encounter again and again. Let my curiosity turn to dirtier things.

But even when I stroke myself to orgasm, it's not enough. It's satisfying.

Sure, I fall asleep. But I don't wake up rested.

I wake up wanting.

Chapter Twenty-Four

SHEPARD

"Shep?" Jasmine's tone is soft, but there's something else there. That assistant voice she uses. The one that masks everything in her head.

"Yes?" My body turns toward hers. It's impulse. I'm too tuned to her. Too interested.

She doesn't want me in her head or heart. I shouldn't be in her head or her heart.

I can't invite her into mine.

She turns. Motions to the zipper of her cocktail dress.

The garment is gorgeous. A deep floral print that skims her chest and falls over her hips.

She's wearing her hair down today. In its usual straight line. The one that makes her look more trendy than traditional.

I pull the zipper up her back. Let my fingers graze her shoulder blades. "Are you supposed to wear white?"

Key was going on about it, but that's a blur. The last few days are a blur.

It's consuming all my mental energy, the horrible thought of my brother ruining everything.

This hasn't even started and I already need a fucking drink.

Bourbon. Neat. Enough to dull every thought in my brain.

That's out of the question. That bastard isn't seeing me drunk and sloppy. He's not thinking he's won.

And I'm not about to lose Jasmine—

"Some people do." She turns. Looks at me. "Are you going to ask me to change?"

"No." I'm not aware enough of the rules here. I need to know them. It makes things easier. "You look lovely."

"Lovely?" She arches her back enough her chest rises into the air. Half pride, half *I dare you not to look*. "Am I allowed to ask if you're okay?"

"Fine."

"This is fine?"

"And you?"

She makes that *eh* motion with her hand. "It's a lot."

"Did your aunts make it okay?" I'm not sure why I ask. Lock picked them up from JFK a few hours ago. He's already dropped them at a hotel and suggested a few places to shop, dine, spa.

"You don't know?"

"Making conversation."

"Shepard Marlowe is making conversation? This is a first." She half-smiles.

She's inviting me to talk to her.

But conversation isn't going to help.

"I'm a little…" My eyes drift to her chest. The curving neckline hugs her enough to invite my hands. I do want her out of that thing. I want to tear the soft fabric in half. Use it to bind her wrists. "Distracted."

That's too much for her. I need to stay away. I don't trust myself.

"And you?" I ask.

"Am I… distracted?" Her eyes flit over my body. She takes in my tailored suit. Then she moves closer. Adjusts my tie. "It matches well."

"Too much?"

"You don't usually ask my approval."

"Like I said—"

"Distracted?"

"Yes." My gaze flits to the window. Still afternoon. The sun is bright.

I'd think it was beautiful if I saw beauty in the world. Instead, I count the minutes we have before we meet my brother and his girlfriend.

Fuck, I've barely considered the girlfriend. I don't regret what I asked of her last year. It was necessary. But I'm sure she holds it against me.

Some people—

Most people don't see the world the way I do. Whatever it takes, to get what I want, whatever that means for others. Selfish, maybe, but I don't give a fuck. If there's something in the way of Jasmine's safety, I'm not going to ask nicely.

That's about all I can promise.

I can't offer her happiness or love—

I don't understand happiness or love.

People say they're happy when they have certain things or hit certain milestones. Are they really? Or are they telling themselves some story?

Having her here, living in my space, mine in every practical way, but not the ways that matter—

It's fucking confusing. I start thinking ridiculous things. Wanting ridiculous things. Like her heart.

Like her accepting my heart.

That's impossible. There's no heart in my chest.

There's a black hole that sucks in pain and circulates it through my entire fucking body.

I can't offer her love.

I can't offer her happiness.

But I can make her come.

I can unzip her dress, push it to the floor, bend her over the table—

"Are you okay?" she asks again. All her. No assistant voice.

"No."

"Oh." Her eyes meet mine. "We do have time. Before we leave to meet your brother."

"We have time?"

"Yes." Her voice drops to a seductive tone. "It's been a few days."

I nod.

"You've been avoiding me?"

"I'm busy."

She stares back at me with disbelief. "At least an hour. By my count. There must be a reason you're ready early."

Yes, I want to fuck her senseless. But it's too much for her. She isn't ready for that. "You don't know what you're asking."

"I don't?"

"I had patience the other day. I don't right now."

"So?"

"I can't be careful. I can't promise to follow your limits."

Her eyes bore into mine. She stares at me, looking for something.

I'm sure there's plenty on her mind, between her dad and the rest of her family. This is a lot for her too. She has just as much at stake.

She wants a distraction too.

I promised to take care of her.

I turn all my attention to her. "I can't promise I'll stay in control."

"What does that mean?"

I don't know. I don't let it happen. "I might hurt you."

"You won't."

I will. That's what she doesn't understand. She still sees the boy she loved. Not the man who's embraced the darkness in his core. "I can't promise that." I push a breath through my teeth. "I don't want to hurt you. I care about you."

"You care about me?"

"Yes."

She laughs. "I guess, coming from you, that's a lot." She turns toward me. "I care about you too." Carefully, she rests her hand on my chest. "And I care about this. I want to play. I… I like that you won't be careful."

My balls tighten.

"I don't want you to be careful." Her cheeks flush. "I want you to be rough."

"You remember the safe word?"

"Coffee bean." She licks her lips again.

I suck in a deep breath. Does she really know what she's agreeing to?

I don't want to hurt her.

But I can't turn this down either. "Are you sure?"

"Yes." Her voice is confident.

I close the distance between us.

Then I slip my fingers under her necklace. I tug it hard, bring her body against mine.

"You have no idea what you're getting yourself into, princess."

Chapter Twenty-Five

JASMINE

Shep holds my body against his. My head against his neck, my back against his chest, my ass against his cock.

He's already hard. I can feel him. Even through all the layers of chiffon. Through the Italian wool of his suit.

He tugs at my necklace again. Hard enough the silver chain digs into my skin.

When I slink forward, he pulls the chain until it breaks.

The metal clatters on the floor. It should bother me that he just broke a necklace with a four-figure price tag, but it doesn't. It's not even that it's his money. That he probably bought it specifically for this purpose.

I wouldn't care if it was my money. If it was some priceless family heirloom I'd sworn to protect.

I only care about his firm touch. That sharp edge to his voice. The feel of his breath on my neck.

He wraps his fingers around my throat. Not hard enough to cut off my airways. Just hard enough to know he can hurt me.

There are so many ways Shep can hurt me. He can snap his fingers and destroy my entire life. That scares me.

This—

This makes my entire body buzz.

I love that he can hurt me. It turns me on so much more than it should. There's some part of me that cares, but it's too far away, too fuzzy.

I want his threat. I want his power. I want his command.

I arch my back, stretching my body over his, pushing my ass against his cock.

"Are you trying to tease me, princess?" His voice is rough. Angry even. But, under that, he's daring me.

"If I am?"

In response, he reaches for my zipper. It's not the slow, gentle gesture of earlier.

He tugs it down my back. Yanks my dress over my torso.

My breasts spill from the fabric.

He keeps one hand around my neck. Brings the other to my chest. Runs his thumb over my nipple.

God, it's been so long since he's touched me. This is the first time he's really touched me. It makes my entire body buzz. It wakes up something deep inside me, some part of me that's been dormant for far too long.

"Fuck," I breathe.

He runs his thumb over my neck with one hand. Rolls my nipple between his thumb and forefinger with the other. "You like when I play with you, princess?"

"Yes, sir."

"Is that why you wore this dress?"

I suck a breath through my nose.

His touch gets firmer. Hard enough it hurts in the best

possible way. "Did you wear it to tease me? To make me think about your perfect tits."

"No… Maybe." My chest heaves with my inhale.

He presses his palm into my neck, pulling me closer. It's hard. Rough.

For a split second, I struggle with my inhale. It should scare me. It does. But in a way that makes me ache for more.

Every molecule inside me screams for him.

He switches to his middle finger. Draws slow circles around my nipple. Then faster. Harder. "You know what happens if you dare me, princess?"

"No." I almost add sir, but I don't. I want to tease him. I want to dare him. I want to make him rough.

"No?"

"No." I say it again, more firmly, so my intent is clear.

He pinches my nipple so hard I see white.

In one swift motion, he bends me over, pinning me to the dinner table.

My forehead bumps the wood. Ow.

I turn my head until my cheek is against the cherry surface. It's strange and uncomfortable and sexy as all hell.

Shep doesn't wait for a response. He pulls my dress over my hips and ass. All the way to my thighs.

The fabric is soft, but it's tight enough it binds me. I can barely move my legs.

I'm at his mercy.

"Shep—" I reach back for him. For something I can hold on to. I'm not sure what I'm asking. Only that I want it more than I've ever wanted anything.

"You know what happens when you dare me, princess?" His voice stays rough and demanding.

I turn my head enough to look up at him. He's

standing over me, fully dressed, every hair in place. But those blue eyes are on fire.

It's all there, in his eyes. Somehow, he's out of control and in control at once. This is what he needs.

And, somehow, it's what I need too.

I should probably call a therapist. Ask her what the fuck is wrong with me. But I don't care about anything but this game.

"Should I take your silence as a no?" His voice gets rougher. Firmer. More in control. He's slipping into his role. Into this game we're playing.

I don't quite understand the rules, but I know I like it. I really fucking like it.

"Do you?" He places his palm between my shoulder blades. Not hard or soft. Just enough I feel the pressure. Just enough I know he could stroke me gently or push me into the table.

"No." Again, I drop the sir. "What happens?"

Without warning, his hand comes down on my ass. His palm against my flesh. Hard enough it stings.

My sex clenches. My nipples perk. My nails dig into the table. I'm going to leave a mark. I'm going to want this every time I see it.

The place I marked when Shepard spanked me. It's so dirty it's wrong. But it feels too good to be wrong.

He does it again. Only harder. Hard enough I gasp.

"Fuck," I breathe. I can ask him to stop. Beg him to stop. Use the safe word. But I don't want that. I want more.

He does it again. That same impact. Enough my cheek bounces against the table.

Again.

My nipples pang.

Again.

My thighs shudder.

Again.

My body screams *more*.

I'm halfway out of my dress, pressed against the dining room table, taking spankings from a man who has the power to destroy me.

And I love every second of it.

What the hell happened to me? And why don't I care?

"Bad girl," he growls. On anyone else, it would sound ridiculous, like a line out of a bad porno. But on Shep?

Fuck. "Yes." I push the words through my teeth.

He tugs at my thong. Runs his fingers over the soft fabric, tracing the waistband. Then the line over my ass and sex. Finally, his fingers skim my clit, over the fabric.

It's smooth. Too smooth. I need *his* hands on my skin. I need *him* touching me properly.

But I still haven't begged. Is he still waiting for me to beg? Does something deep inside him need that?

I can't say I understand it. But I can still play. I can still give him what he wants.

"You wore this to tempt me." Again, his hand comes down hard on my ass.

"Shep—"

"Yes?"

"I… Yes. I did."

He spanks me again. "Was this what you wanted, princess?"

"Yes."

"What else?" *Smack*. His hand hits my flesh.

"You."

"How?"

"Your hands on my chest. My ass. My clit. Your cock. In my hands. My mouth. My sex." Fuck. It's like some dirty version of myself is in control. "I want you to fuck me."

"You think about it?"

"Yes."

"How often?"

"All the time."

"You touch yourself?"

"Yes."

"I'm not giving you enough? You want more?" he asks.

"Yes."

"Yes?"

I try to read his voice. He doesn't want the defiance anymore. He wants obedience. But I haven't had enough yet. I need more. "Yes."

He spanks me hard. The sting of pain tightens the ache inside me. Makes everything feel sharper. Hard enough my entire body screams *more*. And clearer.

I expect another. A threat. A demand. But he surprises me. He pushes my thong aside. Drives two fingers into my sex.

I gasp. "Shep—"

"Is this what you want?"

I nod into the table.

He drives his fingers into me again.

"More," I breathe.

He does it again and again. A steady rhythm that winds the tension inside me tighter and tighter. "You get what I want, princess."

That already feels so good. His digits inside me. His body inside mine.

"When I decide you want it badly enough." He pushes his fingers into me again and again. He drives his fingers a little deeper. A little harder.

It hurts for a moment, then the hurt fades to pressure. Then pleasure. So much I have to close my eyes. So much I have to bite my lip.

I reach for a response, a dare, something. But the only thing I find is a moan.

Words are fuzzy. Far away. The rest of the world is fuzzy and far away.

I only experience what's here and now.

The slick cherry table. The orange light falling over the apartment. The ruffle of chiffon against my skin.

Shep's hand on my back.

My dress at my thighs.

His firm fingers driving into me, winding me tighter and tighter.

Again and again.

Almost—

"Come for me, princess." He pushes his palm into my back a little harder. Just enough I know I'm his.

Then he brings his thumb to my clit. Up and down in the tiniest, softest movements until—

"Fuck." With the next brush of his fingers, I go over the edge. The tension inside me unwinds, flows through my pelvis, my torso, my limbs.

I dig my nails into the table. Into my thighs.

I groan his name as I come.

I expect him to release me. Order me onto my knees. Shove his cock inside me. But he doesn't. He keeps running his finger over my clit.

Again and again.

My sex whines. It wants more, but it can't take more. The pressure is too intense.

Again.

It's not enough. It's too much.

But it's bliss too.

He digs his nails into my back. When I groan, he growls. "Good girl."

It pushes me over the edge. Everything gets fuzzy.

Everything except the bliss washing through my body. Making the world into someplace pure and beautiful.

This time, he works me through my orgasm.

Once I'm finished, he releases me. But only for a moment. For long enough for him to adjust his clothes.

He loops something around my wrist. His tie.

"One palm on top of the other," he commands. When I do it, he cinches a knot. Loose. Then just tight enough I know I'm bound.

My wrists by his tie. My thighs by my dress. My entire body splayed over the table.

I'm completely at his mercy. His, to use however he sees fit.

And, God, I want it so badly. Even though I came twice, I want more. I'm achy and empty and utterly in need of him.

"Shepard," I breathe. "Please."

"Please what, princess?"

"Fuck me. Please." I can't remember our game. What I'm playing. If I'm trying to rile him or soothe him. But I don't care. I only care about getting his cock inside me.

"Please?"

"Please, sir. I want you inside of me. I want to feel you come."

He reaches back and unzips his slacks. "You want to feel me come?" he asks it again, but with a clearer voice. Almost a break of character.

It takes a moment to catch his meaning. We've talked about being safe. How we don't need a condom. But we haven't specifically outlined that. "Yes. Nothing else. Just you." My sex pangs. "Please. Sir."

He brings both hands to my hips, pulls them up, into the air. "You're greedy, princess."

"Yes, sir," I breathe.

He pulls me a little higher as he shifts a little closer. His cock brushes my sex. Just barely.

My entire body whines. I've never been so empty. I've never needed anything this badly.

He pulls back and does it again.

And again.

Then, without warning, he drives into me hard enough he pins me to the table.

I reach for something, but my wrists are bound. I try to spread my legs, but my dress is at my thighs. I try to arch my back, but he's already driving into me again.

Fuck. That feels so good.

His nails scrape my hip. Then the other hip. He holds me in place as he drives into me again.

My sex whines for more. But the table against my face? Ow. I turn my head to the other cheek, but it's no help. The same slick surface.

Shep shifts, doing something to his clothes.

He tugs at my wrists, at the tie holding them together, then he slips his suit jacket onto the table, and lowers me onto the fabric. "Turn your head."

I do.

He bunches the jacket, making a softer padding.

He sets me down gently.

Then he thrusts into me hard.

How can he be so tender and so rough at the same time?

How can I want both so much?

How can I—

Fuck.

His cock stretches me to my limit. Between the pressure and the promise of his words-

This is already more pressure than I can take.

He rocks into me again.

My body stretches to take him. It's a lot. Almost too much. But then that's not enough.

He does it again.

Harder and harder.

Until I groan loud enough to wake the neighbors.

He keeps that same perfect rhythm. He fills me with deep, steady thrusts. Winds the tension in my sex tighter and tighter.

My eyes close. My nails dig into my palms. My legs go slack.

Again and again.

Until I'm there.

I groan his name as I come. I reach for him, for anything, but the tie catches my wrists.

It pushes me further. Heightens the pleasure flooding my body, so I feel every bit of it in every single molecule.

Shep thrusts through my orgasm with that same steady pace, then he goes harder, faster.

His groans run together like he's part animal. Like he's completely out of control.

Then he's there, spilling inside me, growling my name as he comes.

He thrusts through his orgasm, giving me every single drop.

When he's finished, he undoes the tie binding my wrists. He peels my dress to my legs. Then he lifts me, holds my body against his chest, carries me to the bathroom in the hall.

He helps me clean up. Helps me into my clothes.

Kisses me hard. Kisses me like he loves me as much as he needs me.

My head spins. But, right now, I don't care. Right now, my entire world is a place of pure ecstasy.

Because I am his. And he is mine. It's only like this. But that's all I want.

It's all I can want. Because it's all I can have.

So I find my footing as I take his hand and follow him to the elevator and into the limo.

And I smile as he rolls up the privacy screen and looks at me with that fire in his eyes.

"Get on your knees, princess. I'm going to come in that pretty mouth."

Chapter Twenty-Six

JASMINE

"**Y**ou look so pretty." Lizzy jumps from her chair. Then skips—actually skips—to meet me. She throws her arms out in a hug.

"You too." I squeeze her tightly. "Grown up."

She releases me with a smile. Smooths her dress. It's pure Lizzy. A deep purple fit and flare that's equal parts cute and sexy.

It's also… affordable. From one of those trendy sites that sells vintage inspired clothes for a hundred-something dollars.

Sure, that's beyond the budget of most college students. But it's not exactly the four-figure price tag of the dress I'm wearing.

Nick doesn't seem to notice. Or maybe he doesn't care. I can't tell. He's always been careful about appearances. And about following rules.

When I worked for him, he was very clear about the line between private and professional. He refused to discuss personal matters at the office. Or to discuss work matters after hours.

He offered me a job at his start-up because he knew I needed it. But once I got there, he treated me like I was any other employee. Not like I was an old friend. Not like I was his brother's ex-girlfriend.

Lizzy was one of our programming interns. I was surprised when he started mentoring her personally. It wasn't like Nick. He stayed out of things. And he certainly didn't take an interest in pretty young college students.

I never, once, thought he'd cross that line. He's not that type.

When I realized they were fucking—

I was angry. Disappointed even.

He's better than that. He's better than risking everything for his dick. He's certainly better than taking advantage of a subordinate.

But when I saw them together… I don't know. They're too right to be wrong.

He needs her. And she needs him. I don't know how it happened, but the reclusive tech mogul is madly in love.

His eyes light up as Lizzy spins on her heels—well, her black wedges. She's even shorter than I am, but she has some kind of back issue, as a result of being in the car accident that killed her parents. She lives in cute yet practical wedges.

And she…

I guess she and Nick have that in common. The loss. It must be nice to be with someone who understands. Who's willing to share that pain. Who doesn't look at you like you're defective because you still miss your mom.

"Kat always says that." She mentions her sister, an artist studying at Columbia.

"Is she coming?" I supervised the guest list, but my thoughts are still fuzzy. Dulled by pleasure.

Lizzy nods. "To an engagement party?" Lizzy pushes

her dark glasses up her nose. They're perfect for her. They scream *cool computer geek*. "Are you kidding? Kat never misses the chance to celebrate love." She holds her hand to her heart, imitating her sister. "Isn't it beautiful?" She leans back. "Two people joining their lives forever?"

Nick rushes to Lizzy. Holds her steady.

She shoots him a knowing look. One of those couple looks.

Something passes between them. Something only they understand.

It makes my heart pang. I'm happy for them. Really. I'm not sure I've ever been happier for anyone. Nick is like a brother and I love him like a brother. I want the world for him.

Lizzy—she's basically the world, in his eyes.

She's his perfect opposite. Lively, loud, unapologetic about what she wants. No regard for lines or rules or order.

She's always dragging him to a sci-fi movie or a walk in the park or a night of dancing.

And they, well… the walls at Odyssey were thinner than they thought.

It's strange, hearing a man you consider your brother order his subordinate out of her dress. That's just—

It is strange, that Shep and Nick share some of the same tastes. If I knew more about psychology, I'm sure I'd be able to explain it better. Maybe it's a coincidence. Maybe it's shared history. The pain of losing their mother so young. The abandonment by their biological father.

Something their stepfather—

"It's nice to see you, Jasmine." Nick, always a proper gentleman, extends his hand. "You look beautiful." His gaze shifts to his brother. He raises a brow. *Beautiful and just-fucked*.

Or maybe I'm imagining things.

I shake Nick's hand. If it was anyone else, I'd insist on a hug. But Nick is firm when it comes to propriety.

"You too." Nick turns to his brother with a smile. "You look especially lovely."

It's still strange, seeing Nick joke. He does it all the time now that he's with Lizzy, but I'm not sure I'll ever get used to it.

"I try." Shep's tone is almost friendly. He turns to Lizzy and nods hello. "Ms. Wilder."

"Mr. Marlowe." She nods back. "I guess that will get confusing, with both of you here."

"Baby, when's the last time you called me Mr. Marlowe?" Nick asks.

She rises to her tiptoes to whisper in his ear. He's still so much taller than her. He has to bend to bring his ear to her mouth.

It's adorable. Then she blushes and he gets this *oh, I'll fuck you properly later* look and it's—

Well, it would be hot if it was anyone else. As it is, Nick is practically my brother. The brother I never had.

"Yes, you're very charming." Shep motions to the table. We're in a private room above an exclusive restaurant. A room big enough for twenty. Right now, it's just a small round table and four chairs.

Lizzy and Nick already have drinks. Dark liquid in ice. Soda or soda and some brown liquor?

I don't ask. Even after scouring the Internet for tips on living with recovering alcoholics, I don't have a real sense of what's appropriate. Is it better to abstain in Shep's presence? Or better to treat him like a normal person who can take care of himself?

Shep pulls out my chair for me. I sit. Then Nick does the same for Lizzy, and the men sit, and we're all one big happy family.

At least, from the outside.

Before we can discuss anything, the waiter arrives to take our drink orders. Mineral water for Shep. The same for me. Even after he insists that's not necessary.

For a moment, I consider a gin and tonic. The buzz of pleasure is wearing off more every second. I need to calm my nerves. Quiet the voice in my head asking if this is a good idea.

But it feels wrong. Not with him so close. Not in such a small space.

"Just the water, thanks." After the waiter leaves, I turn to the table. To my old friends. Do they believe this engagement? Do they suspect ulterior motives?

They look… friendly. Excited. Happy. For us. And just happy.

"I know what you're thinking," I say. "But I'm not pregnant."

Lizzy laughs. "It crossed my mind."

"Were you going to ask?" Nick asks.

"Fifty-fifty," she says.

He shakes his head. "One hundred percent." He looks to her with love in his eyes. "Who is going to teach you some manners?"

"Yes, you're very cute," Shep says. "But I would appreciate if you'd save the bedroom stuff for later."

Nick chuckles. "Fair."

Lizzy blushes and mouths *sorry* to me. Her gaze flits to Shep. She studies him. Looking for something, but I can't say what.

Have they had a lot of interaction? Or is she just curious about her fiancé's brother?

Shep isn't exactly a nice guy. Caring, yes, in his way. But also cut-throat. If she was standing between him and something he wanted—

I guess I should ask him. It's really not the time. We need to look like one, big happy family to my big, happy family and Shep's friends and colleagues.

"I heard you got fired," Lizzy says. When Nick chuckles *baby, you're terrible*, she waves him off. Continues. "Because of your engagement. You know Nick almost fired me because of my sister."

"You were living with her," he says. "And her husband, who owns a competing company."

"Technicalities," she says. "It was bullshit then. And it's bullshit now. I'm sorry you had to deal with that." She looks to Shep. "Are you making it up to her?"

He raises a brow. "Making it up to her?"

"Not with your dick," she says. "Though, you better bring it on that front. No one disrespects my future sister-in-law."

Shep actually laughs. It's a big laugh. Warm. Real. "Good to know."

"So?" Lizzy leans forward. "Are you?"

"I'm trying." He turns to me. "I'm still not sure what Jasmine wants to do with her time." His eyes meet mine. He looks at me like he loves me. Like he wants the world for me.

I feel it everywhere. "Me either."

"I can find you a job at one of my companies." He holds out his palm. "But something tells me you'd prefer to find something on your own."

I place my hand on his. "Yes."

"Take his job," Nick says. "It's how the world works."

He's right. Like they say, it's who you know. But I don't want to stay on that particular career trajectory. "No, I don't think I'm going back to finance."

Shep's eyes fill with surprise. "You're not?"

"No." It's been in the back of my mind for a long time.

Since Shep's offer, it's been pushing forward. "Last night, Lock took me to an off-Broadway show. It was this little play, put on by a grad student, a cast of three, in a room with bad ventilation. And I loved every minute of it."

Shep's eyes bore into mine.

My stomach flutters. It's not just him. It's everyone. All those expectations. I'm supposed to achieve big things. Not off-Broadway plays attended by six people.

But this is what I want. And after everything…

I'm not sure if Dad will understand. But he does care if I love Shep. Maybe… maybe he gets it.

This is easy. Practice. The challenge is telling my family. "I want to act. I know I'm a little old to start. And incredibly untrained. But it's what I want. I want to be an actor."

Lizzy's eyes light up. "That's amazing."

"It would suit you." Nick nods.

My stomach twists. Then Shep runs his thumb over the space between my thumb and forefinger and my anxiety fades.

I really do believe everything will be okay.

"You'll be great." He looks at me with all the love in the world, then he leans in and presses his lips to mine.

It feels real. Like he loves me and I love him.

Like before, I'm dizzy. Only it's so much worse than before. Because it's not washed in a wave of pleasure.

It's just my heart pounding against my chest, screaming *Shep*.

If I'm not careful, I'm going to fall in love with him.

Chapter Twenty-Seven

SHEPARD

Nick is less reserved than usual. He teases Jasmine. He gushes over Lizzy. He shares a silly story from our childhood about the time I was too scared to jump into the ocean.

Mom had read us this book about a boy who fell off a boat and met all sorts of strange sea creatures. Some were nice. Others were evil. I thought we'd meet some of the latter.

But Nick went in first. He showed me that it was okay. That I didn't have to worry about a giant octopus or a talking crab.

It was fun, running around the waves, splashing, swimming.

At the time, I would have followed him anywhere. I would have ran into the ocean even if I thought there was danger. He was my big brother. The smartest, coolest, bravest person in the world.

At the time, I thought he was right. There was no danger of an animal attack.

There's a bigger risk. The ocean itself. The current, the dark water, the limitless depths.

But that was Nick. He never did warn me about the real danger.

My therapist says I shouldn't blame him. Not for *that* and not for rehab. Nick was always trying to help. In his way. I should respect that.

I should forgive him. For my sake.

But then I only talk to the fucking therapist because of Nick. So I suppose it's what he has to say.

It is a nice dinner. And Nick is softer. He has two drinks. Lizzy has three.

She gets giggly and friendly and a little too open. She accidentally spills some details about their sex life. What they did before they left.

Usually, that would annoy me. Today, it makes me think of Jasmine. Her gasp, her cry, her moan. The sweet sound she makes when she comes.

I should invite this stupid panel to watch us fuck. So they can see we give each other exactly what we need.

That bastard would love it. Another chance to fuck with me. More proof he's left a mark.

I nod along with the conversation, tell my own stories about Nick, make Lizzy and Jasmine laugh until they can't take it anymore.

Then we finish. Lizzy offers to take Jasmine to the venue, to help with setup. So I can talk to Nick alone.

He nods back to her, a knowing nod that makes it clear they planned this earlier.

It shouldn't annoy me—I need to speak with him privately—but it does. Who does he think he is, planning conversations? Does he believe he's earned back his right to act like an older brother?

He hasn't.

He waits until they leave, then he finishes his last sip of rum and coke. Stands. Moves to the window. "This is what you've always wanted."

That's one way of putting it. "It is."

"You don't seem happy."

I stand. Move around the table.

It's a big room, but there's still not enough space. I don't want to be near his implications.

I go to the other window. Take in the view. Yellow lights against the blue sky. New York at night. The city that never sleeps. It's most alive at night.

"Shep?" he asks.

"Was that a question?"

"Yes."

"I'm happy." I hate that he's right. I'm not capable of happiness, but I need to pretend. I need to convince everyone I'm madly in love with my fiancée. That she's madly in love with me. I need that glow Nick and Lizzy have. The one that screams *we're in love and the world loves us because of it.*

"You don't have to lie to me." His voice is soft and firm at the same time. That parental voice that means *you can trust me with anything, because I will take care of you.* "I'm not going to tell anyone."

"You lost the right to say shit like that a long time ago."

"I know. I'm sorry."

My chest tightens. He's sorry? Does he think that makes a difference? Does he think I didn't hear him the first three thousand times?

Sorry isn't enough.

Sorry doesn't erase what happened.

Sorry only brings it back.

I don't need that. I need it gone. Dissolved.

He took that from me. Took the only thing that helped.

Fuck him and fuck his sorry.

"I know that doesn't mean anything, but I am. If I had known… I would have killed him," he says.

"I don't want to hear it."

"I know. But you need to."

"Fuck off."

He takes one step toward me. "He's going to be at the wedding?"

I turn to my brother. Take in his posture.

It's all soft, comforting, like he really believes he looks out for me.

"Are you going to say something?" I ask.

His face screws with confusion. He considers it a ridiculous question. "No."

"Lizzy knows."

"Yes."

"Is she?"

He shakes his head. "She wouldn't."

"She's drunk."

"She's been drunk before."

"Encouraging."

He tries to hold my gaze. "She won't say anything. I promise."

"You can't make promises for other people."

"Do you want to talk to her? She'll promise."

My skin crawls. No, I don't want to talk to her. Lizzy is fine. I'd go so far as to say I like her.

She's a good fit for Nick. A great conversationalist. Witty and smart with a repository of knowledges when it comes to film, TV, or tech.

She can talk business or culture or food. Or fucking life.

But I don't want to think, for a single second, about the horrible truth.

Someone else knows what happened.

Someone else could tell the entire fucking world. Does her sister know?

Her sister's friends? Classmates? Every student at Columbia?

Every one of their parents?

Every employee at every company one of their parents owns?

Gossip travels fast. Especially something like this.

"This has something to do with him?" Nick asks.

"Is that why you wanted to talk to me?"

"Not exactly." He goes to move closer, but he doesn't. "I know you're still angry with me. That you'll always be angry with me. I'd feel the same."

Great, another speech that ends in *I'm sorry*. "Shit happened. You fucked up. You were just a kid. You shoved me into therapy because you were worried. You're still worried. Now, I'm a dry drunk. I've heard it before. Let's not do it again."

"Covered a lot of ground in ten seconds."

I barely stop myself from rolling my eyes.

"I am sorry. For not protecting you. For not coming forward. For not stopping him. I am sorry, but I'm not going to ask for your forgiveness again."

"Good."

"I'm not going away either."

"Do you have a point?" I turn to the window. Press my palm into the cool glass. It does nothing to temper the anger raising my body temperature. I want to throw a fucking chair through this window. Then throw my brother through that.

Fuck his *I'm sorry*.

Fuck his talk.

Fuck the entire world.

"I know Jasmine, Shep. We still talk. I see her father once a week. I'd know if you'd been dating."

"And?"

"I remember the two of you. What it looked like when you were in love."

I push a breath through my chest. Stare at my brother like he's the stupidest person on the planet. Because, right now, he is. He knows what I'm about to say. And fuck him for making me say it. "I'm not capable of that anymore."

"I thought the same thing."

"Good for you. Now, if you don't have a point, I'm going to leave." I need a drink. Bourbon. Neat. An entire fucking bottle.

Immediately.

I close my eyes. Press my forehead to the glass. Will it to cool me somehow. To calm me somehow.

It doesn't. It's not bourbon. It's not a woman tied to my bed. It's not Jasmine bending to my will.

It's fucking glass.

Useless for anything except letting in the light.

"He does have something to do with this?" Nick asks. He takes my non-response as a yes. "Whatever it is, you're not winning anything by playing this game. You'll never win. You'll only prove he can control you."

"Thanks, Dr. Phil."

"You think I don't feel the same way? Really, Shep? Do you really think I wouldn't kill him if you asked?"

I say nothing.

"Ask now. I'll do it. I don't care that I'll spend the rest of my life in jail. It would be worth it."

"You've never hurt anyone."

"Even so."

I have no doubt he would. And no doubt that bastard

will still find a way to come out ahead. "He'd still control your life."

"He would. But if I believed it would release you, if you'd finally feel free, I'd do it."

"You'd be under his thumb for your entire life."

He nods *yes*. "You've thought about it too."

"Of course."

"And this… it's his doing?"

"Are you going to state obvious facts like they're questions?"

"Lizzy told me what happened last year. You were willing to do a lot for Jasmine."

"I was angry." About rehab. And everything else.

"You do care about her."

"Of course." If I could love anyone, it would be her.

"So why are you doing this to her?"

"She's getting what she wants too. Her father—"

He nods, understanding immediately. She wants her father to die happy. Believing a lie. The same way our mother did. "Lizzy believes you two reconnected after all this time. She hates how much she loves it. She's still not a big fan of yours."

"I imagine."

His chuckle dissolves the tension in his shoulders. But only for a second. His jaw tightens as soon as he speaks. "I won't let on that you're… what, paying her to marry you?"

"It's the best tool I have."

He nods *true*. "And I won't let on that… whatever it is you're doing to win his favor."

"I don't want his favor."

"You do. And that's all he'll ever think. That he's still controlling you. Because he is."

My fingers curl into fists.

"The only way you'll get out from under it is if you stop

playing this game. If you admit it to yourself. Deal with what that means."

"I've spent the last year dealing with what that means. Thanks for taking the only thing that helped."

He raises a brow *have you?* "Like you said. We've had this conversation before. I won't put you through it again."

That's clearly not the case.

He continues. "I'll say one thing."

"Yes?"

"You should tell Jasmine. She deserves to know. And she's a smart woman. She'll find out sooner or later."

She won't. That won't happen. It's out of the question.

"It's better if she hears it from you. Otherwise… it's another way he can control you."

"I appreciate the advice."

He shakes his head *we both know that's bullshit*, but he still offers his hand. "Shall we?"

I shake my head. "I need a minute."

He nods, looks to the table, making sure the drinks are empty.

Asshole.

I don't even bother to curse him as he leaves. I just pick up a glass and hurl it at the fucking wall.

It shatters into pieces on the ground. Tiny bits of glass that will cut anyone who tries to help.

Tiny bits of glass that can never be put back together again.

Fuck Nick. Fuck him more for being right.

I won't tell her. I won't let her find out.

I can't protect her from much, but I can protect her from this. And I will.

Whatever I do, I'm protecting her from the ugly truth.

Chapter Twenty-Eight

JASMINE

L izzy bounces around the room, holding her older sister's hand, nodding *yes, of course, listen to her* as Kat helps the caterers set up.

Years working at a restaurant. Then more years as a rich man's wife.

I suppose I shouldn't be so cynical. I spent years working at a restaurant. I'm about to do time as a rich man's wife.

Really, I should ask her for tips. *How do you deal with suddenly having enough? How do you swallow the resentment you have toward your husband, when he has everything and you have nothing?*

What's it like, knowing he still has the power to destroy you?

Do you really trust him not to?

"Ms. Lee." Lock pulls me from my thoughts. He's like me. The old me. Good at being invisible. I don't realize he's here until his British accent flows into my ears. "Your aunts are about to arrive."

Oh.

"They're at the coat check." He motions to the

entrance. "I thought I'd warn you before I let them in. In case you need a moment. Or a drink?"

"Can I ask you a stupid question about England?" I ask.

He nods *yes*. "As they say, there are no stupid questions."

"Wait until you hear it."

He just smiles. That same smile he always has. Like he finds my company charming. I think he does… but maybe it's a put on. Since he's paid to find my company charming.

"Does everyone there know a good gin and tonic? Or is that some way Shep is making fun of Ian?"

Lock's laugh is easy. "Mr. Marlowe and Mr. Hunt have a certain repartee."

"Is it?"

"Our standards are higher, yes. But it's the same as here. Students drink vodka that costs four pounds a bottle. Others only sip Belvedere. Your fiancé—"

"Right." I'm not sure what he's going to say about Shep —that he's always had expensive tastes, that he would drink whatever he got his hands on, that he no longer drinks—but I don't want to hear it. For an hour, I want to pretend this isn't so complicated.

"Would you like one?"

"Yes. I'd like the best you've got. If you know what that is. Or… is Ian around? I can ask him."

Lock shakes his head. "Leave it to me." He nods a *thank you* then moves to the bar.

He's thanking me for asking him to bring me a drink.

Being rich is weird.

I sneak a quiet minute in the bathroom. Check my reflection for signs of our tryst.

A few stray hairs, but the jeweled clip pulling it back

looks intentional. Another coat of lipstick and a few dots of concealer and I look…

Well, like a rich man's fiancée.

Thankfully, Lock is waiting at the wall. He hands me a short cocktail glass, nods his goodbye, leads my aunts into the room.

It's still mid-setup. A dozen caterers. Lizzy and her sister. A few people from Shep's company.

And now Mai and Quyen.

"Honey, you look beautiful." Mai holds her arms out for a hug. She doesn't wait for a response. She jumps in. Holds me.

"Too skinny though," Quyen says.

I take a long sip of my drink. The flavors shine. Quinine, lime, gin. Not just sugar.

Mai waves her away. "You think everyone is too skinny." She motions to her sister's boxy yellow dress. "If you care so much, why don't you show off your curves?"

Quyen responds in Vietnamese. The same argument about fashion they always have. Mai is practical to a fault. She'd rather spend money on family, food, education. To her, fashion is a waste.

Quyen is an art teacher. She loves everything visual. Considers fashion another extension of her personality.

They make arguments about their kids. Which is smarter, with a better future ahead of them. They've each got two, but their kids are younger. Barely teenagers now.

I ask about Van and they're off, talking about an expensive summer camp, and how Van wants to take a film class and whether or not that's a good use of time. Film making is an expensive hobby. Not a practical skill. Van isn't like Allison (who now goes by her English name), the smart, responsible teenager who's ready to study optometry.

She's known since she was tiny. The way some people know they want to act or sing or write, she knew she wanted to study eyes. But it wasn't passion so much as practicality.

It drives Quyen crazy that she has the practical daughter. It drives Mai crazy too. But then…

They're just crazy.

I can't help but laugh at their argument. It's so silly. They're like teenagers, not women in their forties.

"Where is this handsome fiancé?" Quyen asks.

"Tell the truth." Mai leans in close. "Is it the money?" she stage whispers, though I'm pretty sure she intends it as a real whisper. "Or is it the sex?"

"What?" I nearly spit out my gin and tonic.

"Please, Jasmine," she says in Vietnamese. "We have to say this before your father gets here. But it's obvious. You have the glow of a woman whose needs are being met."

Quyen nods *you do*. "These things are important in a husband."

Oh God, please don't let them continue.

"I know you think I'm old and traditional, but it wasn't always that way."

"You're in your forties," I say.

She nods *I know, so old now*, completely missing my point. "I was your age once. Younger even," Mai says.

"I, uh… thank you. For the advice." I take another sip. Fight a blush. They never talked to me like this when I was younger. I guess a first-class ticket and an afternoon at a fancy hotel change things. Or maybe it's losing Mom. Maybe they want to make sure I have good, motherly advice. "We are… compatible in that way."

They laugh and exchange whispers.

My blush deepens. At least… well, is it so bad if they think I'm marrying him for the sex? Better than thinking

I'm rushing down the aisle so Dad can attend my special day.

Or that I'm doing this for a seven-figure payout.

But I can't consider those possibilities right now.

This is… maybe tonight doesn't have to be an overwhelming exercise in faking it. Maybe I can laugh with my aunts and my dad. Maybe I can celebrate love and marriage and forever.

I want to have that one day. A real love, a real marriage, a family of my own. This is just… a dress rehearsal.

They order their usual drinks and start competing on who can give the best advice about marriage.

Never go to bed angry.

Never go to bed in flannel pajamas, always something sexy.

Never go to bed in something sexy, always leave him wondering. Besides, flannel is very practical. And the plaid is cute.

And on and on.

I nod with them as the room fills with Shep's colleagues and friends.

Nick finds Lizzy immediately. It's been half an hour, an hour maybe, but he still kisses her like he's going to war. Like this might be the only chance they get.

My heart warms. My thoughts get fuzzy. Or maybe that's the gin.

I order another round anyway. I don't want to think about how Shep will never love me. About how I'm destined for an eternity with a man who will never hand me his heart.

This is a good deal. I'm coming out ahead. Even if it's with a broken heart.

Mmm. The second is better. It dulls the voice whispering *this is a bad idea*. Then my eyes flit to him.

Shep walks in with my dad. Dad's in a suit and tie and he's walking fine on his own. He's a little pale, sure, but he looks good. Healthy.

And Shep… he looks happy. Over the moon even. His eyes find mine. He smiles and my heart melts.

Mai whispers something about Shep being handsome.

"You're a lucky woman," Quyen agrees. "If he's half the lover he is the looker—"

They giggle like schoolgirls.

I let Shep and Dad meet us here. I don't even fuss when Dad orders whiskey. This is a party. He deserves to have a little fun too.

"I didn't know you were picking up Dad," I say.

Dad shakes his head. "He sent a limo. Very fancy." He holds up his drink. "To Shepard taking care of my daughter."

"I promise, I will try my best." Shep offers me his hand.

When I take it, he squeezes my palm. It's not the steady gesture of earlier. It's frantic. Rushed. Like he's trying to cling to something stable.

Or maybe I'm imagining things.

Shep's eyes go to my drink. They fill with a hunger. Then they move over my body and the hunger shifts to something baser.

"She's a lucky woman," Mai says again, though this time it's a question, directed at Shep. "To have such a devoted man."

"No." He rises to meet her challenge. "I'm the lucky one." He pulls me toward him. "I count my blessings every day."

My body melts into his. My hands go to his shoulders.

Has he always been this tall? Or does he seem bigger

today, like he takes up more space, commands more of a presence?

I let my fingers curl into his neck. Not the rough gesture of his touch. Something soft. Gentle. Inviting.

His eyes meet mine. He stares down at me like he's madly in love with me. Then he brings his palm to my skin. He cups my cheek as he leans down to kiss me.

For a second, the rest of the world fades away. I forget my family is behind me. I forget Shep's colleagues are in front of me.

I forget our deal, the timeline, everything that makes this complicated.

For a moment, I'm in a perfect kiss. Like something out of a fairy tale. The moment where the prince claims the princess. Where the couple declares happily ever after.

True love.

Forever.

My lips part.

His tongue slides into my mouth.

It's not like before. He's still claiming me, but it's not just my body. It's my heart, my soul, my everything.

My fingers curl into his skin. Then his short hair.

His hands go to my lower back.

He holds my body against his as he kisses me a little deeper, a little longer.

Then he pulls back with a smile. One that screams *I love you*.

My knees knock. My head spins. It feels so real. So true. So pure.

My aunts cheer. My dad shakes his head.

Shep's gaze shifts to the door. To two men standing near the entrance, watching us carefully.

Two older men. One in a simple grey suit. The kind of

guy who blends into the background. Or who would, if he wasn't rich enough to make people notice.

And a man I never thought I'd see again.

Shep's stepfather, Lucien.

What the hell is he doing here?

Chapter Twenty-Nine

SHEPARD

The room gets hot. Stuffy.

Jasmine looks up at me, confusion in her dark eyes. She doesn't know why that bastard is here. She doesn't think he has anything to do with this.

She never liked him. She couldn't explain why. It was a bad feeling. An intuition.

I tried to convince her it was nothing. That she was imagining things.

I tried to convince myself.

Failure on both counts.

She knows something is off. She shouldn't have a fucking clue—most people invite their parents to their weddings. The bastard never adopted me officially, but he is the man who married my mother.

Most people would call him my father.

She should expect him.

But, somehow, she knows this is wrong.

Nick's words echo through my head. *She's a smart woman. She'll find out sooner or later. Better if she hears it from you.*

No doubt, the last part is true. But he's wrong about the former.

She won't put the pieces together.

She won't find out.

Not sooner. And not later.

Not as long as I'm drawing breath.

I shrug my shoulders, trying to loosen the tension in my back.

It doesn't help.

I try to soften my expression. To stare into her eyes like I love her.

But that's not enough either.

It's still there. In my head. He's here. He's watching. He's probably getting off on it.

I close my eyes. Let my thoughts drift to better places. Dragging Jasmine to the coat check, pinning her to the wall, tearing off her dress.

Licking her until she's come so many times she begs me to stop.

Ordering her to get on her knees and—

I pull her into a deep kiss. It's not like before. Not the sweet, patient kiss of a groom.

I'm not a loving fiancé, right now.

I'm a fucking beast. And she's my prey. And I'm going to have her any way I can.

Her lips part for my tongue.

She groans against my mouth, melting into me as I claim her body. She likes me rough. She likes me aggressive. She likes me completely out of touch with my limits.

She shouldn't. It should scare her. She should realize that some things are beyond her control.

Some things are destiny.

And I—

Maybe my brother can find happiness. Maybe he can

shake off this curse. But I know better. I know what happens to men like me when women trust them.

She pulls back with a heady sigh. Her entire body is tuned to me, like I'm the only thing in the universe.

It soothes something inside me. Something raw and primal.

Nick is right. She deserves better. She deserves someone who will truly love her.

But I'm selfish. I want her anyway. I'm taking her anyway.

"Save something for the honeymoon." Jasmine's Aunt Mai giggles. She says something in Vietnamese, no doubt something about me.

Everyone laughs. Even Jasmine.

I don't mind being out of the know. It doesn't matter what language they're speaking. I won't understand them either way.

The happy family brimming with love—

That's far beyond my comprehension.

"I'm afraid I need to borrow my fiancée." My fingers curl around her wrist. It's tighter than it should be. Too obviously possessive.

But no one seems to mind. If anything, Jasmine's aunts approve. They whisper something else. I don't have a clue what they're saying. Only that their tone is positive.

Jasmine says a goodbye to her family then she follows me across the room. Her eyes flit from her family to mine —first that bastard, then Nick and Lizzy, who are in the corner of the room.

He glances at our stepfather. Then at me. His stare says everything. *You're making a mistake. Letting him control you.*

Then he turns to Lizzy. He's pretending something. Protecting her from this.

She doesn't know what Lucien looks like. She doesn't know he's still breathing. Still infecting the world.

She doesn't know he's here. And he's trying to keep it from her.

Where the fuck does Nick get off telling me about honesty?

Asshole.

"Mai was saying you seem like a tiger in the sack. Well, it sounds a little different in Vietnamese, but that's the best translation." Jasmine's voice is nervous. "She um… I think she recognizes Lucien. It's been awhile though."

"Yes," I say.

"I didn't realize you were still in touch."

"Here and there." That's a nice way of putting it.

"Oh. I thought… I'm not sure, actually. It makes sense. He was your father for a long time. Of course, you're in touch." Her eyes meet mine. They're soft. Loving. Like she's inviting me to lay my heart bare for her.

That's not going to happen. "Yes." Not the entire truth, but enough.

Despite the disbelief in her eyes, she nods. "And this arrangement—"

"He needs to believe it. Everyone needs to believe it. Nick is the only one—"

"Oh." Surprise streaks her expression. "He didn't let on."

"He has a good poker face."

"Have you ever played him?" she asks. "He's a shark."

My brother *is* an expert poker player. He places in tournaments all the time. Some high stakes, some for a few hundred dollars. I'm sure he could destroy me in a game.

He knows the odds.

And he bluffs better than I do. He's cooler. Calmer. He took all that pain and turned it inward.

Whereas I'm ready to throw a fucking table out the window.

I squeeze Jasmine's hand.

She squeezes back. It's comforting. More comforting than it should be, given the circumstance.

"Mr. Marlowe." Charles, my stepfather's second in command, extends his hand. "It's always lovely to see you." Technically, Charles is someone on the board I can impress. But it's unlikely he'll vote in my favor if that bastard doesn't. Better to focus those resources elsewhere.

Like throwing that bastard out the fucking window.

Deep breath. Poker face. "You too." I release Jasmine. Shake his hand. Turn to her like I'm ready to marry her. No, I am ready. And I am proud to introduce her. She's the most remarkable woman I know. The most remarkable person I know. "Have you met my fiancée?"

"Jasmine Lee." She extends her hand. Shakes his. "I'm always happy to meet a friend of Shep's. But I have to admit, now that I've left finance, I can't stand to hear about it."

"You can't?" I ask.

She shakes her head, leaning into the explanation. "It's so tedious. All the terms, all the rules, all the numbers. Like a board game that doesn't make any sense." She turns to me. Stares up at me like I'm the only thing in the universe that makes a lick of sense. "I'm not going to miss that."

"Ever?" I ask.

She shakes her head. "Never." She turns to Lucien. "I'm sorry. I shouldn't be so rude. I just get caught up talking to Shep." She offers her hand. "It's been a long time."

"Please." He ignores her request for a handshake. Holds out his arms, inviting her to hug him.

She looks to me for approval, but he's too fast.

He swoops in. Pulls her body into his. Holds her like he'll never let go.

My blood boils. This suit is too stuffy. This tie is suffocating me.

I need to take it off, wrap it around his throat, pull tight. So he never breathes again.

But Nick is right. If I kill him, I'll be under his thumb forever.

He'll win again.

The bastard always finds some way to win. He knows rules I don't. He invents new ones.

I don't breathe until he releases her. Then I grab her too hard. Pull her too close. Hold her too tightly.

"Careful." My voice is a threat. "I get jealous."

I won't hesitate if he hurts her. It will be the last mistake he ever makes. I don't care what it means for me. Or for this bullshit game he's playing.

No one hurts her on my watch.

"You've always been such a beautiful girl." Lucien's voice is a dare. *What are you going to do? We both know you're not man enough to stop me. You weren't then and you aren't now.* "And, now, such a lovely young woman."

Charles nods. "My wife would love that dress."

Jasmine smiles and names some boutique in midtown. "Tell her Jasmine sent you. And maybe she'll give me a discount next time."

Charles raises a brow. "Are you lacking cash?"

"Never too rich for a good deal." She turns to me. "Right, baby?"

My balls tighten at the term of endearment. She hasn't called me that since we were kids. And then—

Fuck, this is confusing.

I want to hold her.

I want to fuck her.

I want to kill him.

"Smart too," Lucien says. "I always liked that about you. I couldn't believe my son was ready to settle down so young."

Where the fuck does he get off, calling me his son?

"It was surprising, but I wanted it to be you." His eyes meet mine. "I didn't think you had it in you, Shepard. To win back a woman you hurt so thoroughly."

She replies before I can. "We all make mistakes. Shep realized that. And he... well, the truth is, I never stopped loving him." She turns to me. Runs her fingers through my hair. "He did hurt me. He broke my heart. I wanted to stop loving him, to stop thinking about him, to stop knowing he existed."

She stares into my eyes, asking for something.

I don't know what it is. But I nod anyway.

And she continues. "I tried. I was with other men. I was even in love with one. But when I saw Shep again... when he walked into the Odyssey office in his grey suit, his navy tie bringing out those gorgeous blue eyes." Her fingers brush my neck. It's soft. Comforting. "I knew then. I was always going to love him."

"For that long?" I try to find the truth in her eyes, but I can barely breathe. Truth is beyond my capabilities.

"Always." She rises to her tiptoes and presses her lips to mine. It's quick. A stage kiss. For the benefit of that bastard and his friend.

It doesn't soothe me. It twists the knife in my chest.

I have to pull back. To release her.

I can't stand here anymore. I can't watch him smile and think *look at how I've made him grovel. Look at what I've made him do. Look at all the strings I pull.*

"It helps when they have money, doesn't it?" Lucien asks.

Jasmine smiles, completely unfazed. "It helps when a woman is beautiful. What's the difference?"

Charles nods *true*.

Lucien just smiles. This sick smile that means *I know what you've done and you're not getting away with it*. "Yes, it does. Better when you find someone who's also smart and articulate. What is it you do, Jasmine, now that you aren't in finance? I'd love to help any way I can."

"I'm an actress." She smiles. "Well, in training. I was studying in college, but I had to put that on hold. Now… I'm still working out the details, but I'd like to go back to that."

"Acting. How interesting." Lucien's voice is knowing. "I wonder what people will think."

"I know." She doesn't miss a beat. "Rich men are always buying their wives careers. I'm not going to turn down Shep's connections. But I'm not letting him do this for me either."

"He won't buy you a theater?" Charles asks.

"I suppose I can't stop him, but I hope not. I don't want everyone putting me on a pedestal simply because I'm Shepard Marlowe's wife." She forces a smile. No doubt, she means everything she's saying. But I can't grasp the implications.

I barely manage a breath. "Excuse me, gentlemen." I'm not letting him look at me with that smug smile. I'm not letting him win. "Princess, we should do this."

"Princess?" Lucien raises a brow.

He and Charles exchange some look. One I can't begin to contemplate.

I don't wait for Jasmine's response. I take her hand. Lead her to the stage.

The room is full now. A few dozen people. Her family. My colleagues. Some mutual friends.

And press.

All the people we need to convince. And the bastard who's sure he's controlling me.

I step to the mic. "Thank you all for coming. I know it's sudden, but sometimes, when you know, you know." I squeeze her hand. "The truth is, I've always known. I've loved Jasmine since the first time we kissed, all those years ago. I've always wanted to marry her."

"Why haven't you," someone calls.

I laugh. Play my part. "I've been trying. But I just convinced her." I turn to Jasmine. Stare into her eyes like she really is everything I want. "I love you, darling. You're the smartest, most beautiful, most tenacious woman I've ever met. I'm lucky to have you. And I can't wait for you to be my wife."

She stares up at me like I really am everything she wants. "I can't wait for you to be my husband."

Someone cheers. Someone else claps.

I dive in before the audience can take over. "When I say I can't wait, I mean it. We're going to be married two weeks from today. And everyone here is invited." I turn to the crowd. "Please, join me as I celebrate the most wonderful woman I've ever met." I make my voice teasing. "I have to do it fast. Before she changes her mind."

Everyone laughs.

Jasmine too.

She smiles at the crowd like she's well aware of my surprise announcement.

Everyone smiles back. Happy. In love with our love.

And there's Lucien. Happy. That I'm playing his stupid fucking game.

Happy. Firm in his knowledge that I'm faking this.

Somehow, that bastard always knows.

Chapter Thirty

SHEPARD

J asmine smiles as we make rounds. Shake hands. Accept congratulations.

She plays the blushing bride well. Or maybe she's nervous. Or embarrassed by my speech. I don't know.

He's still here.

I'm still unable to breathe.

I play my part the best I can. Pretend as if I'm so overwhelmed by love I can't speak.

Colleagues believe it. Or they don't care enough to deny it.

She's beautiful, smart, determined. Who wouldn't want to marry her?

It's easier when we meet her family. She declines another drink, but she doesn't protest when her father orders a glass of whiskey. She just laughs along with her aunts. Lets them tease her about her duties as a married woman. The lingerie they'll buy her for a honeymoon. The need to make lots of grandchildren.

It's a bizarre thought, having children with Jasmine.

Once upon a time, I wanted that. A family of my own. A normal life. A job, a car, a house in the suburbs.

Then that bastard changed everything. Now, it's impossible to imagine.

What if I followed in his footsteps?

It's out of the question. But then that doesn't matter. Her family doesn't need to know the terms of our arrangement.

So I nod and say something about how beautiful our children will be if they get their mother's eyes.

And she says something about how ruthless they'll be if they get their father's negotiation skills.

And her aunts say something about how cute they'll be. The first bi-racial kids in the family. They want to welcome them. Invite them to participate in both sides of their culture.

What is that like? To grow up split in half, not knowing where you belong?

There's no reason to consider it. I can't have children. I can't risk passing on this curse.

Finally, the party breaks up. Lucien and Charles leave without a word. Thank fuck.

Jasmine kisses me goodbye. Insists on riding home with her father. On making sure he gets home okay.

I offer them the limo. Send her aunts home with Lock.

Knowing Lock... I'm sure he'd make that literal if they invited him.

No, he values his job too much for that. Or at least, that's what I like to believe. Money buys a lot of loyalty, but it never gets to one hundred percent. Some things aren't for sale.

Ian tries to invite me out for a drink to celebrate—surely, I can bust out the sparkling apple cider for this kind of occasion—but I decline. He means the shit about the apple cider.

He won't let me order bourbon.

He can't stop me. No one can stop me from walking into the nearest hotel bar and demanding a double.

No one can stop me from throwing this opportunity away.

That's all it takes. One drink and she can leave.

One drink and she will leave.

That can't happen. No matter how badly I need to dull the sharp edges.

I push the thought aside on the way home. But it's impossible. By the time I step foot in my apartment, it's the only thing in my head.

I need a drink.

I need a drink.

I need a drink.

It screams at me. The edges get sharp. My thoughts turn ugly.

Something to stop it. Anything to stop. Anything to make me forget I'm still under that bastard's thumb.

My fucking staff is too effective. There's nothing in the kitchen or my office.

Key's room is locked.

Jasmine's is empty.

But that crimson bed—it gives me ideas. For a way to erase these thoughts. A way to feel in control.

The only way.

I go to my office.

It's easier to breathe. He infects the room less.

But he still infects it.

Knowing he's out there, finding ways to pull my strings, finding ways to lord this over me—

I'm not sure what's worse. Him winning. Proving he controls me again.

Or him deciding that Jasmine truly does love me. Thinking I truly love her.

If he knows he can use her to hurt me—

He will.

I don't know how Nick stands it. I'm sure he'd say something about how I'm letting that bastard control me. How he refuses to do that.

It's a nice idea, but he's wrong. There's no getting around it. That bastard will control me until the day I die. Then after.

Somehow, he will.

I try to work, but it's useless. My head is too full. My thoughts are too sharp.

I don't feel a moment of relief until the front door opens.

Soft footsteps move closer. Then a knock.

"Can I come in?" she asks.

"I'll come out." No one comes into my office.

I stand. Shut down my computer. Lock the drawer where I keep this awful contract.

She's standing there in the main room, moonlight casting highlights on her tan skin.

She looks gorgeous. And worried.

"Are you okay?" she asks.

"It's nothing."

Her eyes search mine. "You didn't ask me about the date. I realize you don't have to consult me given our terms, but—"

"I got carried away." It's still there, in my head, the image of his awful smile. It's still infecting the room.

"That almost sounds like an apology."

"I'm sorry."

Her eyes fill with confusion. "Thank you." She stares at me like I've sprouted horns.

"What?" I turn to the window. Try to find solace in the deep blue water. It's no use. There's no clarity in the river. Or the sky. Or the big silver moon.

"Something is on your mind." Her voice stays soft. Curious.

"Is that a question or a statement?"

"More an invitation."

"I meant what I said, Jasmine. I am lucky to marry you. And you are better than what I deserve. But I can't love you. I'm not capable of loving anyone."

Her eyes fill with hurt, but she says nothing.

"I'm not capable of sharing my heart with you. If that's what you're after—"

"It's only a question, Shep. You can say *I'd rather not discuss it*."

That's not the entire truth, but I don't have the moral high ground here. I nod. Play by her terms. "I'd rather not discuss it."

"Okay, well… if you change your mind, I guess." She motions to her room. "I'm going to shower." Her eyes meet mine. They offer an invitation. A different one.

She wants intimacy however she can get it.

Or maybe my ego is talking. Maybe she only wants my body. Maybe she wants nothing more than satisfaction.

Either way—

I'm not denying her.

"You should." Finally, my shoulders relax.

The thought of tying Jasmine to her bed—That's everything I need.

"After, put on that purple robe. Nothing under it." I firm my voice. So she knows exactly what I mean. "Then sit on your bed and wait."

"Wait?"

"Yes. Until I'm ready." My eyes meet hers. "That is what you want."

It's not a question. She nods anyway. "Yes. But… are you sure you're okay?"

"Is this what you want? Yes or no?"

"Yes."

"Then go. Before I lose my patience." I let my voice get harder. "You won't like what happens if I lose my patience, princess."

Chapter Thirty-One

JASMINE

It's official. I'm not only insane. I'm—what is it men say?

Thinking with my dick.

I'm thinking with my clit.

I'm completely out of my head.

But I don't care.

Everything is shaded with pleasure.

My shower is illicit. Like the warm water is his fingertips. Like his hands are the ones in my hair. Like he's standing on the tile, watching with wide eyes.

I should be wondering why he's pushing the wedding, what his stepfather was doing at our party, if my dad really is okay—

But I'm not.

I'm buzzing with anticipation.

Thinking *more, more, more.*

It's the only thing in my head.

And, fuck, that feels good. I'm not listening to my better judgment. Or my inhibitions. Or the voice nagging *make sure he's okay.*

Maybe he's not.

But I'm not either.

And this is all he can offer me.

I'm not a fool. I'm taking it.

I turn off the water. Step onto the cool tile. Pull a violet towel around my chest.

Soft fabric against my skin. Thick. Sturdy.

It's like he's the one touching me.

My breath leaves my body as I step into my bedroom.

The air is crackling with electricity. Everything is charged.

The hardwood floor is smoother. The silk robe is sleeker. The night sky is bluer.

I press my knees together, trying to contain the anticipation coursing through me.

It's not enough.

My sex is already aching.

It's hard to believe we had sex earlier today. The memory of bliss is crystal clear, but I'm still desperately in need.

Like it's been a million years since anyone has touched me properly.

I pull my robe a little farther down my thighs. Tie it a little tighter.

But I don't feel right covering up.

I want to be exposed. I want to drive him as crazy as he drives me.

I undo the sash. Let the smooth fabric roll over my thighs and breasts.

It falls outside my hips. It leaves my body on display for him. My breasts, stomach, pelvis, thighs.

Then I spread my legs a little wider, so I can show him everything.

It makes me achier. Emptier. I need him touching me, holding me, fucking me.

I need him looking at me, his blue eyes wide, his lips parting with a groan.

It's strange. I've never needed someone looking at me before. But I need it so badly I can taste it.

The air buzzes as footsteps move closer.

A hard knock.

The door opens.

Shep steps inside. He moves down the short hallway, into the main room.

Closer to the bed.

Only five feet away.

He's in his suit and tie, but he's not a buttoned-up businessman. No, right now he's wild and fierce.

Barely contained.

Ready to use me however he sees fit.

It should scare me. Instead, it makes my sex clench.

Use me, baby. Make me your toy. Fuck me until I can't breathe.

My inhibitions are gone. I'm not sure if it's the gin or the night or the look in Shep's eyes. But I don't care.

I only care about getting what's mine.

Giving him what's his.

"Bad girl." His voice drips with approval. "Teasing me."

"You don't like it?" My voice hitches. It's some tone I've never heard before. Some tone I need.

His eyes roam my body slowly. They start at my shoulders, work their way down my chest, stomach, hips, legs.

All the way to my bare feet, then back up. He stops at my sex. Then my breasts.

"You want me to see what's mine?" he asks.

"What's yours?"

"Your body." His voice gets firmer. "It's mine."

"Here."

"Yes. Here." He shifts back into character. Harder. More demanding. "Your body is mine and I'm going to do whatever I want with it."

It should terrify me. Instead, it makes me ache.

"What do you want me to do, princess? Do you want to come on my hand? My face? My cock?" He moves closer. Until he's close enough to place his hand on my cheek.

His fingertips skim my chin. Then they dip lower. Over my neck, along my collarbones, down my breast.

"You want me to come inside you? Or maybe here." He runs his finger over my nipple. "On your perfect tits?"

"Yes, sir."

"Yes, to what?"

"Everything. All of it." My eyes find his. "Whatever you're willing to give me."

His pupils dilate. His touch gets harder. Hard enough to hurt in the best possible way.

He rolls my nipple between his thumb and forefinger. Then he's drawing slow circles with his thumb. Again and again. Harder and harder.

Until I have to close my eyes.

Until I have to groan.

He slips his other hand into my hair. Cups the back of my head. It's more gentle than I expect. Loving even.

I blink my eyes open. Try to find some meaning in his expression. Some clue to what he's thinking. What he wants. Who he really is—

I don't see the boy I loved. Or the man I hated. Or even something in between.

Instead, I see the wild animal, contained in his tailored suit, waiting to break free.

He hasn't been naked with me. He hasn't had the space to toss me on the bed, pin my knees to the sheets, dive between my legs.

Is that what he wants? Does he want to make me come? Or does he want to use me like I'm some toy that exists only for his pleasure?

The thought shouldn't make me ache, but it does. I want to be his plaything.

"I want to feel you." I look up at him. "I want to wrap my hands around you. Pump you. Take you into my mouth."

His fingers dig into my scalp. "You want to suck me off?"

"Yes, sir." I study his expression. Try to find what he wants. I can't. But that promise, that dare he made… It still sets me on fire. "Please." I arch my back, letting my robe fall off my shoulders. "Please, Shep. Fuck my mouth. Come on me."

His grip tightens.

"I want your cock. I want your cum. I want you. Everything I can get."

Then tighter.

Until I have to moan. "Fuck."

"You don't set the terms." His voice is a growl. "I set the terms."

"Yes, sir. But you did ask."

He almost smiles. "I did."

"I wanted to provide a thorough answer."

"Clever." He draws one more circle around my nipple then he drags his hand back up my neck, over my chin, along my bottom lip. He slips his thumb into my mouth. Nods *yes*.

I suck on his digit. It's strange, how much I want to

suck on his thumb. How good it tastes. How desperate I am for more.

I've always considered myself a generous lover. But I've never craved a man's cock. I've never been desperate to get my lips around him.

"Good girl." He pulls his thumb back. Then he takes a step backward. Just enough to give me room. "On your knees."

I slide off the bed.

"Keep the robe on." He pulls it up my arms, drapes it over my shoulders. "I like you half-undressed."

I nod.

"Next time, I'll have you like that in public."

Fuck.

"Take you to a restaurant with a secluded balcony. Pull your dress aside. Play with your tits until you beg to climb in my lap."

Climbing in his lap, looking into his eyes, being that close—hell yes. I want it so much it scares me.

But he can't promise that. He's very explicitly not promising that. So I'm not going to ask.

This is all he can offer me.

And, right now, this is all I want.

I adjust my robe so it's just barely revealing my breasts. "Yes, sir." I look up at him. "I would like to be on display for you. I would like to be your plaything."

His pupils dilate. Right now, I'm the one who has him where I want him. I'm the one making him react.

Then he knots his hand in my hair and tugs hard enough I forget about making him do anything.

He's the one in control.

I'm the one following his demands.

He releases my hair for long enough to do away with his suit jacket.

Then it's his belt.

His button.

His zipper.

"Take out my cock, princess." He says it like a promise, not an order. Like it's a gift I've wanted for a long, long time.

It is. My hands go to his slacks. I push the fabric aside.

He springs free.

I wrap my hand around him immediately. Soft skin but he's so hard. And he feels so good. It's the only word I have to describe it.

It's not the first time I've touched him, but somehow it feels more intimate than ever. Like he's giving me something.

I look up at him, asking for permission.

He nods and I run my thumb over him, testing his reactions, exploring every inch.

There. The bottom. A little to the right. I run my thumb over him again. Then harder. Hard enough he shudders.

Again and again.

Until his hand goes to the back of my head and he tugs at my hair. "Open your mouth."

I do.

He takes my hand. Slides it down his cock, so I'm gripping his base. "Firmer."

I tighten my grip.

"Keep it there, princess. I'm not going to be gentle, but I can't wear you out until I'm done with you."

My sex clenches. He's too good at this. I'm going to ignite. All the sparks flying through the room—

It's dangerous.

This is the most dangerous thing I've ever done. Giving my body to Shepard is one thing.

But my heart?

He presses his palm into the back of my head. It's just hard enough to say *you're mine*.

I want it more than I should.

But I don't care about should right now

Slowly, he shifts into my mouth.

Fuck, he tastes good. Like salt and like Shep. I don't wait for instruction. I swirl my tongue around his tip. Then I go to that spot he likes—

He groans as I flick my tongue against him.

I do it again.

Again.

Until he's shaking.

Until I'm the one in control.

For a moment, his eyes close. His fingers curl into the back of my head. His lips part with a groan.

For a moment, he surrenders to me.

Without warning, he pushes hard on the back of my head, pushing my mouth over his cock.

He goes deep. Deep enough I gag. Even with my hand wrapped around him.

He doesn't wait. He pulls back and does it again.

His hand stays firm. He's keeping me in place. Reminding me he's in control.

It makes my sex clench.

It fills me with feminine power.

Yes, he's in control. But I'm what he wants. And this is what I want too.

I'm not sure who's bending to whose will.

No, it's not like that. We're satisfying each other. It's perfect. The only time the two of us have ever been perfect.

Hell, it's the most perfect relationship in my life.

A groan falls off his lips as he slams into my mouth. It's hard enough it hurts. Hard enough I gag. But that only winds me tighter.

I swallow to relax my throat. When he slams again, I take it a little easier.

Then easier.

He tugs at my hair. "Fuck, princess." He rocks into me again. "You're too good with that pretty mouth."

I wrap my lips around my teeth.

He cups my cheek. A soft, tender gesture as he thrusts into my mouth.

Then his hand is on my shoulder, my neck, my breast. He toys with my nipple as he thrusts into me.

My sex pangs with every brush of his hands. With every rock of his hips.

It's so fucking sexy, being on my knees for him, surrendering to his demands, his force, his body.

His brow knots. All that tension winding in him. Tighter and tighter—

Because of me.

I'm making him come.

I'm driving him wild.

With his next thrust, I suck on his tip.

"Fuck," he growls. Then he thrusts into me again. Harder. Faster.

So fast I barely keep up.

Shep tugs at my hair, pulling my head off his cock. He growls my name as he spills onto my chest.

It makes my sex ache, watching him come, feeling him mark me.

Once he's finished, he helps me up, wipes me off, brings me back to the bed.

I expect him to leave, but he doesn't. He moves to the

corner of the bed and pulls out something I've never seen before—

Restraints.

Then he motions to the center of the bed. "Lie down, princess. I'm going to make you come until you beg me to stop."

Chapter Thirty-Two

SHEPARD

Jasmine shudders as I tighten the restraint around her wrist.

She looks up at me, waiting for me to react. To hold her down. Or climb on top of her. Or fuck her without warning.

All brilliant ideas.

I sling my legs over her hips. Shift onto her body, so I'm straddling her.

Both hands on her shoulders, I press her into the bed. Not hard enough to hurt. Not even hard enough to threaten her.

Just enough to promise.

She looks up at me with hunger in her eyes. Hunger. And nerves. This is a lot for her.

I'm moving fast. Too fast maybe.

I need to be careful.

I reach for the other restraint. Slide it over her wrist. Pull tight.

My fingers skim her soft skin. She turns to the touch.

Watches as I run my index finger over the outside of her thumb.

Then back, over the restraint, down her forearm, over her elbow, along her upper arm.

She shakes as I press my lips to her collarbone. It's gentle. Not like me. I need to ease her into this.

I drag my lips down her chest. Take her nipple into my mouth and suck softly.

Then harder and harder—

Until she lets out the world's most perfect groan.

She reaches for me. Finds the restraints tugging her. Groans even louder.

My balls tighten. It's still hard to believe that she wants to be tied to my bed. That she likes it rough.

Buttoned-up good girl Jasmine Lee likes it when I fuck her throat.

When I tie her to my bed.

When I flick my tongue against her nipple.

When I scrape my teeth against the tender bud—

"Fuck." She tries to reach for me again. "Shep… please."

"Please what, princess?" I start gently. Sucking on her sweet skin. Then drawing circles around it. Back and forth. Right to left.

The scrape of my teeth.

Again, she groans.

Again, she reaches for me.

Again, she shakes when the restraints catch her arms.

Under the bed restraints. She's being pulled to the top corners of the bed. Not the most sophisticated. But enough she knows she's powerless.

Enough she has to take whatever I give her.

I tease her with hard flicks of my tongue. Again and again until she's digging her nails into her palms.

Then I bite her softly.

Harder.

Hard enough her groan is equal parts pain and pleasure.

Then harder.

"Fuck." Her exhale is quick. Her inhale is sharp. "Shep, please."

"Please?" I bite her again.

A groan falls from her lips.

Her head falls to one side, taking her wet hair with it.

She looks so fucking beautiful like this. Brimming with anticipation. Lost in this world of pleasure.

Where all she wants is release.

I bite her again. Then I move to her other nipple. Tease it just as mercilessly.

She tastes good. Like the soap in her shower. Like salt. And like Jasmine.

That taste that's uniquely her. That brings me back to all those years ago.

I'm not going there.

I'm here. In this moment, where I'm in control. Where I understand exactly what she wants. Where I'm the only one who can give her exactly what she wants.

Her toes squeeze the sheets as I scrape my teeth against her. She rocks her hips, trying to find some kind of contact.

I press my palm against her hipbone, pinning her to the bed.

Which makes her groan even louder.

I hold her in place as I toy with her nipple. Pain and pleasure mix together, until her groan is a beautiful jumble.

"Shep," she says it again. "Please. Fuck me. Please."

My cock whines. It's ready to be inside her. To feel her sweet softness.

But I'm greedy.

I need more. So much more.

"No, princess." I bite her one more time. "We aren't even close to ready for that."

Her exhale is a whine. A plea. A *fuck me now*.

But I don't relent. After one more scrape of my teeth, I drag my lips down her stomach, below her belly button, the top of her pelvis.

Without warning, I press my palms into her thighs, pinning her to the bed.

She gasps as her knees hit the crimson sheets. "Fuck."

"Beautiful." I take a moment to savor the sight of her. Jasmine, tied to my bed, splayed wide, ready for me.

It's perfection.

She's perfection.

I bring my lips to her thigh. She's so soft, so pliable, so mine.

Right now, in this moment, she is mine.

Right now, in this moment, the two of us are completely free.

Right now, in this moment, her bliss is the only thing that matters.

The rest of world doesn't exist.

It's the best feeling in the entire fucking universe.

She shudders as I kiss my way up her leg. Higher and higher and higher until I'm almost—

"Shep." Her hands tug the restraints. "Please—"

I don't give her the chance to finish her sentence. I bring my lips to her clit.

A soft brush.

Then harder.

Hard enough she tries to reach for me again.

I pin her legs to the bed as I lick her up and down. She tastes so fucking good. Like honey and peaches. Like Jasmine.

I take my time tasting every inch of her. Exploring what she wants. I suck on her clit. Scrape my teeth against her outer lips. Plunge my tongue inside her.

Then it's soft, slow flicks of my tongue against her clit. Enough to tease her. To wind her tight. To keep her on the edge.

I do it again and again.

Until she's panting and shaking and tugging at the restraints.

Until I'm the only thing she sees.

The only thing she wants.

Then I find the place where she needs me. A little higher. To the left. And harder.

Harder.

There.

"Fuck." She groans as I lick her right where she needs me.

I do it again and again.

I push her closer and closer to the edge.

Then over it.

With the next flick of my tongue, she comes. She groans my name again and again, fighting my hands, rocking against my mouth.

Fuck, she tastes good. Sweeter.

My cock begs for more. It's desperate to be inside her. I'm desperate to be inside her.

But this first.

I don't give her relief. I work her through her orgasm. Then I scrape my nails against her thighs.

Hard enough she gasps.

"Shep." She tries to reach for me. Moans as the restraints catch her. "Fuck."

I keep her pinned as I work her through another orgasm.

She comes fast this time. Hard.

She rocks against my mouth, letting out a groan that's equal parts agony and ecstasy.

It's music. Better than music. Because who gives a fuck about melody when there's Jasmine's groan?

"Fuck." Her breath hitches in her throat. "Fuck me, please. I want to come on your cock."

My balls tighten.

"Please." She looks down at me. Makes her voice soft. Obedient. "Please, sir."

Fuck. I can't resist that. It's impossible.

Still. I make her wait. Stand as I undress. First my shoes and socks. Then the tie. Shirt.

She watches carefully as I slide my slacks off my hips.

Then the boxers.

She stares at my cock like it's her favorite meal. Maybe it is. Maybe she feels the same way I do. I need to make her come. To watch her, feel her, taste her.

I shift onto the bed. Place my body between her legs. But I don't fuck her.

I slip a finger inside her. Then two. Three.

She groans as I stretch her wide.

She wants to fuck me. I want to fuck her.

But she needs to earn it first. "You're going to come on my hand, princess."

"I… don't know if I can, sir."

I arch a brow.

"Physically. If I have anything left."

"You do."

"I do?"

I nod. I can tell by the way she pulses.

I pull my fingers back then drive them into her again.

She arches her hips. Just barely rising to meet me. Just barely pushing me deeper.

A few more thrusts and I bring my thumb to her clit. I draw slow circles exactly where she needs me.

Her head falls back.

Her lips part with a groan.

Her nails dig into her palms.

"Fuck. Shep…" She gasps as I drive my fingers deeper.

Something in her posture changes. She stops thinking. Starts melting into my touch. Trusting me with her entire body.

Trusting me to give her what she needs.

I draw those slow circles.

Drive my fingers into her.

Again and again.

As I wind her tighter and tighter.

She doesn't pant or beg for more.

She lets her lids flutter together. Lets her hair fall over her eyes. Lets her thighs hit the sheets.

Then she's there, groaning my name as she comes on my hand, looking up at me with lazy eyes, sure I'm going to finally free her.

I push her legs apart. Then I pull her closer. Closer.

Until her cunt brushes my cock.

She groans at the contact. The promise of bliss. Of our bodies joining.

Of the entire universe making sense.

I push into her slowly. One sweet inch at a time, she envelops me with her softness.

It's like coming home.

This is where I'm supposed to be. Where we're both supposed to be.

She's surrendering to me. She doesn't even need the restraints. She's already there.

She's already mine.

I pull back and push into her again. Slow and steady. Feeling every inch of her.

She looks up at me, her dark eyes hazy with pleasure, affection, trust.

Here, I understand her perfectly.

I grab a pillow, lift her hips, place it under her ass.

My fingers curl into her thighs.

She hooks her legs around my waist.

Then I drive into her with slow, steady strokes. Again and again. Until pleasure is gripping every one of my senses.

Until she's dizzy with bliss.

Until we're completely connected.

I keep her there, so close to release, so tightly wound, until her groan is equal parts agony and ecstasy. Until it's more agony than ecstasy.

Until it's all agony. All plea. All *please, Shep, have mercy*.

This time, I do.

I move exactly how she needs me. Hard thrusts as deep as I can go.

Just fast enough.

There.

She groans as I drive into her. A groan that's all anticipation. All bliss.

My eyes fall closed. My fingers dig into her thighs. Harder. Hard enough she yelps.

I scrape her skin as I thrust into her.

As an orgasm overtakes me.

Fuck.

My cock pulses so hard I see white. No sign of the room around. Of the beauty splayed before me. Of anything but pure, deep bliss.

Then she's coming, her cunt pulsing around me, pulling me closer and deeper.

Then she collapses, completely and totally spent.

I untangle our bodies. Help her out of her restraints. Lie next to her.

She snuggles into my chest, resting her head against my shoulder, draping her arm over my waist.

It feels good, having her so close. Better than it should.

For a moment, it feels like we really can be more than this.

Chapter Thirty-Three

JASMINE

I wake up alone. And sore.

My body is still buzzing. But the coldness of the empty bed—

This is confusing.

No, it's simple. Shepard will fuck me. He won't love me. I need to find a way to understand it.

Sure, I say the words again and again, but—

I need to believe it. To know it the way I know the climax of Macbeth. The way I know I love my father.

I go through my morning routine, dress in comfortable clothes, move into the main room.

Key is waiting with breakfast and tea. Oolong, perfectly steeped, a new pairing that enhances the flavors of both items. Eggs with scallions. Toast with chives and goat cheese.

Simple, strong, creamy.

She has a note too. From Shep. He's busy today, doing God knows what. But he wants me to pick a location for our trip. We need to visit one of Jeff and Marcus's chocolate factories. To prove we appreciate his gift.

And we need to sell it too. To seem like the most happily engaged couple to ever live.

That's a stretch.

But I guess it's not so bad picking between London, Paris, Rome, and Tokyo.

There are certain perks to this arrangement.

Orgasms. Fine tea. Trips abroad.

The only thing lacking is love.

Just that one little thing.

———

"Jasmine, you have thirteen days," Mai says. "You need to find something now."

"You only get married once," Quyen argues. "She can't wear a dress that's all wrong."

They look to me to pick a side, though I'm not sure why. They've been having this argument for the last twenty minutes. For our entire ride from their hotel (my first stop after breakfast) to this row of shops.

This is the first shop of many options. From the current status of conversation—

It's going to be a long day.

"This is beautiful." Mai points to one of the dresses in the window. A lace mermaid gown by a famous designer. With a five-figure price tag. "But so much money. It's a waste."

"Her husband makes that in a day," Quyen argues.

"More like a few hours," I say.

They look at me with wide eyes. It's like they're characters in a cartoon with exclamation points over their heads. "It's that much?"

Did they not realize?

"I knew Shepard was from a good family, but wow."

Mai looks at the price tag. Her posture changes as she looks around the store. It's no longer out of reach. It's well within her grasp.

Money changes things. It always changes things. I don't want it to change the way they look at me, but I guess I don't have a choice.

"It's his money," I say. "Not mine."

"His money you can spend on a dress. On your wedding." Realization spreads over Mai's face. "Who is planning this?"

"One of his assistants." I'm not helping my case.

Quyen shakes her head. "An assistant? Jasmine, you trust his assistants to plan the most important day of your life?"

"This is the most important day of my life?" I ask.

She nods *of course*. Picks out a dress that's much more ornate. Lace flowers cover visible boning, a trumpet skirt, a bow at the waist. It's couture. High fashion. Weird.

"You're bold." She motions to the dressing room. "You deserve a bold dress."

Mai waves it away. "Bold is another way to say ugly. When was the last time someone called a new haircut bold as a compliment?" She looks at me, her thoughts visible on her face. *Besides, no one thinks Jasmine is bold. She's a good girl. Studies hard, never complains, sacrifices for her family.* "Why not wear that?" She points to another gown in the window. One an even, ahem, bolder design.

A tight bodice, a peacock tail, and no skirt. Like a superhero in an impractical bridal outfit.

But Quyen loves it. "She has great legs."

Mai laughs *that much is true*. She scans the rows of dresses, looking for something more… normal.

She finds something aggressively normal. A simple ivory sheath with no detail.

Quyen shakes her head *not in a million years*. She joins her sister at the rack. Finds a more exciting version of the same dress.

Still a simple sheath, covered in thick lace. "Have you picked a style?" she asks. "Or a venue? We need to know what's appropriate."

That's a great question. One that should be on my mind. What is our venue? If I had all the time in the world, I'd pick…

I don't know. I've never thought about *where* I'd get married. More about who and what happened after.

Immediately, my head fills with images of Shep's home back in California. The park where we used to spend our time. The giant redwoods we'd visit a few times a year.

The fancy hotel in San Francisco where we tried to order drinks.

The pictures of my parents wedding. A simple ceremony in the park in traditional Vietnamese attire.

It is spring.

But does the park represent some deep part of me? And which park? Which says *Jasmine Lee is more than a rich man's wife?*

Does that even matter?

It's not a real wedding. We aren't really in love. We aren't really professing our desire to stay together forever.

"We're still deciding," I say.

My aunts exchange a look. One that means *that's not good*.

"Are you sure you're not pregnant?" Mai asks.

"It's okay if you are," Quyen adds. "You wouldn't be the first—"

Mai cuts her off. "Your dad would be so happy."

"I know." I laugh, despite the awkwardness. "He's very excited about grandchildren."

They exchange another look I know well. One that means *is that really going to happen? Or will he be gone first?*

Not something I can consider at the moment. It's enough to plan this wedding.

"What do you want, Jasmine?" Mai takes both dresses and leads me and Quyen toward the dressing room. My aunts wave the attendant away.

Quyen comes into the stall with me. Though stall is selling it short. It's a huge space, the size of my old bedroom, with a three-panel mirror and half a dozen hooks.

"I will pick out a few more options," the saleswoman says. "And you have undergarments?"

"She doesn't need a fancy bra with this figure," Quyen says in Vietnamese.

Mai laughs and tells the salesgirl we're settled. Then she goes off with her, no doubt to help her pick dresses that don't demand too much attention.

"My sister is a good sister. A good aunt." Quyen helps me out of my boots, sweater, jeans. "You're like her. Practical. Smart. But you're like me too. Romantic." She smiles softly. "Mostly, you're like your mother. Pragmatic with this idealism you don't want to admit you have."

"I don't know about that."

"See." She unzips the fancier sheath. "You don't want to admit it. But I know it's there. This rushed wedding… it's because you… well, if you ask me, it's because you love the sex."

"Oh my God." I turn bright red.

She motions for me to raise my arms. Once I do, she steps onto the chair and pulls the dress over my head. "It's okay. It always starts that way. Your uncle… he's quite the—"

"Please don't finish that sentence."

She laughs. "It started that way. Physical. But it's not possible for it to stay that way. You learn to understand each other. Trust each other. Love each other."

"I…" Well, I can't tell her *no, he'll never love me, but you're right, the sex is great*. "We do understand each other." Kind of.

She helps me into the dress. Steps off the chair. Pulls the zipper. "It's the passion that pushes you. And the practicality that keeps you there. You are a smart woman, Jasmine. You see a good thing when you have it." She turns me to the mirror. "Beautiful."

"What do you mean?"

"You do have the frame. With taller shoes."

"About seeing a good thing?"

"He's rich and handsome and he looks at you like you're a princess. Of course, you're marrying him."

"I…" Still can't tell her *no, no, it's about money, but not the way you think*. "He looks at me like I'm a princess?"

She nods. "Maybe it's your body. Maybe he's thinking about what he'd like to do to you later—"

"Oh my God." Somehow, my blush deepens.

"But he does. When no one else is looking—"

"If you see him—"

"When he thinks no one else is looking."

"Oh." I try to focus on my reflection. To assess the dress objectively. To think only of how things appear. "Really?"

She nods. "I may not know much, but I know the way men look at women."

"You know a lot."

"It's true." She laughs. "I know a lot. Everything. Including this."

"I, uh…" Is it possible? That Shep really does look at me with devotion? That he's not just pretending?

Maybe she's seeing what she wants to see.

Maybe he's a better liar than he seems.

Maybe he's thinking with his cock.

He's devoted to making me come. And that's not a bad deal. It's really not.

I turn. Focus on the dress. Elegant. Simple. Boring. "I don't think so."

Right on cue, the saleswoman knocks on the door. "We have more options, Miss Lee."

"Come in," I say.

Quyen opens the door. The saleswoman hangs two dresses. Then four more. She places white shoes on the carpet, next to one of the ornate chairs (it's more throne than chair, really). "To see how it fits with heels. Or if you wear flats and hem. Some women want to look up at their groom."

"He's very tall," Mai says. "She will."

"He's not that tall," Quyen argues.

"You don't think anyone is tall." Mai shakes her head. Tells the story of a Warriors player coming into her restaurant. He was so tall he bumped his head on the door. But Quyen still thought he wasn't tall.

Quyen returns with her own story, about the time they met a famous actor who is known for standing on boxes so he's eye to eye with his leading ladies. But Mai thought he was tall.

It warms the room. Eases the tension in my mind. I've heard these stories so many times. They're home.

The whole not knowing where I'm getting married thing... I can deal with that.

No, I can pick a place. I'm not sure what I want, what says Jasmine Lee, not just a rich man's wife, but there's one thing that comes to mind.

The place that's been my sanctuary the last few years.

I change out of this dress. Find my cell in my purse. Text Shep.

Jasmine: Can we talk about the location for the wedding?

Shep: I reserved a theater.

Jasmine: A theater?

Shep: Yes. A two-thousand seat one. We'd have to do it Monday, when the show is dark. But it's not a problem.

Jasmine: Oh.

Shep: Oh?

Jasmine: Yes. Oh.

Shep: You don't like it?

Jasmine: No. I do. But since when do you enjoy theater?

Shep: Is there some place I do enjoy?

Jasmine: Besides the bedroom?

Shep: Unless you'd like to invite our guests there.

Jasmine: It's almost big enough.

Shep: They'll get a certain idea.

Jasmine: It's what my aunts think. That I'm marrying you for the sex.

Shep: Every man's fantasy.

Jasmine: Really?

Shep: I know it's not my sparkling personality.

My lips curl into a smile. He's actually teasing me. It's rare. Precious.

Jasmine: Not the money?

Shep: There are other rich men.

Jasmine: There are other skilled men.

Shep: You're treading dangerous ground there.

Jasmine: Will it hurt your ego? If I suggest you aren't the best I've ever had.

Shep: What do you think?

Jasmine: It's probably the only way I can hurt you.

Shep: There are lots of ways you can hurt me.

That's hard to believe. Shep is so guarded. His heart is behind a five-thousand-pound safe.

It's how he wants it.

I respect that.

I want to respect that.

He isn't going to love me. No use in daydreaming of pillow talk and walks on the beach.

Shep on the beach… that's a funny image.

Jasmine: The theater is perfect. Do we have a plan for the honeymoon?

Shep: It's a surprise.

Jasmine: Will I like it?

Shep: I'm not sure it will matter. Since we'll spend all that time in bed.

Jasmine: Is that a no?

Shep: You didn't answer the question.

Jasmine: Which one?

Shep: If I'm the best you've ever had.

Jasmine: Don't tell me you're insecure.

Shep: No. But if you don't answer, I'll have to force you to admit it.

Jasmine: Is that supposed to loosen my tongue?

Shep: No.

Mmm.

Yes.

So much yes.

All the yes.

"Send your dirty texts later," Quyen says. "You've barely started."

My blush spreads to my chest. Is it that obvious? How do we get to dirty so fast? I guess it is the only way we connect.

"Excuse me." I drop my cell in my purse. Slip into the heels. Let her help me into the next dress.

It's her pick. An enormous princess dress. The skirt is the size of my old shower. The bodice is fitted. It even has that v at the bottom.

The light fabric twirls as I spin. It's the kind of dress. One that demands movement.

"How will he kiss you?" Mai laughs. "You can't barely move past the thing." She tries to move closer, to reach for my hips, but the skirt is in the way.

"It's beautiful. Let him strain himself," Quyen says.

It is beautiful. And I do feel like a princess. But not like me. "It's not it."

They exchange a look of victory. Somehow, they both take this as a win.

They help me out of the dress. Then they move to the wall. To something behind the stack of dresses.

"This is just an idea," Mai says. "I think you should stay modern. Wear something new. Practical. But your father—"

"He would love it," Quyen says.

She holds up a black dress bag. Unzips it to reveal a traditional Vietnamese wedding gown. Like the one in my mom's pictures.

It's not modern. Not here. Not even in Vietnam. Nowadays, most women wear a white western dress for the ceremony. They may change into their Ao dai later. But they keep the opulence for the pictures.

Still… it looks so much like what my mom wore.

I nod. Let them help me into it.

So much like the sheath. Soft red fabric that skims my skin. Long, elegant lines.

Beautiful. Traditional. Bold.

"It's too modest," Quyen argues.

"And you look like one of *those* girls." Mai mutters

something about a friend of hers who just refuses to assimilate.

"But like your mother too." Quyen blinks back a tear. "So much like her."

"She would want modern," Mai says. "She wanted you to fit in. Like a normal, American girl."

"She would want something grand. Something big. That makes you feel like royalty." Quyen turns to me. "What makes you feel like royalty, Jasmine? It's your dress. It's your day. It's your chance to stand in front of everyone and declare your love for your fiancé. Do it in a way that feels honest."

For once, Mai agrees.

I can't stand up and scream *this is a normal marriage, really*. Or *for God's sake, stop telling me how my wedding dress should make me feel. And don't add the pressure of pleasing my late mother on top of it.*

Well, I can. But I'd rather not hear their frustration.

I can find a compromise. Something that honors my history, and my mother, without looking like I'm in a costume.

"I have an idea." For the first time, my heart swells at the thought of the wedding. It's perfect. "I think you're going to like it."

Chapter Thirty-Four

JASMINE

Lock works with me immediately. He whisks me to visit with a designer. I explain exactly what I want. My aunts start issuing orders to the designer—their mom, my grandma—was a seamstress. I let them run with it. As long as they promise they won't tell my dad until it's ready.

The designer promises three days.

I spend most of my time with them. We walk around the Met, take in the sights of Times Square, watch *Wicked* and *Phantom of the Opera*.

We eat real New York pizza. Good bagels. Vietnamese iced coffee and pho from a place in Chinatown. Of course, Mai hates it. She hates everything that isn't from her restaurant.

We even manage to bring Dad out one day. And walking around the park with him, seeing him laugh with his sisters-in-law, listening to them reminisce about his and mom's wedding—

It's worth everything.

The quiet dinners I have with Shep are nothing.

The three-day trip we plan to Rome is—

Well, I'm not exactly dreading it. Even if I'd rather not leave my family. Even if I have no idea why we're jumping through these hoops to impress someone as bland as Jeff.

I can't imagine his business partner Marcus is any more interesting.

Why do we care what they think?

I suppose it's above my paygrade.

For once, I don't worry about it. I enjoy the fresh air, the strong tea, the sunny skies.

For once, life is good.

Easy.

And when the dress finally arrives and I bring it to Dad's apartment and show it off to him—

He cries and hugs me and says, "Your mother would be so proud of you."

And I believe him.

If she knew the truth… It's like Quyen said. She would be proud of me for doing the practical thing, even if she secretly wanted me to follow my heart.

But hearts are silly things.

Sometimes, it's better to ignore them.

Chapter Thirty-Five

SHEPARD

"You look awful." Ian holds up his mug as if to toast.

I keep my cup of drip exactly where it is. Awful isn't the right word. Torn in half is more accurate. Too much of me craves Jasmine's company. Every time I think this might get easier, that bastard reminds me it won't.

These constant updates on Marcus and his fucking factory—

Like anyone cares he overcharges tourists in a dozen different cities. Even I know his bars aren't worth what he charges. They're not the single-origin craft chocolate he claims.

They're fine.

Maybe I'm blinded by my hatred.

Maybe I don't know good chocolate anymore. Maybe I'm still incapable of truly savoring food.

That doesn't feel right... I can taste the flavor quality of this coffee. A little burnt, too acidic, not strong enough.

Mediocre.

But I know good is out there. I've had great before.

And Rome...

The thought of sipping espresso as Jasmine shakes her head *it's horrible, how do you drink it* makes me smile.

Then I think about why we're heading to Rome and—

"It's not lack of sex." His voice is teasing. "I know what you look like when you aren't getting laid. It's not pretty."

He's not wrong. Though *getting laid* is hardly the language I'd use. "What do you know about pretty?"

"Are you claiming I'm not beautiful?" He lets out an easy laugh.

It's ridiculous. Ian is an attractive man but no one would call him beautiful. Handsome is a much better fit. As Key likes to remind me.

As Lock likes to remind me.

Sometimes, they even argue about the words that best suit Ian. And whether or not the rumors are true. Is he really fixated on virgins? Introducing women to domination? Picking up strippers and offering cash for a night at a hotel?

I never ruin their fun with the truth. Well, what I know of it.

"Jeff sent over your itinerary," Ian says. "Heading to Rome this weekend."

I'm not even going to ask how he knows. Ian always knows. "Do you have a point?"

"It's a romantic city."

"It's the center of Catholicism."

"And pasta."

"And wine." Really, the entire world revolves around booze. Mezcal in Mexico, Souchu in Korea, wine in Italy.

"Should have gone to London," he says.

"So *you* could woo her?"

"You can't handle a little friendly competition?" He rests his back against the wall. Looks out on the empty office. It's early. Just the two of us here.

We're always the first two here. I'm not sure how he does it. If my information is good—and I'm pretty sure it is —Ian has a lot of late nights. But he always makes it here at the crack of dawn. And he never looks worse for wear.

"A man your age shouldn't strain himself," I tease back.

He just laughs. Another easy laugh. "That's a low blow."

"Can you reach it? Or do you have back problems? I hear these things happen."

His smile gets knowing. He's only ten years older than I am, but it's enough I can tease him. "Did she pick Rome? Or did you?"

"Marcus."

He nods *of course*.

"I'm sure there's some bullshit reason."

"You want me to find out?"

For a moment, I consider it. Ian has his ways. Not all of them are legal.

If Jeff and Marcus are planning to spring a visit from that bastard, I need to know.

But that won't happen. Jeff hates him. Jeff hates playing these little games.

"I realize I'm the last guy you'd ask for advice on marriage," Ian says. "But I do know women. And I can tell Jasmine trusts you."

"I'm aware."

"Whatever you're after… maybe she really wants to give it to you."

"You're right. I'm not looking for your advice."

"Go to London after. There's no good tea in Rome." He nods *goodbye*, turns, leaves.

I guess he's right about that. I can't fill most of Jasmine's needs, but I can make sure she has tea to drink, food to eat, a comfortable place to stay.

I can't do anything for her heart.

But I know how to care for her body.

Chapter Thirty-Six

JASMINE

First class is quite the upgrade. Wide seats. Soft pillows. The friendly skies so many airlines promise.

The flight attendant smiles like she dreams of fulfilling my every desire. She's happy to bring me a sparkling water. My enjoyment of dinner is her only craving. And do I want the ice cream dessert? Vanilla or chocolate? Maybe some coffee or tea to go with it.

She wishes she could be of more help. They only have the one tea. Tea. She understands there are more options out there, but she's not really familiar. In Italy, the culture is all coffee.

It's strange.

Three weeks ago, I was this woman, smiling at strangers, pretending as if I lived to fill their needs.

Don't get me wrong. I like being helpful. I always enjoyed getting things done. Even trivial things, like fetching the Americano at *that* coffee shop instead of *this* one. Because God forbid it's not perfect.

But doing it with a smile, pretending as if it was effortless, as if it was truly fulfilling my deepest desires—

That, I didn't like.

That, I don't like.

And this whole trip to Rome…

I'm not really sure what to do here. Shep knows how I feel. He knows I appreciate his help. He knows I resent the imposition.

But that doesn't feel quite right.

Sure, our reasons for flying to Rome are unclear. I wish I was in the know. I wish he trusted me enough to explain this.

But, right now, I don't resent a single thing.

Right now, I'm… happy.

I don't care about the awkwardness of first class or the shitty tea or the vague explanation.

Only that Shep is sitting next to me, his lips in a half-smile, his eyes bright.

He's so handsome.

And I'm so screwed.

Because I really do like him. More.

The speech I gave about how I never stopped loving him—

It's way too true.

But it can't be too bad. Because I *do* care about this shitty tea. Ugh. It tastes like nothing. "Is this really what passes for tea?"

"Ian says you're out of luck in Italy."

Again, I stick my tongue out. Like I'm sixteen again, complaining about my dad's cooking.

"You can try espresso."

Again, I stick my tongue out. Coffee is a club to the senses. Sure, I appreciate the Vietnamese Iced Coffee Mai serves in her restaurant… if I want something that makes a Frappuccino look subtle. Black coffee... no way.

"Too strong?"

"Way too strong."

"They have milk and sugar."

That is... true. And there's something about his easy tone... it's just right.

All this is so easy. Like we're kids in love. Like our biggest concerns are midterms and what we're wearing to Spring Fling.

His fingers brush mine as he takes the cup. He brings it to his soft lips. Takes a small sip. "It tastes like tea."

I shake my head. "It's an abomination."

"What happened to the oolong"

"I drank it."

"All of them?"

I nod. "The bags are barely better. There's no room for the leaves to breathe."

His smile spreads a little wider. "Is that right?"

"Yes." I reach for a visual aide, but my cup is long gone. The flight attendant took it the second I finished. She's exactly like I used to be. Everywhere and nowhere at once. Only visible when people want to see her.

"I have something for you," he says.

"Is it appropriate?"

Shep's wicked smile lights up his blue eyes. It's that beautiful, dirty *I don't know what I'm going to do to you, princess*. Then it's more. Something deeper.

Or maybe I'm imagining things. Oxygen deprivation. Tea deprivation. Inability to think because of the proximity of Shep... syndrome. If that's a syndrome.

He's not wearing a suit today. He's in jeans and a navy t-shirt.

Jeans.

I haven't seen Shep in jeans in years. We went to private school. We wore uniforms. He only donned jeans on the weekends, but it was all he donned.

And now—

Shep *wears* his suit. How can he look just as good in casual attire? It's not fair. It's wrong.

But I guess it's in my favor. So I can't really complain.

He undoes his seatbelt. Stands. Reaches for something in the overhead compartment.

His shirt goes with his arms, revealing inches of taught skin. Abs. The perfect v. The soft hairs that disappear beneath denim.

It's the jeans. They're mixing me up. Turning me into a sex maniac.

Or maybe I'm just a sex maniac now.

We sleep in separate rooms. And we've been busy. He's been busy with work or world domination or whatever he does when he's at the office.

I've kept busy too. With my family, acting classes, evenings watching movies.

It's been days since he's touched me.

Four days.

Four days without his cock and I'm ready to join the mile high club.

I'm so far beyond insane.

His shirt falls as he lowers his arms. He holds out something, presenting it to me.

A box of tea. Bags of milk oolong. Not the one I requested from Key. A new tin.

My fingers brush his as I take the tea. It's such a small thing. It shouldn't mean so much. But it does.

He's trying to meet me halfway. In his way.

"Thank you." My stomach flutters. It's like I'm a

teenager again. Like I'm waiting for him to kiss me for the first time.

"Should I ask for hot water?"

I nod then immediately regret it. I don't want the flight attendant here. Even if she knows how to be invisible.

I don't want the reminder of how things used to be. How things will be for me again if this doesn't work out. I'm not naïve. I'm twenty-four and I'm not white. Even if I gain talent fast, I'm not going to have a lot of options.

The world sees me as the help.

Even after I marry Shep, the world will see me as the help. A different kind of help. The pretty trophy wife who fills her role in exchange for security.

Still smiling, still effortless, still *thank you, I'll get right on that, sir*.

I don't want to remember that. For a few days, I don't want to feel like I'm stuck inside that box. I want to believe my life is like the sky—

Bright, expansive, full of possibilities.

The flight attendant drops off the hot water with a smile. "What a sweet husband, bringing your favorite drink. I wish mine was that sensitive."

"Not yet," he smiles. "But soon."

Her eyes go to the enormous ring on my left hand. "An early honeymoon." She smiles. "Very smart. Hold on to this one. He's a keeper."

"He is." I wrap my fingers around my paper cup.

Shep turns his body toward mine, blocking the rest of the plane. He has the aisle seat. I have the window. He asked which I wanted. He asked where I wanted to be.

He unwraps the box. Opens it. Pulls the bag from its plastic seal.

He's careful. Like this is precious cargo.

Slowly, he slips the bag into my cup of water.

"Thank you." My eyes find his. I can't look away. His eyes are so beautiful. A deep blue that demands all my attention. "She's right. You are a keeper."

"She means rich."

"Maybe she means handsome."

He actually smiles. Full-on smiles. "Is that so?"

"Or she can sense your… raw sexual energy." Did I really just say that?

His smile gets dirtier. "Princess, you know what happens if you dare me."

"Right here?"

He nods *right here*. "Under a blanket."

"They'll kick us out."

"How? We're halfway over the Atlantic."

More like a quarter of the way, but I don't correct him. It feels good, letting him tease me.

"Are you happy?"

"Happy?" That's a big question.

"With the wedding?"

"Your team is handling it well." My laugh is nervous. "Do you ever get used to that? Having a team?"

"Eventually."

"I can't imagine. It's strange, waking up to tea and breakfast. Key ready to fill my every need. That used to be me."

"I know."

"When you're the help… people look at you, but they don't see you."

"I know what you mean."

Does he though? Shep has always been well-off. He's always commanded attention.

"I know you think otherwise, but I've always seen you, Jasmine. The first day at school, in Honors American

Literature. You were chewing the end of your pencil as you read *Huckleberry Finn*."

"You remember that?"

"I remember everything. The way you rolled your eyes at me. Then blushed, because you couldn't help but invite my stare. You thought I saw you as a scholarship kid. But that wasn't it."

"You were thinking about what you wanted to do to me?"

He nods *exactly*. "Even now… when I see you in that pencil skirt. I'm sure there are people who look through you. But all I can think is that I need that skirt at your waist."

"Oh." My chest warms. My tongue twists. He's so handsome. And sexy. And the look in his eyes… there's desire, yes, but there's affection too. "I meant more… that people don't think you matter. You're not a person to them. You're a tool. Like a word processor or a coffee machine. It's the same as when I worked at Mai's restaurant."

"You're invisible."

I nod. "I thought I hated it. But this…" I hold up my left hand. "It's a whole different challenge."

"It's a lot of attention, the spotlight."

I nod.

"It will pass. We'll marry, people will talk about it for a few weeks, then they'll lose interest."

"And we'll just…"

"Live."

"But what will that look like?" I dunk my tea bag three times. The water gets a little darker. A slightly deeper brown. More flavor.

I take a sip. It's okay, not great. The water isn't warm enough for a proper steep. The tea isn't ready to unfurl. It isn't ready to reveal itself to me.

I swallow another sip. "Will you keep working late?"

His eyes stay on mine. He studies my expression, looking for something. "I always work long hours."

I'm not sure what I want, really. If this was real, I'd want it all. Happy dinners, long walks in the park, lazy afternoons on the couch. A family.

But this isn't real. I haven't spent time picturing my perfect fake marriage. "Do we sleep in separate rooms? Do you visit me to fuck me when it's convenient for you then leave?"

His gaze softens. "I don't want to give you the wrong idea."

"You can spend the night in my bed without giving me the wrong idea."

He studies my expression, deciding if he agrees. "Okay."

"Okay?"

He takes a sip of his coffee. "I'd like that."

"Oh." My heart thuds against my chest. He'd like that. It shouldn't mean so much, but it does. "And I… are you only going to take me out when you need to show me off?"

"Is there something else you'd like to do?"

"It would be nice to have dinner without worrying about what image I'm projecting."

He nods *of course.*

"Or we could go to the theater. Spend an afternoon in Central Park. Do you go to the park? Or is there too much mud?"

He half-smiles. "I'm not sure I've ever seen you covered in dirt."

It's true. I've never been the type to garden or hike or play with paint.

"I'm not sure I've ever seen you in flat shoes." He motions to my wedge sandals.

"I'm short."

"You're not." He shakes his head. "The average woman is five four."

"I'm average? Wow, I've never heard such a compliment."

His chuckle is easy. "Slightly above average."

"Stop. You're making me blush."

His expression shifts to something I can't place. Some look that screams of love and affection. "We'll be away from prying eyes soon. Then, we can do more. I… I want to protect you as much as I can." He motions to the aisle and the seats across from us. "Usually, I'd charter a private plane. More time to myself. Or ourselves." His intention drops into his voice. *More time to tear off your clothes and fuck you senseless.*

Or maybe it's the sex maniac who's taken over my brain. "Have you done that before?"

"Do you really want the answer to that?"

He might as well say yes. I bite my tongue.

"I like you jealous. I've never seen it on you."

"I'm not—"

"You are," he says. "I am too. I want to kill any man who's ever touched you."

"Oh." My cheeks flush. His possessiveness shouldn't soothe me, but it does.

"You were my first."

"You were mine."

His smile shifts. More nostalgic. Sad even. "After I got sober, sex was the only thing that made sense. It wasn't solely physical. Not exactly. But it wasn't personal either."

"You don't have to explain. You didn't owe me anything."

"But you're still jealous."

I nod.

"My tastes were always there. But I was afraid to give into them. I was afraid I'd scare you. That I'd scare myself."

I'm not sure what to say. Would I have accepted his need for control at sixteen? I doubt it. Even if I was interested—and I would have been—I would have been too shy.

"With other women... it was easier. I didn't care what they thought of me. And there were so many who wanted that. Who helped me figure it out."

I bite my tongue.

"I did care for some of them. But not the way I care for you."

"Oh."

"I always thought about you. Tying you to my bed. Pinning you to the wall. Wrapping my hand around your throat as I fucked you."

My thighs shudder. "You're teasing?"

"A little."

"To distract me?"

"Myself. I don't want to think about the other men. I hate that someone else has made you come. I hate that someone else has heard your groan."

"You still..." I swallow hard. I should hold on to this. Make him sweat it. But I can't. "I was never with Nick. I wouldn't. Even if I wanted revenge. He's like an older brother."

His eyes glue to mine.

"I... could have said something earlier—"

"But you wanted to keep me jealous?"

I nod.

He smiles, impressed. "You've always been shrewd."

I'm not sure I should be flattered by his compliment—he's calling me manipulative—but I am. "Thank you."

"So, I imagine I don't have to explain this to you. That we had to let Marcus pay for this trip. Buy our tickets, pick our hotel, arrange our plans."

I nod. I may not know the details, but I know rich men. It's always a power play.

"I wish it was easier. I wish we were in a private plane. I wish your father was well. I wish we were marrying because we're madly in love. I wish this wasn't complicated. But it is."

"I know." *Do you think it's possible? That you could love me? That this could be simple?* It's a silly question. But it keeps echoing in my head.

"I will need to show you off." Shep does nothing to mask the desire in his voice. "I'm sure it will feel objectifying at times. Men see a beautiful woman and they make assumptions. They expect things. I'll protect you as much as I can, but I can't stop what's in their heads." His voice shifts to something honest. Vulnerable even. "Sometimes I forget you're only here because I've paid you."

"That isn't exactly—"

"I know. But I also know how the world works." He shifts into his seat, his eyes on the seat in front of his. "You're a romantic at heart. You want to marry someone who will love you. You want to have kids your dad can hold. And you want to show them what it means to follow your dreams. But you're a smart woman. You understand the world doesn't always allow that."

Since when does everyone think I'm a romantic?

He looks to me. "I can't give you that. But I can be… softer. I can try."

"Thank you."

His fingers slide over his paper cup. It's a mindless gesture. Something he doesn't realize. "You need to promise me something."

I nod *of course*.

"You need to tell me you understand I'm not capable of loving you. It's got nothing to do with you, Jasmine. It's me. This curse I'm under..." He shakes his head. "I'll love your company. I'll love your wit, your beauty, your determination. I'll love the way you respond to my touch. But I'll never fall in love with you."

"Of course," I lie. "I understand completely."

Chapter Thirty-Seven

SHEPARD

Time zones aren't on our side. We arrive a few hours after midnight.

Still, someone greets us at our apartment. They smile as if it's the middle of the afternoon and happily show us around.

It's nicer than what I expected from Jeff and Marcus. An apartment in an old building—Rome is all old, three or four-story buildings. One bedroom, a den, a small kitchen. The food and appliances we requested.

When Jasmine sees the electric kettle—the one her father covets—she nearly jumps into my arms.

I wait for the attendant to leave, then I make the mental image in my head a reality.

I lift her into my arms, carry her to the bed, push her skirt to her waist.

She writhes under me as I stroke her to orgasm. It's so fucking beautiful, watching pleasure fill her dark eyes. Watching her back arch, her toes curl, her lips part.

It's even better when she relaxes in the afterglow. She

wraps her fingers around my wrist, sinks into the sheets, falls asleep.

I stay with her for a while. Watch her chest fall with her inhale. Help her out of her soft dress and her lacy bra.

Then I unpack, shower, join her in bed.

It feels too good, lying next to her. It fills some part of me that's empty.

I fall asleep at peace.

Then I wake up a few hours later, in the middle of a nightmare. All those sharp edges. All the reasons why this will never work.

It's nice believing I'm capable of loving her, but that's a fairy tale.

The truth is far too ugly.

————

AFTER A QUICK BREAKFAST, WE WALK TO JEFF'S CHOCOLATE factory. Though factory is the wrong word. It's more a processing center. A place to sell overpriced bars to tourists.

It's on the edge of the city's shopping area. Jasmine stays close on the long walk. She squeezes my hand as she takes in the sights.

Cobblestone streets, open plazas, four-story buildings with faded paint and wide balconies.

Ruins every few blocks.

Rows and rows of pastarias, cafés, gelato shops.

Novel things in old buildings. Ruins filled with tourist groups. A museum run by the Catholic church with a line that spans city blocks.

My job takes me to cities all over the world. As much as I hate to admit it to Ian, London is one of my favorites.

The old and the new are balanced. The city has history but it still looks forward.

Rome is trapped in time. All memories. All yesterday. All relics of the past.

Even when they're in shambles.

The damage is what draws people. Come, look at these crumbling pillars, the remains of what was once great.

Why would anyone want to see that?

I try to put the thought aside, but it lingers. This trip belongs in Rome. Marcus and his partner are here for the same reason.

So they can marvel at the sight of something in shambles. Something that will forever be preserved in its half-destroyed state.

Never rebuilt. Never fixed. Never released.

"This is it." Jasmine squeezes my hand as she stops in front of a tall building. Marcus and Jeff's shop. It's repainted. A brighter shade of cream than most of the buildings. It's just a little off. Just enough it stands out. "You think he'll have tea?"

"No."

"I uh…" Her expression gets sheepish. "I'm sorry I fell asleep last night. I wanted to—"

"Don't be. I've never had a better compliment."

Her cheeks flush. "I just, uh… I guess we should look happy here?"

No, we should fuck against that wall. Take off your panties. You're coming on my cock. Now. "We can get away with tired."

"Right." Her eyes pass over me slowly. It's different than the way other people look at me. More like she sees me. Like she sees something beyond a ruthless business-man. "I did appreciate the kettle. Thank you."

"Of course."

"And that oolong. Did my dad recommend it?"

I nod.

"Do you talk to him? Just the two of you?"

"Only about you."

She raises a brow.

"And Mariah."

"He deserves better—"

"She's a widow."

Oh.

"Her husband is her late husband. She hasn't been able to—"

She nods, immediately understanding. "Do you think they're… oh my God. Is it okay for her to work for him? Is that totally wrong? Should we find someone else?"

I can't help but smile. "Don't ruin his sexy nurse fantasy."

"That's my dad!" Her face turns bright red. Like she's a teenager, embarrassed by her parents kissing.

"We do mostly talk about you."

"He's probably having sex with her."

"Is that so bad?"

She looks at me like I'm crazy. *How can you ask that!?!?!?*

It erases the tension in my shoulders. Takes me back to a lazy Sunday afternoon, on the couch, watching one of those old movies she likes. "He did lecture me about treating you well."

"Well… in a normal way? Not a sexual way?"

I can't help but chuckle. "He didn't specifically mention that."

She stares at me like she's going to kill me. "You're evil."

I brush a hair behind her ear.

She shakes her head *true, pure evil* as she shakes the bell.

The softness fades immediately. No more memories of quiet afternoons or easy kisses or sunny skies.

We're here. Preparing to impress board members two and three.

If we don't manage this, I lose.

Worse, that bastard wins.

We need to impress them. Whatever it takes.

A moment later, an assistant opens the door. She smiles at us and asks us to follow her.

I motion *after you* and help Jasmine up the steps.

She stays wide-eyed as she takes in the interior of the building. It is beautiful. Like a church. Tall ceilings, marble floors, walls decked with paintings.

A bit much for a factory.

And there's Marcus. And his second in command. Diablo.

Did his parents realize they were giving him such an apt name? No, that's not quite right. Diablo is a saint compared to my stepfather.

I suppose he's more like Charles. A lapdog who does whatever his owner commands.

That, I understand.

What I don't get is Marcus and Jeff. What the hell do they get out of playing these games?

Maybe that bastard has something on them.

Or maybe they're assholes who like to watch fresh meat squirm. I wouldn't put anything past them.

Marcus smiles. *I can't wait to watch you suffer*. He holds out his hand. "Shepard." He ignores formalities despite the nature of our relationship. "It's always wonderful to see you."

"Yes." I shake his hand as firmly as I can, but I don't have a grip. The room is spinning. "A little early though."

"The time difference is hard on people." He releases my hand. "Maybe you'd like some espresso?"

"Sure." I suck a breath through my nose. Push it

through my teeth. Then Jasmine's hand is on my wrist and I'm capable of inhaling. "But my fiancée prefers tea."

"I'll see if we have anything," he says, as if he will personally check every room for tea. As if it's him, not his assistant, who does the heavy lifting.

"You must be the fiancée." Diablo extends his hand.

"I must." Jasmine releases my wrist to shake. "Jasmine Lee."

"It's lovely to meet you, Miss Lee." He smiles. "I was hoping you'd pick Madrid." He launches into a discussion of the merits of authentic Sangria.

She listens carefully. Or convinces him of it.

I try to stay a part of the conversation, but it's impossible. What the hell is Marcus doing? He could have a direct line to that bastard.

Or he could be fetching tea.

There's no way to know. Jeff is easy to read. Marcus—

I haven't got a clue what he wants.

"I'm sure you'll do well as an actress," Diablo says. "A woman as beautiful as you are won't have trouble finding work."

She turns to me, looking for something, but I'm not sure what it is.

"She was amazing as Ophelia in high school," I say.

"Your high school put on *Hamlet*?" he asks.

She laughs. "It was an advanced school. We were very competitive."

"And you played Juliette the next year?" he asks, genuinely interested. Or pretending.

She smiles. "If only… I didn't make the cut. I was the nurse."

He nods knowingly.

But I haven't got a clue what he knows. And I don't care. I hate these assholes.

I can't let it show. I can't feel it, think it, see it.

There must be something else. Some way I can find a quarter of her charm.

That's it—

"She was better than the lead. But I am biased." I turn my body toward hers. Take her hand. Then the other. My next inhale is easier. Then I pull her closer and my exhale is effortless. "I can never take my eyes off you."

"Shep…" Her voice gets breathy. "This isn't the place—"

"I don't care." I pull her body into mine. Her pelvis, her stomach, her chest, her lips.

She tastes good, like tea and honey.

Her hands go to my shoulders. One curls around the back of my neck. Then it's her fingers in my hair.

Her touch is soft. Tender. Loving.

Fuck.

My body gets light.

She pulls back with a heavy sigh.

For a moment, it's just the two of us. The desire flowing between us.

And something more. A need for something deep inside her. Not just her admiration, respect, obedience.

Her love.

Then Marcus interrupts and I'm a lead weight again.

"We found something." He claps his hands together. "Is Earl Grey all right?" He says it like it's some sort of exotic tea, not the most popular scented black tea in existence.

"Yes, thanks." She smiles, takes my hand, turns to the main room. "Where does this tour start?"

"Of course." Marcus beams. "This is one of my favorite locations." He motions *follow me*.

Diablo stays behind us.

Jasmine stays glued to my side.

I let Marcus speak as he leads us down the hallway, around the corner. To the room where his staff melts cocoa.

A giant silver machine—like some kind of oversized mixing bowl—spins dark chocolate in slow spirals. The entire room smells like cocoa. Rich, sweet, a little floral.

This isn't where they make the chocolate itself. No, they melt big blocks from a factory in Belgium. They take pure blocks of cocoa, add sugar, press them into bars with candy, nuts, essence of orange.

Sometimes, they make shapes. Hearts, roses, tiny little Coliseums.

"We're going to make bars," he exclaims, like a teacher trying to convince students their homework is fun. "I had my assistant refresh me last night. I'm ready to give the lesson myself."

Diablo nods his approval. "My wife adores your chocolate." He practically drops to his knees to kiss Marcus's ass.

"Oh, I hate to say I'm not familiar with your brand." Jasmine holds a perfect poker face. Despite the logo plastered in every conceivable location, she sells her lack of knowledge of their company. "I have to admit. I have a soft spot for a local brand." She names a craft chocolate brand in San Francisco. "Do you know them? Well… local to the Bay. I haven't been there in some time."

"I do." Marcus frowns. "They make an excellent bar. A lot of unique flavors. Do you have a favorite?"

"Oh, I'm not sophisticated. I like everything." She smiles. "As long as it's dark."

"As dark as my soul." I try to lighten the mood.

She follows my lead. "Do you sell one hundred percent cocoa?"

"Yes." Marcus forces a smile. He's not all that amused.

But he is looking at us differently. Like he believes us. "But only for baking."

"Is there something different about it? That prevents people from eating it?"

"Only the bitterness," he says.

"I'm used to that." She laughs and squeezes my hand.

I squeeze it back. "You can't even drink coffee. How will you have pure cocoa?"

She turns to Marcus. "We can have a taste test. What do you think? Which is more bitter: espresso or chocolate?"

"I'll have my assistant bring espresso when we make bars," he says. "Though, in my opinion, it is the espresso. I can tolerate pure chocolate more easily."

"Will they kick you out of Rome for that?" She looks to Diablo. "Do you like your coffee sweet?"

"Like I like my women." He smiles. "As sweet as pie."

She turns to me. "I like my men… tall, dark, and strong… But I can't stand coffee. With cream and sugar, it's tolerable. But I have to add so much it barely tastes like coffee."

"Strong?" I ask.

"You aren't?" Her fingers curl around my wrist. She motions to my arm. Telling me to put on some display of strength.

I nod. Shift my arm, so it's around her mid-back. Then the other under her knees.

There.

She shrieks as I lift her into my arms.

"Save something for the honeymoon." Marcus smiles. Is he actually charmed? Or is it something else?

He and Diablo exchange a look.

I hold Jasmine against my chest. "I like having you here."

She stares up at me with a smile. But is it for me or them?

"At my mercy." I lean down enough to kiss her. Then I set her down. Wrap my arms around her. Hold her close as I kiss her hard.

She groans against my mouth. Pulls back with a shy expression. "I suppose we should save something for the honeymoon."

"Where are you going?" Marcus asks. "I'm sure I can score you an excellent deal. I have resorts all over the world."

Is that it? He wants to show off? Impress us? Get us to say *why, you certainly are an amazing man. I'm so glad to know you and have you on my side.*

If it's that simple…

I'm not sure I can kiss ass. But I can thank him for the offer. And Jasmine—

She is used to convincing rich men she thinks they're fascinating. She's good at it.

"Do you have a favorite chocolate, Shepard?" Marcus asks. "I'm partial to beans from Ecuador. But a lot of people prefer the ones from Peru."

Diablo nods.

"I can't say I know the difference. My assistant purchases all my food," I say. "Mostly blends."

Marcus shakes his head in horror. "I'll send you a kit right away. You deserve better."

"I appreciate that." I try to make my smile genuine. "Thank you."

"Nothing too bitter," Jasmine says. "Well, something dark for Shep. To match his soul. But something sweeter for me."

"Milk chocolate?" he asks.

"No, I just like the sweetness," she says. "I'm not big on milk."

She never puts milk in her tea. But isn't that how you drink oolong? Or does she pick teas that don't need milk?

I want every detail.

I want to know everything about her.

I always have, but it's different now. Deeper. Fuller.

Marcus leads us into his cooking room.

He motions for us to take our spots behind one of the long white tables. The room is two tables, plus a display in front. Set up for a demonstration.

I press my palm into Jasmine's lower back to lead her to one of the tables.

Diablo whispers something to Marcus then takes a spot behind the other table.

Jasmine looks up at me. *Should I?* She motions to the spot next to Diablo.

I'm not sure. I can't read him well. I lean in to whisper. "Do you think it's what he wants?"

She nods *yes*.

I trust her instincts. "Go."

She smiles. "How about I join you?" She moves to his table. "Since we both like it sweet."

"Your men bitter. Your chocolate sweet?" he teases.

"Maybe not bitter… just… sweet in their own way." She smiles at me.

He whispers something in her ear.

She laughs. It's a big laugh, but it sounds real. Authentic.

Or I can't tell if she's pretending.

I guess it doesn't matter. She's charming them. Of course, she is.

Who could possibly resist Jasmine?

Chapter Thirty-Eight

JASMINE

R ich men and power.

Which came first? The lust for power or the wealth?

All three of the men here are jockeying for position. For some reason. Something to do with this agreement.

I smile like I don't notice. Let Diablo tease me about Shep's reputation. Smile and shrug *I'll never tell*.

That's my job here.

I smile. I charm. I look pretty.

Honestly, I don't mind it. It's closer to acting than my old gig. Less kissing ass too.

Men respect a trophy fiancée a lot more than they respect an assistant.

Marcus goes on and on about the cocoa farming process. It's interesting, actually—the process of growing and shelling the fruit, fermenting the beans, breaking them into smaller pieces. What isn't interesting is Marcus's constant bragging.

His farm is the greatest and his farmers are the greatest and his beans are the greatest.

At least he insists on paying his people well. Even if it's for the bragging rights.

I have to admit. The melted chocolate is amazing. Better than any I've ever tasted. Sweet and nutty with the perfect texture.

I lose myself in sculpting it into adorable shapes, adding essential oils, creating a signature bar.

Ginger and dried cranberries.

Of course, it's not what I really want. What I really want is an oolong chocolate. It's possible too. As Marcus explains, I need to keep a finished bar in a glass container with leaves. The fat in the chocolate pics up the flavor through the air.

Apparently, it's easy to scent chocolate.

It even picks up people's perfume.

I guess we're similar that way, absorbing everything around us. Holding on to it. Giving it away later.

But this…

I don't want to hold on to the memories of rich man bullshit. No, I'm holding onto the site of Shep with his sleeves rolled to his elbows, his gloved hands covered in melted chocolate.

A dollop on his nose.

The taste of his skin under the cocoa.

The way he smiles as I lick it off.

This is perfect.

Everything else surrounding it is complicated. But, hey, I'm in Rome with my fiancé, nibbling gourmet chocolate.

That's good.

That's really fucking good.

———

After three bars, we call it a day.

Marcus walks us to the door. Hands us gold giftbags filled with cocoa treats. Truffles, soaps, lotions, bars, nibs.

He shakes my hand. Shep's.

Then he looks at Shep knowingly. Like he's offering approval. "You're a lucky man."

Shep turns to me. Smiles like he's madly in love with me. "The luckiest."

I shake my head. Try to find something original. Settle on— "I'm the lucky one."

Diablo and Marcus share a look.

They whisper something. Diablo shakes our hands. Then he nods a goodbye and returns to the factory.

Marcus leans a little closer. Close enough to whisper. "I'm sure you have a lot you'd like to see in Rome. I won't take over your trip. But I do insist on one thing." He pulls something from his pocket. A small red envelope with a gold bow. "Trust me. You'll be glad you did."

I take the envelope. Go to open it.

But Marcus stops me. "Don't let him see it. Make it a surprise." He winks at me. Then he takes a step backward. "Enjoy the wedding. And the honeymoon. I hope everything after will be… peaceful."

What the hell does that mean?

Marcus smiles, turns on his heel, disappears in the building.

I move away from the door, then I open the envelope.

Shep smiles. "Impatient."

"I'm allowed to see it." I hold it to my chest. "You're the one who's supposed to wait."

The crease in his forehead softens. The frustration in his eyes fades. He's feeling better. More present. "You're making me wait?"

I nod.

His voice drops. "*You* are going to make *me* wait."

Ahem. "Yes."

"Is that a dare, princess?"

"Yes," I bluff. No. Not at all. I don't want to wait. I want to jump into his arms and have him right here, in the middle of this quaint cobblestone street.

Well, maybe not the middle.

More against the building.

Him pinning me to the wall as I—

"You won't last five minutes." He brings his hands to my hips. Pulls my body into his. "Besides." His lips find my ear. "I know what's in the envelope."

"Oh?"

"He's done this before."

"You've brought other—"

"To men I know. And a few women." He runs his fingertips along my chin. Then down my neck. Over my collarbone. "It's a gift certificate to La Perla."

"Oh."

"If you want to be generous, you can say he's—"

"Big-hearted?"

He nods. Brings his lips to my neck. A soft kiss. It's tender. Gentle even.

Then it's harder.

Still tender but with a raw need beneath it.

"If you want to be cynical, you can say he gets off on knowing he's in our bedroom." Shep kisses me a little harder. "Or you can take my stance."

"Yeah?"

"I don't care about his motives if I can fuck you sense-less in the dressing room."

"Oh."

"Princess?"

Oh. That's an actual invitation. I nod.

His smile gets wicked. That smile that means *you have no idea what I'm going to do to you.*

Chapter Thirty-Nine

JASMINE

The store is unassuming.

Yes, the expensive garments are gorgeous. But the place looks like any upscale lingerie shop in Manhattan.

Slick robes in black.

Lace bras with floral print.

Panties with mesh butterflies.

An impossibly tiny thong that looks as expensive as it is.

Functional bodysuits in beige, tan, black.

A garter belt with a several-hundred-dollar price tag.

It's like something out of an old movie. Completely unnecessary for the weather here—it's far too warm and sunny for thigh highs—but still inviting.

A secret sex appeal. Something that hides under good girl clothes.

I guess that's everything here. No one will know I'm wearing a sheer black bra and panty set under my simple sundress.

They're even the same color.

They're our secret.

Or they will be.

Shep whispers a command. "Pick out anything you want. Go to the dressing room. Change into it. And wait." His lips brush my neck. Then he pulls away. Goes to the saleswoman. Smiles as he slides something into her palm.

Enough cash for her to look the other way?

Or just the gift card from Marcus?

I ask myself if it matters. If her presence makes a difference either way. Do I want her listening? Do I want her gone?

The truth is, I don't care.

As long as I have him, I don't care who else is in the shop.

This is our dirty secret.

I try to take my time. To make him wait as I pore over every available garment. But this is an expensive shop. There are only so many options.

There.

That's perfect.

I take my new attire into the dressing room. Slowly, I strip out of my sundress and my more reasonably priced bra and panty set.

This isn't my usual thing. It doesn't even make sense with my wedding dress.

But it feels right, donning sheer white lace.

This thing that screams innocent, virgin bride. I haven't been innocent in a long time. But I still want him corrupting me.

My gaze shifts to the mirror. Three panels in the corner. Another on the door. It gives me a perfect view of my back, ass, legs.

I don't usually focus on how my body looks. Yes, I dress to impress. I style my hair. I make sure my clothes fit.

Yes, I take care of myself with healthy food and long walks. Sometimes, I manage an actual workout.

But I don't obsess over my looks. I'm slim, sure, but I'm also too short, with a barely there waist, and rather, erm, limited assets.

When I was younger, I hated my lack of T&A. I wanted to look like a Victoria's Secret model. Tall and long with full breasts and a round ass.

Over time, I stopped caring about my undefined waist and my lack of T&A. But I didn't love the way I looked. I didn't stare and think *damn, I'm hot shit.*

Right now?

Right now, I'm the sexiest woman in the universe.

I have the same figure, but I look different. I feel different. Like a sweet angel waiting for a devil to corrupt her.

A vision.

A goddess.

Here, playing the good girl, enticing him to defile me—

Good thing I'm buying this thong. I'm already wet. I'm already shaking.

I brush my hair behind my ear. Apply an extra coat of lipstick. Something to drive him even more crazy.

He likes when it marks his skin. I can tell from the way he growls. From the way his eyes light up when he spots the stain.

He's out there. In the room. I can hear his footsteps. I can sense his presence. Somehow, I can feel him. It's a new ability.

A Shepard sense.

Or maybe it isn't new. Maybe it's something that's been dormant for a long time.

He is a part of me. Whatever happens after this year, he'll always be a part of me. Though, right now—

I'm past insane. Because, right now, I want more than the year. I want the forever he requested.

I want all of it.

Love. Marriage. Family.

Mr. and Mrs. Marlowe and all their adorable kids.

That's not in the cards. He can't promise to love me. But he can make my entire body buzz. And that's—

Fuck.

His footsteps move closer. Then it's his knuckles against the stall door.

"Yes." My words are impossibly high-pitched. I'm light. I'm floating.

"Open the door."

I unclick the lock.

He pushes it open then presses it closed. His eyes go wide as he looks me up and down. There's no more tension on his face. There's no uncertainty to his expression.

Only desire.

Pure, raw, primal need.

"Princess." He presses his palms into the mirrored door. "Or maybe I should call you angel?"

I shake my head. I like him calling me princess. It's ours.

"My bride."

My chest warms. My sex clenches.

"You wearing this under your wedding dress?"

"Maybe."

His fingers curl into the mirror. "Turn around."

I shift on my heels.

His voice gets gruffer. Firmer. "Put your hands on the floor."

I spread my legs a little wider. Then I reach for the floor, one inch at a time.

He lets out a low groan as my fingers graze the carpet. "You trying to drive me crazy, princess?"

"Isn't that the idea of lingerie?"

He responds by pushing off the door. He takes a step toward me. Then another.

His cock brushes my sex. His slacks and my panties are in the way, but I can still feel him. All the heat and hardness.

The pressure of the lace.

He leans over me just enough to wrap his hands around my arms. Slowly, he pulls me up. Holds my body against his.

My eyes go to the mirror. There's something about seeing him behind me. About seeing his hands on my skin.

It makes my sex clench.

Fuck, I need him so badly. It's hard to believe I've ever needed anything this badly.

He traces the waistband of the thong over my stomach and hip, then back to my other hip, then again, again, again.

Through the mirror, his eyes find mine. "Watch."

"Yes, sir." I don't want to push him today. I want to coax him into giving me everything.

He presses his lips to mine. Then he steps back. Releases me.

Slowly, he undoes the knot of his tie. He moves back to me. Pushes me against the wall. Raises my hands over my head.

Loops the silk fabric around my wrists and cinches it to one of the hooks.

I'm tied up in a dressing room.

Watching him—

I don't care what I'm watching. As long as he's doing it to me.

Shep looks me up and down slowly. Like he's savoring every single inch of my skin.

His lips find mine. He kisses me hard. With raw desire *and* soft affection.

It's not like our first few kisses. It's deeper. Purer. Better.

His need pours into me.

My need pours into him.

And something else. Something from deep inside my core. I'm offering it to him. Asking for it in return.

I don't have a word for it. Maybe it is love. Maybe I'm in love with him. Maybe I've never stopped loving him.

Before I can properly contemplate the matter, he breaks our kiss. His lips go to my neck, collarbone, chest.

Stomach.

I watch as he lowers himself onto his knees. As he peels my panties aside. Brings his lips to my clit.

Fuck. He doesn't tease me today. He licks me just how I need him.

My eyes close for a second. It's almost too much. My body is already buzzing. My skin is already sensitive.

Everything feels deeper, harder, sweeter—

More.

He slides his hand up my stomach. Over my breast. Then his thumb is against my nipple, scraping the lace against my tender skin.

Fuck. It's such soft lace, but like this, it feels rough in the best possible way.

He does it again and again.

A little softer. A little harder. Slower. Faster.

I force myself to open my eyes.

The sight of him, on his knees, between my legs, his hand on my breast—

It's the hottest thing I've ever seen.

He has me tied up. He's in control. But he's bending to me too. Giving me what I—

Fuck.

The pressure of his soft, wet tongue winds the tension inside me. He works me exactly how I need him too.

Then a little faster.

A little faster.

Until it's perfect.

I reach for his hair, but the tie catches on my wrist. I'm bound. At his mercy.

It pushes me over the edge. With the next flick of his tongue, I come. I groan his name again and again.

I don't care that I'm too loud. That someone might hear. That we might end up in an Italian prison.

He tugs the lace thong a little harder. Pushes it into my thigh. Then he's there, sucking on my clit, sending waves of pleasure through me.

"Shep—" I let the tie tug at my wrists. Fuck, the soft silk, the light pressure.

He pulls the lace cup of the bra aside. Then it's his thumb against my nipple. Slow circles that drive me wild.

The tension winds quickly. Until it's too much. More than I can handle. I'm so close. I'm almost—

He pulls back, leaving me on the edge. "Say my name when you come, princess."

I stay impossibly taut. So, so close to unraveling but not there yet.

Then he brings his mouth to me and I'm there.

I groan his name as I come.

My eyes close. My universe goes white. As pure and sweet as the bridal lace.

I am an angel and he is corrupting me and I love every fucking second.

He works me through my orgasm. Then he pulls back. Takes off his suit jacket. Undoes his top two buttons.

Unzips his slacks.

His cock springs free.

He doesn't wait. He brings his hands to my thighs. Pushes my thong over my ass.

For a moment, it stays at my knees. He holds my gaze as he slides two fingers inside me. He pushes them deep.

Then he does it again.

Again.

Harder.

"Shep—" My head falls back, hitting the wall. "Please. Fuck me. Please, sir. I need you."

"You need me?" His voice stays firm, but there's something else in it. A curiosity. Like he's asking how much I need him.

Right now, more than anything. But I really can't say if I need his lips, hands, cock, respect, affection, love.

All of it.

But especially—"I need your cock inside me, sir."

He lets out a low groan. Drives his fingers into me again. Then again. Again.

I shift my legs so the thong falls to my ankles. Then I kick it off.

He's merciful. He brings his hands to my thighs. Lifts them. Wraps them around his waist.

My weight shifts off the ground. To his hands. The wall. The hook.

It creaks. It's not made for this.

He pins me to the wall as he lifts me up. Unhooks me. Brings my arms to him, so they're hooked around his neck.

My wrists are still bound, but I can feel his skin. He's so close. As close as he's ever been.

He holds my gaze as he pushes into me.

Fuck. At once, I'm whole. I'm pure. I'm exactly where I need to be.

He rocks his hips, pinning me to the wall, filling me again.

My fingers curl into his neck. His hair. Then it's my nails against his skin. I'm at his mercy. He's holding me up. With the help of the wall, yes, but it's flimsy.

I have to trust him.

And he… I'm barely bound. He trusts me too.

He pulls back and rocks into me again.

My thoughts disappear. Pleasure takes over my senses. That overwhelming fullness.

"You feel so good, baby." The words fall off my lips. "Fuck me. Please. Come inside me."

He doesn't correct me. Ask me to call him sir. He looks into my eyes for a moment. Then he moves closer, so his head is in the crook of my neck.

He thrusts into me again.

I watch him move until I can't take it anymore.

I have to close my eyes.

To soak in every sweet inch.

Deep, steady thrusts.

Again and again.

Until I'm wound so tight I might burst.

Then tighter, tighter—

There.

I breathe his name as I come. My head falls back. My nails dig into his skin. Hard enough he growls.

My sex pulses, pulling him closer, taking him deeper. It's so much. So intense I'm sure I'm going to swallow him whole.

It pushes him to the brink.

He rocks into me again. Then he comes.

He groans my name, thrusting into me as he spills every drop.

Mine.

For this perfect moment, he's mine.

And I'm his.

And we understand each other completely.

When he's finished, he sets me down, unties my wrists, cleans me up, helps me into my clothes.

Fixes his.

We emerge to an empty room. A locked door. I don't ask how much he paid the saleswoman for the privacy.

I don't care.

This is perfect.

Nothing is knocking me off my high.

Chapter Forty

JASMINE

Technically, Rome isn't the city of love. But it feels like it.

We spend our days walking around the quaint streets. Eating fresh pasta. Licking gelato from cones. Tossing coins in the Trevi fountain.

We find the best espresso shop in Italy. Shep groans over the subtle chocolate notes.

I add an extra bag of sugar. Even then, I barely make it through my tiny macchiato.

He insists I try again, so the next day, I order a latte. Add only a single bag of sugar.

Ick.

He laughs at my expression. Presses his lips to mine. Says he's never seen anything better. Well, not while I was dressed.

I force him to order a weak tea from the café where we grab lunch, but it doesn't really make my point. The tea is bad because it lacks flavor. Not because it scalds the taste buds.

Still, I try the coffee again. Let him buy me pistachio gelato to make it up to me.

Let him make it up to me in much more interesting ways.

I insist on a trip to the Coliseum, but the enormous ruins aren't enough to keep me away from the hotel. When Shep asks if I want to stay or go—

We spend the afternoon in bed.

He gets naked with me.

Yes, he holds my arms over my head. Yes, I come the second he brings his hand to my throat. Yes, I love how he's in control.

But there's something about him trusting me like this. About feeling every inch of his skin against mine.

Raking my nails against his back.

So, when we arrive home after dinner and take off our clothes, I offer him my hand. I let him lead. I let him show me where to touch him.

Then I stop waiting for his permission.

I run my hands through his hair. I dig my nails into his back. I bring my lips to his neck.

I kiss him like I'll never get enough.

Because I won't.

I really won't.

———

EVEN OUR RETURN FLIGHT IS HEAVENLY. SIX QUIET HOURS with a book.

Okay, the shitty tea isn't great. But there's something fresh waiting at home.

Oolong, raspberry teacakes, and reality.

All these wedding plans to finalize. Details to figure out. A guest list to double-check.

Shep's stepfather is coming. That makes sense. He is practically his dad.

Or it should.

But when I scour the Internet for hints of Shep and Lucien's contact, I find nothing. No business deals. No social media. No interviews where one mentions the other.

It's like they don't know each other.

And Shep certainly wasn't fond of his stepfather.

So why is he sitting in the front row at our wedding?

Why does Shep change the subject when I ask if he's coming to the rehearsal dinner?

I always thought there was something there, some reason why their relationship was strained, but there's no way...

That's not possible.

Is it?

Chapter Forty-One

SHEPARD

Jasmine draws every eye as she steps into the restaurant. It's not just the rock on her ring finger or the jeweled clip in her fancy updo or the gorgeous gauzy dress skimming her tan skin.

Her smile is radiant.

It's brighter than the sun.

And it's for me.

Sure, this isn't a conventional arrangement. But she's happy. She's beaming at the thought of saying *I do*.

Ian lifts his glass to toast. "Your bride is too pretty for you."

"You need new material." I don't have a better come-back. He's right. She is gorgeous. And she's my bride. Today, it feels like a triumph. All triumph.

It doesn't matter how we got here. Who pulled which strings.

It only matters that she's mine.

Forever.

In two days, it's official.

My body gets light as my eyes meet hers. Her smile

shifts to something softer. Something that promises her body as much as it promises her heart.

Then her father takes her arm and she blushes at her dirty thoughts. Turns to her aunts. Joins them for a drink.

This is a smaller rehearsal dinner. A dozen people.

Her father, her aunts, Nick and Lizzy, Ian.

It almost seems normal, my small display of family.

Fuck. Ian is half of my family. Where have I gone wrong?

I watch Jasmine's aunt Quyen talk her into a gin and tonic. "We have four varieties of Fever Tree."

"I know." He taps his cocktail glass against my bottle of Pellegrino. "You treat me right."

"The best for my best man."

His chuckle is low. "Yes, it's got nothing to do with your issues with your brother."

"He's here, isn't he?"

He gives me that Ian look that means *stop lying to yourself.*

"And you're Mr. Family?"

"I have women who call me daddy."

I can't help but laugh. Of course, he does. "Don't let Key overhear that."

"She'll find me even more irresistible?"

"Don't sleep with her."

"What kind of man do you take me for?"

I shoot him a *really* look.

Ian smiles and taps my glass again. "Fair." He turns to greet Nick as he crosses the room to us. "Always good to see you, Phoenix." He calls my brother by his full name. None of his friends call him Phoenix. It's always Nick. But then Ian is making a point. They aren't friends.

He's actually on my side.

"Always." Nick shakes.

Lizzy practically bounces after him. She's in one of those purple dresses of hers. One that is somehow innocent and dirty at the same time.

She must drive him out of his mind.

Usually, the thought of Nick's sex life would irritate me. Right now, I don't mind. I'm glad he's happy. As long as he doesn't start lecturing me in that *do as I say, not as I do* way of his.

"You don't look nervous." Lizzy's eyes fix on me. "Aren't you nervous?"

"Baby, you're going to scare him," Nick says.

"Just think. Everyone is going to watch your wedding. Everyone has different expectations. After you say I do, that's it. You're with one person for the rest of your life," she says.

"Do you have something to tell him?" Ian chuckles.

"Ian doesn't believe in commitments," I say.

"No. Just short ones," he clarifies.

Nick shoots him a knowing look. "I believe you've met. Ian, Lizzy. Lizzy, Ian."

He leans down enough to shake her hand. "You're the girl who almost convinced the great Phoenix Marlowe to leave artificial intelligence forever."

"Guilty as charged." She smiles, not at all ruffled by his implication. "Though I think Shepard had more to do with that than I did."

Ian studies me the way he studies a mystery he's yet to solve. Like he's figuring out where to start on his search for information.

"Nick was too smart," I say. "He refused to play that game."

"I don't think he realized he was playing," Lizzy says.

Nick leans down to whisper something in her ear.

She nods an *okay* and turns to me with a cutting look.

"Seriously, Shep. You better be good to Jasmine. Or else." She makes that finger across the throat *you're dead* gesture.

"I think she could take you," Ian says.

"Without a doubt." I offer her a toast.

She taps her glass against mine. "Until then… the bride is much more interesting. Congratulations." She shoots my brother one of those *find me in twenty minutes and fuck me senseless* looks, then she joins Jasmine's family.

"That girl is crazy about you." Ian keeps his eyes on my brother. "Congratulations."

"Aren't you supposed to say that to the groom?" Nick asks.

"Jasmine only seems mildly intrigued," Ian says.

"She looks happy," Nick says. "Are you?"

"I am." For the first time, in a long time, it's the truth. I'm happy. Period. End of sentence.

I let Nick and Ian discuss business. Nick has a new project. Machine learning for a bio-tech company. Guessing people's health ills before they realize they have them.

It would be terrifying if I worried about technology.

But computers aren't dangerous. People are. The darkness that lurks in certain hearts, waiting to consume anything that comes close.

Somehow, he hears my thoughts. Somehow, he knows there's a parade he can rain on.

Because the second I join my bride and her family, that bastard walks through the door in his three-piece suit and his easy smile.

"I'm sorry I'm late." Lucien's voice is matter-of-fact. Like everyone expects him to be here. Like we've been waiting for him to really start the party. "I hate to keep a beautiful woman waiting."

Jasmine looks to me for an explanation. Did I really invite my stepfather to this dinner?

No. But maybe Lock or Key... it's what a normal person would do. So I nod. "He is the closest thing I have to a parent." My stomach turns. The words are true. They shouldn't be true, but they are.

This man is the only father figure I've ever known.

The only parental figure I have left.

The only mentor I ever trusted.

And he's here, once again, to ruin everything.

Chapter Forty-Two

SHEPARD

E ven with Jasmine next to me, I can't hear anything but my pounding heart.

This event isn't for us. It's for our families.

I stay quiet as Jasmine's aunts share stories about her childhood. The time she and her mom started acting out scenes from their favorite TV drama. Jasmine's impatience when her mom taught her to cook. She always wanted to eat right away. It was impossible for her to wait for beef bones and herbs to mix into a tantalizing broth.

And, now, she's still impatient. Rushing into marriage. But for reasons they understand.

"He's so handsome. And she's so satisfied. I would rush too." Quyen holds up her drink to toast. "To true love."

"To true love," Aunt Mai says.

Her dad holds up his drink.

Nick holds up his glass too. It's just him now. Lizzy made an excuse to leave.

He told her the truth about Lucien. That's fine. It's his right.

But telling her what happened to me—

It was in her eyes. That look of pity. I'm no longer a monster who tried to destroy her relationship. I'm not even an asshole who needs to watch himself.

I'm a victim.

A pathetic creature who can't fend for itself.

Who doesn't deserve the respect full-fledged humans get.

She doesn't look at Nick that way. It's different. Almost tolerable.

How did he manage that? How did he claw out from under that sickening label?

"To true love," my brother says. "Or true lust." He winks at Jasmine's aunt Mai.

Mai giggles like a schoolgirl.

Quyen shoots Nick a knowing look. "Are you sure you aren't single?"

"There's no ring," Mai says.

"It's not over until it's over," Quyen says.

"What about yours?" Jasmine laughs. She's happy. At peace. She finds Lucien's presence strange, but that's where it ends.

She doesn't know he's here to remind me I'm under his thumb. To make sure I know I'll never escape this curse.

Even if we marry, and the board votes for me, and I beat him in this battle, he'll win the war.

He always does.

I need a drink.

"My husband is getting older. He won't live forever," Quyen says. "I need a younger man. Who can keep up with me."

Jasmine laughs along with Mai and Nick. "Nick is too slow for you."

"Oh?" Quyen raises a brow.

Jasmine nods. "Always working. Or on his computer. The only thing he does for fun is—"

"His fiancée," Ian offers. He eyes me curiously. He knows something is wrong. He knows I'm playing this stupid game with Lucien. But not why. No one knows why. No one but my brother.

Jasmine blushes. "I was going to say poker. But yes—"

"That's good. I need a virile man," Quyen says. "My husband—"

"That's my uncle!" Jasmine's voice raises to a shriek. "Please don't."

Mai jumps in. "Your uncle was a very—"

"Oh my God." Jasmine hides behind her drink. Her third of the night. It's good she's loose.

It's good she doesn't see this.

But if her tongue is as loose as her smile—

I can't let that bastard know the lengths I've gone to. I can't let him have the satisfaction.

"How about we keep the toast to true love?" Jasmine asks. "To love. And finding it where you least expect it." Her eyes meet mine. They fill with all the affection in the world.

For a second, I forget the awful circumstances. The people around us. The restaurant downstairs. The ticking clock over my head.

For a second, I look into the eyes of the woman who loves me. Who I… maybe it's not love, but it's as close as I can get.

For a second, the world is beautiful.

Then that fucking bastard offers his congratulations. "To true love."

He holds up his drink. Bourbon. Neat. To fuck with me, no doubt.

"I miss Liv every day." He twists the knife in my

chest. "She was an amazing woman. So much like you. She saw the beauty in everything. She was always trying to understand more. To find deeper meaning in a painting. To get to know a colleague. To see how someone else lived. She was always searching." He looks to me. "She didn't find everything. But, then, some things are better unfound."

I dig my fingers into my glass.

"I'm sorry." He smiles that sickly sweet smile. "I'm going off about my marriage when this is your day. I have to make sure you know how proud your mother would be, Shepard. And you too, Phoenix. She would be proud of the men you've become."

"Excuse me." Nick places his glass on the table. "I've got to meet Lizzy at home."

Jasmine looks to me for explanation.

I shrug as if I don't know.

But she doesn't buy it.

No one buys my ignorance.

"It's hard to hear about Mom," Nick says. "Painful."

Thank fuck he's helping me for once.

"Shep, I have something for you. A wedding present. But I can't let the bride see." He motions to the hallway. "Can I have a minute?"

"Of course," Lucien speaks for everyone. "But first." He holds his glass a little higher. "To the Marlowe family. They deserve the world. And I hope they get every single thing they deserve." He smiles through the threat. He convinces the room he means it as a fucking compliment.

Nick stands.

I toast. Pray for my sparkling water to turn to wine.

It doesn't.

I swallow it anyway. Follow Nick to the hallway. The stairs. The quiet street outside.

We're at a cozy place near the park. A quiet area for families. A neighborhood for respectable people.

It's warm tonight. Too warm for this suit. This fabric shouldn't feel so confining—I wear this in August, when it's ninety and humid—but it does.

I need it gone.

I need to break the fucking window.

Any window. It doesn't matter as long as I destroy it.

Nick places his hand on my shoulder.

I almost deck him.

He doesn't flinch. "You're still sensitive?"

"Fuck off."

"You know what he's doing."

"What about fuck off is unclear to you?"

He takes a step backward. Away from the restaurant. "I have a car waiting." He motions to a sleek black town car parked across the street. "You should leave."

"I'm fine."

"You're not."

"I'm not leaving." I suck a breath through my teeth. "He'll think he's won."

"He has."

I turn toward the restaurant. "If you don't have a point—"

"Why do you let him hold this over you?"

"Let him?" The world goes red. I can't see the blue sky or the green trees or the dark pavement. Only righteous fury. "Fuck you." I try to keep my voice down, but it's impossible.

So I cross the street.

That's not enough. We're still in view of the upstairs window. That bastard can still see me squirming.

I go past Nick's car.

He follows me around the corner. "I'm sorry."

"Don't—"

"You're right. It's not a fair accusation. You're the victim—"

"Don't call me that."

He just stands there, five feet away from me, his posture strong and in control.

How does he do that? He should be crumbling. Or throwing something. Or destroying the nearest car.

How can he stand there and speak softly?

"What are the terms?" he asks.

"The what?"

"You think he hasn't tried to do this to me?"

"What did he—"

"I wouldn't hear it," he says. "He fucked up a deal as retaliation. I was angry. After a few months, it didn't matter."

I swallow hard.

"Is that it? A deal he'll ruin?"

I say nothing.

"Is there a deal?"

"You know that's not—" I push the words through my teeth. Reach for something, anything, to keep the world from spinning. All I find is a tiny tree. It's too small, too weak, too thin. It can't hold me. "I can't let him win."

"That's all it is?"

No.

But I don't want to tell him.

I don't even want to think it.

I squeeze the soft bark until it snaps. It doesn't soothe me. Or ease the ache in my stomach. "He has photos."

Nick freezes. No more strong poker face. Just fear. The kind of deep fear that turns the entire world black. "That's a felony."

"Only if he's caught."

"Shep—"

"Don't." I let the tree crack. Let it split in half. Let its top fall to the ground. "I don't need your opinion. Or your apology. Or your bullshit pep talk. We both know he'll find a way to release them."

"There's metadata. You know—"

"On film."

"No one will—"

"They will."

"People will understand," he says.

"Yes, they'll understand. They'll look at me the way Lizzy did. Thank you for that, by the way—"

"She's my fiancée."

"It's my past."

He says nothing.

"They'll understand I'm a victim."

"Shep—"

"Tell me I'm wrong. Tell me people will see past it. Tell me it won't be a black mark by my name until the end of time."

He doesn't.

"Even if I did out him. If I took him down with me. I'd always be, Shepard Marlowe, the man who was abused by his stepfather." I stare at my brother. "Tell me I'm wrong. Tell me people won't whisper about how he touched me. How he forced me to touch him. Tell me it won't hover over me for the rest of my life."

"It already does."

Fuck him.

"I am sorry, Shepard. Really. You're right. People will talk. People will look at you like you carry a darkness that will infect them if they get too close. But the people who matter, who love you… they'll be able to finally see you."

"As a rape victim."

"That's not what I mean."

Yes, it is. He can explain it any way he wants it. We both know what he means.

I should let people in. Share my ugly past. Let them know why I'm a damaged freak.

"I'm glad it worked out for you." I don't wait for a response. I turn and move toward the restaurant.

But there's something awful around the corner.

Lucien is there. And he's talking to Jasmine.

Chapter Forty-Three

JASMINE

"I didn't realize you and Shep stayed in touch." I try my best smile, but it's not there. I'm happy drunk. My inhibitions are MIA. I want to tell Shep's step-father to fuck off. I don't know what his deal is. But he clearly makes Shep uncomfortable.

And he's just…

Weird.

Off in some way I can't articulate.

Too nice, too proud, too shiny.

I didn't like him when I was fifteen and I don't like him now.

But I have no idea why. Or why Shep avoids him.

Maybe it's not anything Lucien did. Maybe it's like my inability to taste lychee jelly without curling into a ball of grief.

Maybe Lucien reminds Shep of losing his mother. I understand that.

"It's uh…" I reach for something that will convince Lucien I'm a doting fiancée. And get him to leave. "I appreciate that you came."

"Of course." He takes my hand in his. "Young love is so beautiful."

"Right."

"I was older when I met Liv. I'd been with other women. But it was different when I fell for her. As if the stars were finally shining." He makes a show of looking to the sky. "I suppose it's hard to convey to a New Yorker. You never see the stars here."

"I'm used to it."

"Do you consider yourself a New Yorker now? Or is your heart in California?"

"I love the city." I pull my hand to my side. "It's a little chilly out here." I make a show of rubbing my arms. It's not chilly. Even in my thin dress. It's warm. Humid even. "I should get back. Before Mai gives my dad a heart attack."

He reaches for my hand again. "I shouldn't be talking about myself. I'm sorry. I suppose I just… want you to understand. I'm not proud of what I've done."

What the hell is he talking about?

"I had this hole after Liv died. I needed to fill it. Nick took up poker. I did something similar."

Okay…

"I make wagers. With friends. It started as a New Year's resolution. Charles was trying to lose twenty pounds. I bet him he couldn't. To motivate him."

"Sure."

"He bet me I couldn't close a deal for ten percent above asking. It was little things. Then bigger ones. Then Shep got involved." He reaches into his pocket. Pulls out a folded stack of papers. A contract. "I wasn't going to tell you. But you're such a sweet young woman." He unfolds the papers. "This is all a game to him. You're a pawn to him. You deserve better." He pushes the papers into my hands. "You deserve the truth."

Chapter Forty-Four

JASMINE

W hen I return to our rehearsal dinner, the room is cold. It's not the difference between the air-conditioning and the spring evening. It's something else.

A black hole sucking in the life around it.

Mai and Quyen are still laughing. Making Dad blush.

Ian is still flirting shamelessly with both of them.

He looks to me and raises a brow *are you okay?*

I nod as if I am. I should be. It shouldn't be a big deal. I don't want to believe anything Lucien says.

So what if Shep has a contract? If he's doing this just to beat Lucien at some sick game?

I knew the deal when I signed up. Marriage, selling true love, a year on his terms.

The papers are signed. My fate is sealed. Another eleven and a half months as his.

Only it doesn't feel like a curse anymore.

I want to be Shep's. His wife, his love, his everything.

I manage a smile as I chat with my family. Ian. The host at the restaurant.

Even as I help Dad into Lock's car.

I keep a smile until I'm alone, on the way back to Shep's apartment, walking in the moonlight.

Then I read every tiny detail again.

Is this really all I am? A pawn in Shep's game?

Is he really that good at pretending?

I don't want to believe it.

I don't want to believe a thing Lucien says.

But there is something Shep isn't telling me. And I need to know.

Whatever it is, I need the truth.

Chapter Forty-Five

SHEPARD

At home, Jasmine is sitting at the dining table. She's wearing that same white dress. The same silver heels.

But everything else is different.

It's in her eyes. That look Lizzy had.

That's impossible. Lucien would never admit this. And Nick couldn't have told her.

There's no way she could know.

She can't know.

Anything is better than that.

"What are you doing?" I slam the door closed. It doesn't hit hard enough. The world is too soft, too unable to take the beating it deserves.

Her eyes stay glued to me as she stands. She unfolds the paper. Leaves it on the table. "Your stepfather talked to me."

"Did he?"

"He wanted to tell me about this game you play... how you'd made a bet that you could win me over."

Of course, he did.

There he goes, inventing rules I don't know. I'm too close to winning, so he brings up the game.

Bet makes it sound fun. It's not fun. It's sick. But there's no sense in discussing that. "And?"

"I was thinking," her voice is soft. She's not angry. She's understanding. Caring. Loving. "Why would he tell me that? Not because he has my best interests at heart. Because he wants to put a wedge between us."

I say nothing.

"Why would he want that? Why is he playing this strange game with you? You don't love him. You don't like him. You go pale when you see him. And Nick too. He—"

No.

She's too close to the truth.

I can't let her say those words. I can't let her go there.

"You're right. It's a game. That's all. It's fun toying with people. Especially you." I pull the bottle from the paper bag in my hands. "But I already lost." I set the half-emptied bottle of bourbon on the counter.

"Shep—"

"I drank. You win. I'll have Lock send your first payment in the morning."

"I don't want to win. I want to talk to you."

"It will take a few days to send the rest. He'll arrange the details."

She crosses the room to me. Reaches for me.

I move away. When she follows, I push her.

She stumbles, but she doesn't stop. She holds her ground.

I suck a breath through my nose. I need to hold my expression. To convince her I don't give a fuck about her.

To do whatever it takes so she leaves before she figures this out.

She can't know.

She can't.

"You should go," I repeat it again.

Still, she holds her ground. "I only want to talk."

"There's nothing to discuss. This was a game. And I lost. So go. Collect your winnings."

"We're supposed to get married in two days."

"You'll have your money. That's what you wanted, isn't it?" I move past her. "Let yourself out. I'll change the locks tomorrow."

"Shep—"

I don't respond. I lock myself in my office and blast a metal band I can't stand.

She pounds on the door for a few minutes. Pleads for me to come out.

Eventually, she realizes it's hopeless.

Eventually, she leaves.

Chapter Forty-Six

JASMINE

At home, Dad's on the couch, reading one of those historical fiction books he adores. He sets it down as soon as he sees me.

He doesn't ask what happened. He just fills the electric kettle and motions for me to sit.

When I do, he finds a blanket, fixes a cup of chamomile, puts on a movie I used to watch with Mom.

When I try to protest, to insist I make him something, he shakes his head.

"Let me take care of you for once," he says. "You've been taking care of me for long enough."

Chapter Forty-Seven

SHEPARD

K ey wakes me in the morning. She drops the empty bottle in my lap. "You're better than this."

"Thanks for the advice." It's too fucking bright in here.

She shakes her head. "You know, we can't help you if you insist on keeping the house empty."

I rise. Close the curtains. "You're not supposed to come into my office."

"You're not supposed to drink." She pulls the curtains. "You realize we all know why you request privacy."

"Yes."

"We all know about your... tastes."

"Do you?"

She just barely smiles. "What do you think happened when Lock dropped those young ladies at their apartments? They had questions. And answers."

That's what you get for being a gentleman. "Do you want something?"

"You have a guest arriving in a few hours."

"Tell them to leave."

She smiles *hell no*. "You should clean up. And change your clothes. You're not presenting your best self."

"I'm not seeing anyone today."

"Two hours." She leaves the door open. "You're going to need both of them."

———

A SHOWER AND A CHANGE OF CLOTHES HELP. AS DO COFFEE and breakfast. But they're not enough.

My head is still pounding.

The room is still spinning.

The world is still dark and ugly.

There's only one thing offering a shred of relief—she doesn't know.

But it's ripped away as soon as Key answers the door. Because the guest isn't my brother or Ian or someone else on a misguided mission to talk me out of cold feet.

It's Jasmine.

Chapter Forty-Eight

SHEPARD

"**G**ood morning." Jasmine's eyes meet mine for a moment then they're back on Key. "I'm okay. And you?"

"Okay?" Key's voice is incredulous. "That's one way of putting it." She turns to me with that motherly *what are you doing* look. "Weddings are hard. People fight. It's normal."

"You can tell Miss Lee that she can leave," I say. "There's no reason for her to be here."

"You can tell Miss Lee that," Key says. "She's right here."

"Fine." My fingers curl into fists. My staff knows better than to defy me. They know to follow my fucking orders.

Not that I have ground at the moment. I lost all of it last night. And I...

I'm not angry she's here.

I want to be. I want to throw that empty bottle at the wall. So the shattered glass falls at her feet. So she knows exactly what this is.

But not because I'm angry.

I want her here.

It's ridiculous. She already knows too much. If she stays, she's going to learn more. And I can't—

This can't—

I clear my throat. "Then tell Lock—"

"Who do you think drove Miss Lee here?" Key nearly rolls her eyes. "I'll have tea in a few minutes. Milk oolong? Or gaba?"

"Milk oolong. Thank you," Jasmine says.

"Did you have breakfast, Jasmine? I'm happy to fix something. Or some tea cakes perhaps?"

"Sure, yes. The tea cakes." She nods another thank you and turns to me. She waits until Key is in the kitchen to approach.

I move from my seat. To the sliding glass door. "You should go."

"Maybe."

"Is there a problem with your check? An error? Or is it not enough?" Or maybe Lock's fucking with me. Pretending as if he forgot it. Pretending I forgot a signature.

"Yes." She takes three steps towards me. "I'm not cashing it."

"Don't be ridiculous."

"We have a deal. A marriage. Another year."

"No. I broke our terms. I drank last night."

She shakes her head. "I looked again. If you drink, I can end the deal. You have no say."

Fuck. She's right. I didn't think it would matter. I didn't think I'd be this pathetic.

"Dad is feeling better, but that's not a guarantee. I want him to walk me down the aisle. I want him to know someone is taking care of me. And I'm not going to find some random stranger on the street."

"You're going to lie to him."

She takes one more step toward me. "I know who you are, Shep. I know what you can offer me. Maybe it isn't love. But it's something close."

"It's not—"

"It is. And I want it. I want to fall asleep in your arms. I want to tease you about your coffee. I want to sit on the couch watching movies." She moves closer. Close enough to touch me. But she doesn't. She places her body next to mine. Next to the window. "I want to be your wife. No matter what happened with your stepfather."

I press my hand into the glass. "We don't always get what we want."

"I know. And I know, if you break the contract, there's nothing I can do. No, there is. I can take the ten million. And I will. But I'm not going to tell anyone. I'm not going to spill any of your secrets. Even if I could force you into this, I… well I'm not you. I wouldn't want to." Her eyes find mine. "I love you."

My exhale is too heavy. Too full. There's no air in the room.

It's too hot.

Too bright.

Too fucking loud.

She can't love me. It's not good for her. I need to tell her no, stop, run away.

But there's something holding my tongue. This part of me that's desperate for her love.

And more. Her understanding, her acceptance, her pride.

It wants her to know.

To know and stay.

But it's stupid. She can't know. It's better if she doesn't.

"I won't ask again. About your stepfather. I've never liked him. He always gave me this sinking feeling at the pit of my stomach. I couldn't figure out why. If I think about it… you always clammed up around him. You'd only touch me the days he wasn't around. And when he did interrupt… no matter what we were doing, you always insisted on driving me home."

"Stop," I say. "Don't say it."

Her expression stays soft. "I won't. I won't guess what happened. And you don't have to tell me. I hope you do one day. When you're ready. But if you don't… that's okay."

"I won't."

"Okay." She turns so she's facing me. "It's your battle. I won't pretend I can fight it for you. But that isn't why I'm here. I'm not here to ask you to spill your secrets."

What?

"I hope you do. I hope you trust me one day. I hope you let me shoulder that burden with you. But I can wait."

"You should go."

"No. I love you. I'm not giving up on you."

"You left me—"

"Because you wouldn't stop drinking."

"I had to drink. It was the only way."

Her eyes soften. "I… even if that's true, I'd do it again. I can't be with that version of you. I guess there's an easy out. Find a bottle, tell me it's your new mistress." Her gaze shifts to the clear blue sky. "I won't beg you to change again. I won't beg you to love me. I'm just going to ask one thing. Marry me tomorrow. Marry me, like we planned, and give this a chance. A real one. With no one watching."

"I can't."

Her eyes turn down. "Why?"

"What he did… where do you think he learned it?"

"He was—"

I can't let her finish that sentence. "Don't feel sorry for him."

"I don't."

"He passed that curse to me. And now I... I'm a monster, Jasmine. Don't you see that?"

She holds her ground.

"I'm going to hurt you one day. I'm not going to be able to stop myself." I already want to. I want to pin her to the wall, tear off her panties, fuck her until she's not asking questions.

Until she's mine and I'm the one with all the cards.

It's the only bright spot in an ocean of darkness.

"You won't," she says. "I trust you."

"That's a foolish decision."

"It's not a choice. I wouldn't choose to love you. I wouldn't choose something this complicated. But I do love you. I've tried, for a long time, to stop loving you. But I can't." She stares into my eyes. "Maybe you feel like a monster. But you're not. I can see you better than you can. And you're not some beast who can't control yourself."

"I am."

She presses on. "Even if that's true, if you are out of control... that's my choice. I can trust you or not."

"Jasmine—"

"You can decide you're not ready for this. That you won't be with me. But don't tell me it's for my own good. I know what's good for me. I know what I want. I want to marry you. And I'm going to be ready, tomorrow. I'm going to be there." She places her hand next to mine. Just barely. Just enough our pinkies touch. "Don't make me wait too long."

Chapter Forty-Nine

JASMINE

I suppose with my insanity official, it's hard to describe my current mental state.

I'm in a tiny room backstage, pretending as if I'm contemplating my makeup, struggling to pace.

This dress is too snug. These heels are too high. My hair is pinned too tightly.

Everything is in place for the wedding. Everything except my groom.

It's a hell of a play. Under different circumstances, Shep would be proud. Nick would shake my hand. Lizzy would gush.

As it is...

Shep's status is still unknown. And everyone else believes the wedding is going on as normal.

Men are spoiled. They only need a clean suit and tie. Neat hair. Bam, they're ready.

It isn't the multi-hour extravaganza of bridal styling.

Has anyone ever worn this much makeup?

Mai watches me pace and shakes her head. "You had too much tea. You should have some champagne."

Maybe. I am shaking. But I don't want Shep to taste alcohol on my lips. Not after last night. Not ever. "I'm okay."

She shoots her sister one of those *what a difficult child* looks.

"Everyone is nervous on their wedding day." Quyen squeezes my hand. "You look beautiful. And you're doing the normal vows. All you need to do is walk and smile."

"Maybe." I struggle to walk to the other end of the room. I blame the soft carpet. Even if it is my cloudy thoughts.

This is bizarre. Three weeks ago, marrying Shep was the worst fate imaginable. Now, it's the only thing I want.

No, that isn't true. I want Dad to be okay. I want to practice my acting. I want to build a career.

But right now—

Where the hell is he?

I check my cell again. Nothing from Key or Lock. Nothing from Nick. Nothing at all.

No one knows where Shep is. If he's coming. If he's on his way to the Cayman Islands.

I tap out text after text. Erase every one.

Please come.

Don't make me wait.

I love you.

You made this stupid deal, don't be the one to renege.

You don't have to come. But talk to me. Tell me we can do this.

Let's go somewhere else. Somewhere small. Just me and you.

Anything.

Anywhere.

Mai pulls my phone from my hand. Turns it off. Slides it into her purse. "It's not the time for distractions."

"You do look beautiful." Quyen smiles. "Just like your mother."

"Older though," Mai says.

"Why point that out?"

"She is older."

"She's still young."

"Not that young. Only so much time for grandchildren."

"It's her wedding day! Let her enjoy it."

"You should—"

A knock interrupts them.

The officiant's voice. "It's time."

How can it be time? I don't know if he's here. What if he's not here?

I suck a shallow breath through my teeth. Struggle through my exhale.

The officiant pulls the door open. And there's my dad, in a clean black suit, smiling the world's widest smile.

"Jasmine," he says in Vietnamese. "You look even more beautiful than your mother did."

My heart melts immediately. "Yeah?"

"So much like her." He offers me his arm.

I hook mine with his. "Is he…" I can't ask if he's here. That gives too much away. "How does he look?"

Mai shoots him a *zip it* look.

For once, he listens to her. He steps back to allow Mai and Quyen to go forward. My bridal party. Walking with his.

But that must mean—

People wouldn't be walking if he wasn't—

The music wouldn't be playing if he wasn't—

Or maybe this is some elaborate prank. This whole thing was a ridiculous game. Can I truly make Jasmine beg?

Maybe Shep is the monster he claims to be.

Maybe—

Maybe—

"You're up, Miss Lee." The planner stresses the *Miss* as if to say *remember this. It's the last time you'll use it.*

I squeeze my dad's arm as I step forward.

Insane doesn't even begin to cover it. I'm completely and totally incapable of knowing my limits.

Why did I dare Shep?

Look what happened last time I dared him. He may not be stronger than I am, but he's a million times more stubborn. If he's sure about getting his way—

He won't be—

Is he—

Oh my God—

Dad pats my hand as we turn the corner.

And there he is.

Shepard. Standing at the end of the long aisle. Waiting with an expression of utter contentment.

So many people are here, but I don't see them.

I only see him.

I practically float down the fucking aisle.

He takes my hands and leans in close enough to whisper. "I'm sorry."

"Me too."

The officiant breaks us up. Says something about how we're too eager.

Shep squeezes my hand.

I mouth I love you.

He mouths *me too*.

It's not quite there. But, for now, it's more than enough.

Epilogue

Shepard

The words flit through my mind quickly. A flash of lightning. Bright enough to illuminate the horizon.

Gone too fast.

But still burned into my mind.

Why now?

There's nothing remarkable about the moment.

I appreciate every second with Jasmine, but I don't go counting the stars. Or thanking some higher power. Or blowing dandelions.

She's mine.

That's my ring on her finger.

That smile on her face—

It's because of me.

Every second is remarkable.

Which means nothing is remarkable. I'm a man of numbers, not words, but I know that much. Special is out of the ordinary.

I wish I had a better word than ordinary. There's

nothing ordinary about her smile. Or the cross of her legs. Or the laugh filling the room.

It's priceless.

Even if it happens nearly every day.

Even if this is an ordinary evening.

We're here, in this quiet restaurant, watching the sun fall into the horizon. Another afternoon tea gone over time. Her lipstick marking a perfect white cup. Her dark eyes filled with joy.

Her fingers brush my wrist. She smiles. "You're thinking something."

It's there again. Those three words. Only brighter. Bigger. A flashing billboard in Times Square. One that demands the entire city's attention.

"Shep? Are you okay? Or did I lose you at 'off-Broadway?'"

No, I'm still hanging on every word. I still want every thought in her head, every feeling in her heart, every inch of her body.

"I did, didn't I? I swear, I'll stop talking about auditions one day. It's just so exciting. It's been six months of nonstop practice. I'm finally going out there, getting rejected nonstop, like everyone else. I know I'm not great yet—"

I can't wait. I bring my hand to her cheek. Pull her into a deep, slow kiss.

For a second, she's stiff. Surprised. Then she melts into me.

My tongue slips into her mouth. I don't claim her. Not exactly. I let her know she's mine.

That I'm hers.

That I want it like this forever.

She pulls back with a heady sigh. "What was that—"

"I love you."

Her eyes go wide. She opens her mouth to speak. Stops

herself. Tapping her fingers against the table, counting the tiny moments that made this possible.

It's there. In the air, the room, the universe. I love her. I have. For a long time. Always. It's just been impossible to explain. Impossible to accept. Impossible to understand.

How can a monster love anyone? Or anything?

But I'm not—

I can't even say that. Sure, I can repeat the affirmations from my shrink—*I'm Shepard Marlowe and I'm not a monster*—but I can't do it with conviction.

I don't believe it.

Not all the way.

Not most of the way.

I'm not healed just yet. Maybe I'll never be healed. Maybe this darkness will always live inside me. Somewhere deep and hidden. Somewhere no one else sees it. But there just the same.

I still flinch when she surprises me. I still churn at the sound of that bastard's name. I still throw the nearest thing when I think about how he—

I haven't told her yet.

But she knows. Somehow, she knows. She knows and I'm sitting here, across from her, staring back at her.

She knows, and I'm not running away.

She knows, and she's here.

I'm not sure when she knew. For how long. Or how she put the pieces together. If someone told her. I never ask. I never ask.

It doesn't matter.

She knows, and she's here.

She knows, and she wants me.

She knows, and she loves me.

That's all that matters.

"I love you." It's easier the second time. Right. Like

music. Or poetry. Or something else I want to understand. "More than anything."

"I love you too." She smiles, not drawing attention to the moment, just reveling in the feel of the words on her lips. "It's a good thing. Because you're stuck with me." She taps her wedding ring. Then runs her finger over mine.

This time, she's the one who pulls me into a slow, deep kiss.

This time, I'm the one who melts into her.

Jasmine

"Come here." Shep's fingers brush my silk robe. Then they're on my wrists. Softly. Then firmer. Not enough to demand.

Enough to request. That's as close as he gets to *please*.

"Why should I?" I tease him. Because I can. Because, even after two years, even on our wedding anniversary, he's never this gentle.

"Why should you?" He looks up at me, affection in his clear blue eyes. "Why should you?" he repeats the words again. A little lower. A lot more demanding.

My body whines. That's all it takes. A hint of bossiness in his voice and I melt. I want to toss this robe aside, slide into his lap, follow his every order. I need to hold my ground. To enjoy every second of teasing him. "Why should I?"

"Do you want to come?"

My knees buckle. He's too sexy. It's wrong. And it's all in my favor. Which makes it very, very right.

"Princess?"

"Right now?"

His lips curl into a smile. The gentleness again. Him. Not the scene. Just my husband, sitting on a hotel bed in London, smiling at me. "Come here."

"*Come* here."

His deep laugh fills the room. Lights up his gorgeous eyes.

Shep is happier than he's ever been, but he's not exactly Mr. Positivity. He's still merciless at work. And when it comes to my well-being.

He nearly killed the last person who crossed me. And it wasn't a big deal. An actor who gave me the wrong time for an audition. To cut down on competition.

It didn't work. I showed up late and irritated and brought all that into my performance. Everyone at the show thought I was a stone-cold-bitch. For a few days. I cracked quickly. I'm not into the whole method thing.

And I'm…

Well, I'm still not an amazing actor. And, after two years of practice and auditions, I'm not sure I'll ever be an amazing actor. I still love the stage, love scene study and improv and line readings.

But the endless auditions, the constant nos, people judging me based mostly on how I look—

I don't want that life.

Six months ago, I realized something. I missed the world of finance. I missed business. I missed checking practical tasks off my to-do list.

I had all that money. And all that drive to help people, spread art, get these done.

So I did something crazy. The craziest thing I'd done since I demanded Shep marry me.

I started a charity. We teach acting to low-income kids.

Bring them into productions. Help them learn how to express themselves. And how to work with others.

Maybe it's not math and science, but it is something that helps them find a better life. And it's satisfying in a different way. A way that fills my heart with love.

I still hone my craft. I still audition now and then. But, mostly, I focus on sharing my love of theater with the entire world.

What could be better than that?

"Princess?" He says it softly this time. Asking, again. Not just for me to sit. For something else too. Something deeper.

His fingers curl around my wrist. He runs his thumb over the outside of my hand. Then his other hand is on my lower back, pressing the smooth fabric into my skin.

I let him pull me into his lap.

My hands go to his shoulders. One curls around the back of his neck. The other finds his cheek.

He leans into my touch as I run my fingers along his chin.

My heart thuds against my chest. After two years, six continents, and countless orgasms, I still crave everything he's willing to give me.

His softness and his hardness. Not that I'm thinking about his hardness. Or his hands around my throat. Or his lips on my thighs.

I'm not…

Fuck, this is important. I need to concentrate. On something besides how badly I want him splitting me in half.

His fingers curl into my waist. He pulls me a little bit closer. Looks up at me with a little more softness. "I've been thinking."

"Did I drag you to too many plays?"

His smile widens. "There's such a thing?"

"Not everyone wants to spend every night of their vacation in a theater." I run my hand through his hair. It's a little longer now. The way he kept it when we were kids. That same gorgeous shade of brown. One that brings out his blue eyes. "I can't imagine it's your first choice."

"Are you in the theater?"

I nod.

"Then it's my first choice."

"But if you could take me anywhere—"

"Besides right here?" He pats the clean white sheets.

My cheeks flush. Somehow, the staff always knows when it's time to change the sheets. They always do it without alerting us. We fuck like rabbits, go out for tea, come back to the suite to fresh sheets.

After two years, I'm used to the conveniences that come with wealth. I'm even used to having a staff. It's nice telling Key *I can't think about dinner. You know what I like. Make something good* then sitting down to perfectly steamed fish and vegetables an hour later.

It's nice never making my bed, cleaning my room, scrubbing the damn shower.

It's really nice knowing someone is taking care of my dad.

But it's also… weird. At heart, I'm a normal girl who fends for herself. I don't exactly miss washing dishes—or flying coach—but I still do double-takes over some of the prices Shep pays.

Even though…

He did make good on his word. After our honeymoon —two weeks in Thailand, half the time in bed, the other half lying on the beach, touring the city, eating enough noodles to burst—Shep transferred ten million dollars to my bank account.

I told him it was ridiculous. Unnecessary. He already took care of every one of my needs. What was I going to do with ten million dollars?

He insisted. Said he owed me the money. Said the contract was clear. He needed to pay me the ten million and terminate the agreement.

So the marriage was ours and ours alone.

No strings, no point to prove, no prenup.

A normal, healthy marriage.

Or as normal as either of us can get.

For a few weeks, I refused to even look at the cash. It was too much. It didn't feel earned. But when Dad got word of the deposit, he talked me into using the money for good.

It took a while to figure out what that meant. Longer to put the paperwork together. But now…

I can't imagine a better use. I give people the opportunity to fully express themselves. I give them a safe space to find their emotions, wants, desires.

To heal.

And Dad…

He still lays on the guilt trips when he deems me ungrateful for Shep's wealth.

It's ridiculous. I'm the only first-generation woman whose parents guilt her for not spending enough money.

Think of what your mother would do? Would she really want you to waste this opportunity?

I'm glad he's still here. Because if Mai and Queyen could use him and Mom to guilt me into doing things their way—

I'm so glad he's here. And okay. Yes, he's not in fighting

shape. He'll never be at one hundred percent again. But he's healthy and happy and alive.

And married to his freaking nurse. I guess she's not his nurse anymore. He doesn't need a nurse anymore. I guess it's a good thing he has a medical professional nearby.

"Princess…" He shakes his head with mock distaste. "Picturing me naked?"

"No." I press my lips together. "Not exactly."

He stares back at me with all this trust. All this love.

It warms me everywhere. It makes my limbs light. If he wasn't holding me, I'd float to the ceiling.

I still might.

I love him so much. More every day. Getting to be this close to him, sharing his space, his time, his life—

Maybe we aren't a normal couple. Maybe we haven't worked out every single one of our issues. But I don't care.

We're happy.

And he's safe. He doesn't tell me everything about his past. Only bits and pieces. He's still working through it. He'll always be working through it.

He's trying to let go. Forgive. For himself.

It's the opposite of the Shepard Marlowe I know.

And it's… well, I'm happy for him. That he's releasing this burden. But I couldn't let go or forgive.

I asked Ian's help. The tech genius found information on Lucien. Nothing about Shep. Or Nick. Or anything salacious.

No, we found ordinary, run-of-the-mill evidence of insider trading.

I took it to Lucien. Told him I'd release it if he ever came near Shep again. He pretended like he had no idea what I was talking about. But he did back off.

I asked Shep's staff to keep an eye on him. To tell me if

they ever get news of any contact from Lucien. Even a fucking Christmas card.

I know, I shouldn't spy on my husband. But it's what he would do. If he knew, he'd be proud.

As it is…

For once, I got to save him. That feels better than anything.

"I'm glad your mind is in the gutter." He pulls me a little closer. So my thoughts return to the room. So I sink into his lap.

"Aren't we going to dinner?" I run my fingers along his collar. Down his tie. I want to fuck him. Okay, to have him fuck me. But I want a quiet dinner too. I want all of it. Everything. "We can't be late."

"We can't?"

I shake my head with absolutely no conviction.

He smiles. "I better make this fast."

I shake my head.

He slips his hand under my robe. "I've been thinking."

"Yeah?"

"About us. Our future. Our life."

I stare into his deep blue eyes. "Something specific?"

His gaze flits to the floor. His cheeks flush. His chest caves.

Is he actually… shy?

Shepard Marlowe, a man with the power to destroy anyone in his way, a man who makes me come so hard I see stars, is shy.

This has never happened.

Ever.

Warmth spreads through my torso. And something else. A fierce need to protect him. From anyone and every-thing. "You've been thinking."

He nods.

I run my fingers along his jawline. To his chin. Gently, I tilt his head so we're eye to eye. "Whatever it is, you can tell me."

He nods. "I'm ready."

"You're ready?"

"Yeah." His blush deepens. "To start trying."

"Trying… Oh." Oh. My head fills. My heart swells. My body screams *yes, let's start right now.*

"I know your charity is taking up a lot of time. If you want to wait—"

"No."

"No?"

"Yes. Now. Let's start. Let's try." My fingers curl in his hair.

"Right now?"

I nod.

"Your IUD?"

"Don't ruin the moment with practicalities."

He mimes zipping his lips.

"We can… practice. Then, when we get home, I'll make an appointment. And we can really start…"

"You think I need practice?"

"Well…" This time my cheeks flush. "You don't always come inside me."

He smiles. "You don't like that, princess?"

"You know I…" My blush deepens. "It's just… the biology."

He reaches out. Cups my cheek with his palm. His voice gets softer. All that gentleness. All him. "Are you sure?"

"Yeah." I nod. "If you are. Because, Shep… I love you so much. I've wanted this for a long time. When Dad got sick, I couldn't stop thinking about it. About how much I wanted him to meet his grandkids. How much I wanted to be a mom. And then he got better and I... I still wanted to be a mom. But I know you—" God, how do I say it?

How do I say *I know you're terrified you're going to follow in the footsteps of your abusive stepfather? But I know you won't. Because it's been two years and I've dropped every one of my limits and even though you have carte blanche, you're always gentle with me?*

I settle on, "I know you're scared."

"I am." His voice stays soft. "Terrified. It's an ugly world out there."

"Sometimes."

"Sometimes." He cups my cheek. "Sometimes, it's beautiful. Full of love. And life. And a woman who would move the stars for you."

"I would."

"I know, princess. I would too."

"You're sure?"

"I am."

"How sure?"

He tugs at the strap holding my robe together. Then, in case I'm not completely sure of his answer, he brings his hands to my waist, flips me over, pins me to the bed.

I lose myself in his command.

In surrendering to the man I love.

In being one with my husband.

———

Want more?

Sign up for my mailing list for a bonus scene from *Dirty Husband*. What are Jasmine and Shepard up to in a few years? Find out!

Ian's book, *Dirty Desires*, is coming this spring. In the

mean time, check out Nick and Lizzy's story in *Dirty Boss*. Turn the page for a sample.

Already read *Dirty Boss*? Get your bossy billionaire fix with *Dirty Deal* (keep turning for a sample).

All caught up on the Dirty series? Keep your alpha hero fix going with *Tempting*. Brooding tattoo artist Brendon is obsessed with his little sister's best friend. He wants to have the bookish virgin every way he can—especially tied to his bed.

Dirty Boss - Excerpt

Buy *Dirty Boss* Now

The elevator doors slide open. I take a deep breath, cultivating every ounce of badass I can muster. Either I nail this interview and get this internship, or I slink back to Stanford for dull classes and three thousand miles between me and everything I love.

Here goes nothing.

The woman sitting behind the reception desk is pure New York City cool. Slick straight black bob. Sleek red dress. Perfect makeup.

"You must be Elizabeth Wilder. I'm Jasmine Lee, the office manager." She shakes my hand with a strong grip.

"Lizzy."

Jasmine smiles. "We mostly go by last names here. It's a lot more formal than the Bay."

She leads me through the modern office. It's sleeker than a typical San Francisco startup. Modern art hangs next to huge windows. The room glows with the soft January light.

We stop in a corner office.

Jasmine motions for me to sit in the leather executive chair. "I'm going to leave you with this programming test. Then Mr. Marlowe is going to come in and ask you a few questions."

My stomach twists. Phoenix Marlowe is the company's CEO, a billionaire programming genius. How am I supposed to impress him?

"He's excited to meet you. He couldn't stop talking about your AI projects." She points to the monitor, now displaying a programming test. "Good luck."

She nods a goodbye on her way out the door.

The second it clicks shut, my attention shifts to the computer screen.

I get lost in the hard but doable questions.

Until I hear his voice.

That same voice I heard that night in San Francisco.

"I hope I haven't surprised you," he says.

That's him. It can't be possible, but that's him. I spin in my chair so we're eye to eye.

What the hell is Nick doing here?

"No," I say. "It's fine."

He closes and locks the door. His gaze drifts to the résumé in his hands. It's like he doesn't recognize me. Maybe he has one-night stands all the time. Maybe it meant nothing to him.

My head fills with the feeling of his body sinking into mine, the taste of whiskey on his lips, the smell of his cologne.

He's wearing the same cologne today.

His eyes flash with something. Anger, I think. He's hard to read.

It's something. Something bad.

He does recognize me. He must.

His voice is rough. "Who is Marie?"

I take a deep breath. "My middle name. And Nick?"

"Phoenix. My friends call me Nick."

"I didn't realize." I press my hand against the slick surface of the desk. "I'm sure this kind of thing has happened before."

His eyes narrow. "No."

"But you're very—"

"I don't go around fucking college students." He places my résumé on the desk and takes a seat behind it.

"I don't go around fucking billionaire programmers." My nostrils flare. My heart pounds. Anger fills my veins. As much as it hurts, meaning nothing to him, I need this opportunity. It's the only way I can stay near Kat. And Kat's the only person I trust. I clear my throat. "Can we start over?"

Frustration spreads across his face. "This project means everything to me."

"Your assistant, Ms. Lee—"

"She's not my assistant."

"Whatever she is, she told me how impressed you were by my board game bots. Is that true?"

"Yes." He stares at me like he's expecting me to back down.

I don't.

"Your programming skills are not up to the standards of Odyssey Industries. Your code is sloppy and inefficient."

"You didn't even look at my programming test."

He taps the monitor.

"You can see the test on your computer, can't you?"

Nick nods. His eyes meet mine, and his expression shifts. It's softer. "You're stubborn and overconfident."

"I am not." Objecting doesn't help my case. But he's wrong.

"I'd like to hire you, Ms. Wilder. You're the only candidate with any grasp of artificial intelligence." Nick stares back at me. "But there are other issues to consider."

"I fucked the boss, so I'm shit out of luck?"

His expression is impossible to read.

"Are you even going to deny it?" I will myself to stay logical. This is a good opportunity. Not worth wasting over a romantic connection, not when there are three million men in Manhattan.

It doesn't help.

I can't look at Nick for another second. How can this be the same man I met last September? That man was calm and collected, but there was warmth in his eyes. His voice was stern and strong, but it was caring too.

This guy is a narcissistic asshole.

I push myself out of my seat. "I'll spare you the awkwardness of explaining it to HR." I sling my purse over my shoulder and march to the door.

"Lizzy, wait."

That's not happening. Not when there's a tear welling up in my eye. This opportunity is everything to me and it's nothing to him.

There's no way I'm staying in New York.

Dammit, I'm not crying in front of him.

Head down, I rush to the elevator. Jasmine says a frantic goodbye, but I pretend I don't hear her.

There are footsteps behind me. I can't bring myself to turn and find out if they belong to Nick. I duck into the staircase and race all the way to the first floor.

I disappear into the Wall Street subway station.

———

My sister, Kat, lives with her fiancé Blake Sterling on the

Upper East Side. He's wealthy. If I tell him about this internship, he'll offer me the money to stay in New York.

But I'm not accepting help from either of them. Kat spent the last four years taking care of me. For once, she's going to live her life. I'm going to stand on my own two feet. Even if it kills me.

I collapse on the modern black couch and scan my streaming options. All the sci-fi movies make me think about Nick's project. The Haley Bot (named for Hal, the evil computer in *2001: A Space Odyssey*) is a virtual assistant far beyond any of its competitors. It's an amazing AI project. It's the best opportunity I'll ever have to learn about AI.

This internship is the only way I can stay in New York without dropping out of school.

I can swallow my pride, apologize, and convince Nick to keep our relationship professional.

But I'm not so sure I can be around him without melting into a pile of desire.

Buy *Dirty Boss* Now

Dirty Deal - Excerpt

Get *Dirty Deal* Now

The manager takes one look at my discount heels and my loose pencil skirt and shakes his head.

"Sorry, but the position is already filled." He leers at my chest. Raises a brow. *Maybe you'd like to fill a different position.*

I swallow the insult rising in my throat. "Do you know when you'll be hiring again?"

"It might be awhile."

"Keep me in mind. I have a lot of experience." Not so much the kind he's looking for. But I do know how to wait tables.

He takes my résumé but keeps his eyes on my chest. "Sorry, honey, but we're looking for something specific."

Yeah, I bet.

I take a not-at-all-calming breath. This guy is nothing. He's not going to make me lose it. I've dealt with a thousand entitled jerks worse than him.

I'll deal with plenty more tonight.

It comes with working at a nice place.

I nod a *thank you* and walk out of the restaurant slowly.

I keep my steps casual. Easy. Well, as easy as I can in these shitty heels.

The air outside is freezing. Even by March in New York standards. The white sky is heavy with grey rainclouds.

Usually, I like the drizzle. I like the temperamental weather—the snowy winters, the rainy spring, the humid summer, the crisp fall.

Right now, not so much.

I dig into my purse for my phone. Lizzy will cheer me up. She always does.

With my next step, I bump into something solid.

No. Someone. Soft wool wraps over a hard body.

My leg catches on his. I think it's a his.

My ankle shifts.

Shit.

I throw my hands in front of my face to catch my fall.

Ow. The concrete smarts. And it's fucking cold.

"Are you okay?" a deep voice asks.

So that's a him. Very him. His voice is masculine. There's something about the steady timbre. Something that makes me forget I'm splayed out on the ground, damp concrete wetting my skirt.

"I'm fine."

His shoes are nice. Leather. Designer. Expensive. His slacks fall at exactly the right place. They're grey. Wool. And they're covering long legs.

His black wool coat falls at mid-thigh. It's buttoned. It's hiding his torso. It's hanging off his strong shoulders.

He's looking down at me, his blue eyes filled with… with something. I'm not sure. It's hard to do anything but stare back at those eyes.

They're beautiful.

And he has this square jaw. The kind of jaw that belongs on a sculpture.

Or a Disney prince.

He's the hottest guy I've seen in months.

And I'm splayed out on the concrete staring dumbstruck.

Awesome.

"I… Um… You should watch where you're going." I pick up my purse and slide it onto my shoulder.

He leans down and offers his hand.

Okay.

I guess he's a gentleman.

That's weird, but it fits him, what with the whole Disney prince vibe.

I take his hand. It does something to me. Makes the air sharper, more electric. Sends heat from my palm, down my arm, through my torso.

It's a strong hand, but it's smooth.

And that suit—

And that *I get what I want* look in his eyes.

I know this guy. Well, I know his type.

He's pure money.

The kind of guy who has the world at his fingertips.

"I really am fine." I pull myself to my feet. Or maybe he pulls me. Either way. I take a step towards the corner— the subway is only a few blocks away—but my ankle isn't having it. Fuck. That hurts.

His grip on my hand tightens. "Sit down." He nods to the bench behind us. "If you can walk."

"I don't need your help."

"Oh, really?" He raises an eyebrow and nods to my shoe as if to say *put it on then*.

Oh.

I'm not wearing a shoe.

For some reason, my foot isn't cold.

None of me is cold.

He's just so…

Obnoxious for telling me what to do.

And incredibly, painfully appealing.

I shift my weight to my other ankle, but I can barely balance. "I have to get to work."

"You'll get to work. Trust me." He slides his arm under mine, like a human crutch, and he sets me on the bench.

His touch is comforting.

It should be scary—this guy is a stranger. I don't even know his name.

But it's not.

It's soothing.

Tender.

But that doesn't mean anything.

It's just that it's been so long since anyone has touched me with any care or attention.

I take a deep breath. It does nothing to slow my heartbeat. "What's your name?"

"Blake. You?"

"Kat."

Those piercing eyes find mine. He presses his fingers against my ankle. "It's sprained."

"I've dealt with worse."

His stare is penetrating. It demands an explanation.

But why?

He doesn't know me.

He doesn't have any obligation to help.

He's someone and I'm no one.

He's not even going to remember me tomorrow.

Still, I want to wipe away the worry in his eyes. "I ran cross-country in high school."

He nods with understanding.

"I can't work on a sprained ankle."

"What do you do?"

"I'm a waitress." And I can't afford to not work.

I stare back at Money Guy. Blake. His expression is still streaked with concern. He's not going to leave me alone until he's sure I'm fine.

And I can't exactly make a quick exit. Not with my ankle this fucked up.

"I'll ice it when I get home. I promise." Ibuprofen will have to get me through my shift tonight. I've played through the pain before, back when I ran all the time instead of every so often.

"I'd feel better if you went to the E.R."

I press my lips into a customer-service smile. "Not happening."

"Where do you work?"

"It's not far. I can walk."

"I'll walk you." He slides my shoe onto my foot.

His fingers graze my ankle.

His touch is soft. Tender. Sweet. Like we're old lovers, not strangers.

It wakes up all my nerves.

I want those hands on my skin.

Under my skirt.

Tearing off my blouse.

Sliding my panties to my knees.

I swallow hard.

I don't think about sex like this. And certainly not with strange, rich men who insist on walking me to work.

Blake.

Money Guy.

He certainly has the tall and handsome thing covered.

If things were different, if Lizzy wasn't home, if I

didn't have to work, maybe I'd invite myself out with him.

We could have dinner. Drinks. A night at a hotel. The kind with security. So it's safe.

I could finally punch my v-card.

But things aren't different.

I can't waste time with strange men.

Even rich ones.

I rise to my feet. "I can walk myself." I take a step to prove it. The first is fine, but the second makes me wince. Maybe I can't work on this. Fuck.

He slides his arms under mine, offering himself as a crutch again.

This time, I take his help without protest.

"You really shouldn't work on that." His voice is steady. Impossible to read.

"It's really none of your business."

He nods and walks with me. "It was my fault. I wasn't paying attention."

"You can admit that?"

"Should I not?"

"No." I take a few more steps. It's not so bad. I'm off tomorrow. With rest, ice, and plenty of over the counter painkillers, I'll be okay. "Just… I serve a lot of guys like you."

"Handsome?"

He… he's joking. I think.

I try to find the meaning in his expression, but I get lost in his beautiful eyes.

"Business types," I say. "Guys who are used to getting what they want."

"And they want you as dessert?"

"Sometimes." I get a lot of phone numbers. But that's normal. All the girls at the restaurant do. "They don't usually take no for an answer."

"And I?"

"I guess you're the same." I manage to put my full weight on my foot. It hurts, but it's tolerable. We turn the corner. It's not too far now. "Those guys... they don't like to admit anything is their fault. Even if they order the wrong entree. Or forget to say 'hold the onions.'"

"I know the type." He raises a brow.

We cross the street. I'm moving faster now. New Yorker fast. I nod to the restaurant two blocks down. "I'm there. I've got it." I step away from him.

He pulls his arms back to his sides. "I'm not different."

He pulls something from his back pocket and hands it to me.

It's a business card.

His voice is that same steady tone. "Give it a few days and let me know how you're doing."

"You mean how my ankle is doing?"

He holds my gaze. There's something in his eyes— some tiny hint of vulnerability. I look at the pavement, then back to his eyes. That vulnerability is gone. Replaced by pure determination.

"That's my personal number. Text or call anytime." He takes a step back. "Be careful."

I nod. "Thanks."

He turns, walks around the corner, and he's gone.

I look at the business card.

Blake Sterling. CEO of Sterling Tech. They're huge. Lizzy is obsessed with them. Uses their web services exclusively.

Blake is the CEO of one of the biggest tech companies in New York.

And he wants to know how I'm doing.

Get *Dirty Deal* Now

Stay In Touch

Sign up for <u>my mailing list</u>. (You'll get first notice on cover reveals, teasers, and new releases, and a bunch of awesome bonus content like a bonus scene from *Dirty Husband*).

You can also <u>like my page on Facebook</u>, <u>join my fangroup</u>, <u>follow me on Instagram</u>, <u>follow me on Twitter</u>, or <u>friend me on Facebook</u>.

Author's Note

Dear Reader,

First of all, thank you for reading. And please bear with me as I spill my thoughts. (If you'd rather hit the main points, <u>sign up for my mailing list</u> for updates on *Dirty Desires* (Ian's book, coming this spring) and a bonus scene from *Dirty Husband*).

Shepard Marlowe made his first appearance in *Dirty Boss* (then titled *The Billionaire's Control*) in December 2015. More than four years ago. At the time, I planned to write his book immediately. But *Rock Your Heart Out* took off and *Dirty Boss* didn't and…

I was intimidated by Shepard. He was a ruthless asshole. Yes, he'd been through a lot, but how the hell was I supposed to write him as a sympathetic character? Why should *I* care about his HEA? Lots of people love books about alphahole heroes who treat the heroine like shit. I'm not one of those people. I don't mind a sassy troublemaker or a gruff asshole as long as he has a heart of gold.

How the fuck was I supposed to write Shepard Marlowe with a heart of gold? The guy… well, I won't spoil anything in *Dirty Boss*, but if you've read it, you know he had selfish intentions. Heart of gold? More like black hole where his heart is supposed to be.

It took awhile to find a way into the story. When I started, it took awhile to find a way into Shepard's head. I tried writing him as the ruthless asshole Lizzy met in *Dirty Boss*. But it didn't work. Shepard was ruthless yes, and he didn't care if he was an asshole or not, yes, but he didn't act out of malicious intentions. He was surviving the only way he knew how. That was how I had to write him. Not as an alpha hole, but as a wounded man fighting for a way to dull the pain. (Readers call me the "queen of broken bad boys" for a reason).

Shepard is still haunted by trauma. He's still living in its immediate aftermath, reacting through the narrow lens of his past experiences. He's hurting so much he can't imagine a future where he feels whole. He isn't trying to heal himself. He isn't trying to find the light. He's trying to hurt a little less. Period. End of sentence.

He isn't healed at the end of the book. He isn't sure if he's ever going to feel whole. He's taken one step, but there's still a long journey ahead of him.

(This isn't the first time I contemplated taking the "all is lost" moment, diving deeper, ending *this* book at that moment, and writing another. To put that more plainly, I almost turned this book into a duet. I almost ended this book at Shepard calling off the wedding. I'm not sure where the next book would have started or went, beyond the eventual HEA, but it certainly would have been interesting. I didn't give into the impulse this time, but I hope to do so in the future. I hope to dive into the healing process and show how difficult and painful it can be. For now, I have to hope that showing Shepard take his first few steps is enough).

It's an unfortunate fact. Many people experience abuse at the hands of their relatives, guardians, lovers, spouses. Many people experience abuse by those who are supposed to care for them.

Most of those people aren't billionaires with the world at their fingertips. I never come into my books with an agenda (other than showing the beauty and frailty of human relationships and how important and fucking difficult and fucking worthwhile it is to find someone who understands you, who you understand). I didn't come into this book with an agenda. But I hope I gave Shepard's trauma the depth and realism it needed. I hope I brought you a hero who was no less masculine or "alpha" because he experienced sexual assault. And I really hope that you have never suffered from abuse. And that, if you have suffered, you will reach out for help.

You can find resources at RAINN.org or call the National Sexual Assault Hotline at 800.656.HOPE (4673)

Take care of yourself and the people you love.

As always, thank you for reading. I hope to see you for Ian's book, *Dirty Desires*, coming this spring. While you're waiting, check out *Dirty Boss* or *Dirty Deal*. Or, if you're all caught up on the *Dirty Rich* series, find another dominant alpha hero in *Tempting*.

Love,
Crystal

Acknowledgements

My first thanks goes to my husband, for his support when I'm lost in bookland and for generally being the sun in my sky.

The second goes to my father, for insisting I go to the best film school in the country, everything else be damned. I wouldn't love movies, writing, or storytelling half as much if not for all our afternoon trips to the bookstore and weekends at the movies.

A big shout out to all my beta readers. You helped give me the confidence to put out a book a little more heartbreaking than usual. And also to my ARC readers for helping spread the word to everyone else in the world.

To all my writer friends who talk me down from the ledge, hold my hand, and tell me when my ideas are terrible and when they're brilliant, thank you.

Thanks so much to my editor Marla, and to Hang Le for the cover design. And to my wonder narrators Lance and Grace for bringing this story to life!

As always, my biggest thanks goes to my readers.

Thank you for picking up *Dirty Husband*. I hope you'll be back for Ian's' book, *Dirty Desires*.

Also by Crystal Kaswell

Dirty Rich

Dirty Deal - Blake

Dirty Boss - Nick

Dirty Husband - Shep

Dirty Desires - Ian - coming 2020

Sinful Serenade

Sing Your Heart Out - Miles

Strum Your Heart Out - Drew

Rock Your Heart Out - Tom

Play Your Heart Out - Pete

Sinful Ever After – series sequel

Just a Taste - Miles's POV

Dangerous Noise

Dangerous Kiss - Ethan

Dangerous Crush – Kit

Dangerous Rock – Joel

Dangerous Fling – Mal

Dangerous Encore - series sequel

Inked Hearts

Tempting - Brendon

Hooking Up - Walker

Pretend You're Mine - Ryan

Hating You, Loving You - Dean

Breaking the Rules - Hunter

Losing It - Wes

Accidental Husband - Griffin

The Baby Bargain - Chase

Inked Love

The Best Friend Bargain - Forest — coming 2020

The First Taste - Holden - coming 2020

Standalones

Broken - Trent & Delilah

Come Undone Trilogy

Come Undone

Come Apart

Come To Me

Sign up for the Crystal Kaswell mailing list

Printed in Great Britain
by Amazon

30447151R00229